THE RIVER WITHIN

Karen Powell

THE RIVER WITHIN

Europa
editions

Europa Editions
8 Blackstock Mews
London N4 2BT
www.europaeditions.co.uk

A catalogue record for this title is available from the British Library
ISBN 978-1-78770-216-5

Powell, Karen
The River Within

Book design by Emanuele Ragnisco
www.mekkanografici.com

Cover image: Hugo Henneberg, *Night Scene - Blue Pond*, 1904.
Private Collection (Courtesy Natter Fine Arts Wien)

Prepress by Grafica Punto Print – Rome

Printed and bound in Great Britain by Clays Ltd, Elcograf S.p.A.

Too much of water hast thou, poor Ophelia
—HAMLET, ACT IV

THE RIVER WITHIN

CHAPTER 1
Starome, North Yorkshire, August 1955

D anny Masters came home one afternoon at the beginning of August. Something stirred beneath the surface of the water, at a point where the river at last quietened and then opened out into a wide pool, bottle-green beneath the canopy of the trees. His movement was slow at first, so that a passer-by might look twice, thinking it the shadow of a bird or a swaying branch above. A billowing next, deep, growing, blurred at the edges, and then up he bobbed as jauntily as a buoy, his one remaining eye widened at the shock of release.

For a time he drifted, undisturbed, his feet nudging the river bank, arms lifted above his head as though relishing the summer warmth after the silt and gloom of the bone-cold cavern where he'd been lodged these past days, with only blind creatures for company. Insects hummed and darted across the surface of the water, feverish in their efforts, sensing a warning of autumn, even on this highest of summer days. Danny's skin began to darken with exposure to the air. Small fish darted around him.

Three figures came along the river path, heading in the direction of the village: two young men, one blond, the other dark, while a little behind them, a girl of about seventeen, with pale hair and a light step. The two men were engaged in a debate, and it was the girl who first spotted the body, now snagged by a reed bed at the edge of the pool, just beneath the path. She stared at a bootless, sockless foot, the sole wrinkled and waxen. A softened toenail swung loose, like a door on its hinges.

Thomas Fairweather, the darker of the two men, must have sensed her pause behind him. He broke off his talk and turned, his gaze following his sister's, beyond the wild roses that grew so dark in this spot that they appeared almost black. Something to do with the composition of soil was all anyone knew or cared to find out.

'Oh Christ!' he said, and then he was in front of his sister, inserting himself between her and the river bank.

'You mustn't look, Lennie.' Thomas stared around him, as if seeking a culprit in the quiet woodland that lay all around. 'You'd best go home.'

Lennie stood hand over mouth, the breeze picking at the hem of her new green dress. It fluttered around her knees. The insects seemed to have paused in their frenzy.

'Go back to the cottage,' Thomas repeated, firm now, taking hold of her and propelling her along the river path, in the direction from which they'd come.

'Isn't it . . . ?' Words stuck in her throat. Eyes still fixed on that sodden mass. Green cloth, one boot remaining. Where did the green stop and the water start?

'He's been dead for days.' Confirming what her senses already knew.

Others came. Workers from the estate helped the two young men haul the body from the edge of the pool and then up onto the river path where it rested, skin slackened from its long immersion.

'Danny Masters!' The word went round and the body, deflating, seemed to sigh with relief at this correct identification: a few more weeks on the riverbed would have slurred his features, rendered him no more than a template.

'He'll have gone in at the Stride,' said Nathan Lacey, the head gardener, standing back and shaking his head.

Under his authority, the men cohered into a purposeful group. The estate outbuildings were to be searched for something that could function as a stretcher, to give the boy some dignity at least, while Thomas set off back along the river path to telephone Dr. Harrison, the line up at Richmond Hall being the most reliable one since the war, even after all this time.

On the river bank, Alexander Richmond made no move to follow either his friend or the estate workers.

A flash of green, bright against darker foliage, caught his eye. 'Helena?'

Never Len or Lennie when *he* spoke to her. 'I thought you'd gone home.'

She stood in the shadow of an oak tree, cheek pressed against its crocodile-hide bark. From the river path, her frame seemed moulded to the base of the great trunk.

Alexander crouched down and stared into the blank socket of the corpse's eye.

'Come and look.' He pointed at Danny's forearm. 'Covered in cuts. And the other one might be broken. See the funny angle. I wonder if he fought *very* hard.'

'Don't.'

The smell was already rising, spreading. Bloated torso, rotten gas. She could see patches of dark skin on an exposed shin-bone.

Lennie's feet moved forwards at Alexander's command, the undergrowth damp against her bare legs.

'How long does it take to drown, d'you think?' A narrow shaft of sunlight broke through the canopy and made a halo of Alexander's blond hair.

'You know what the Stride's like,' said Lennie. 'The current doesn't let go until it's done.'

She had seen the river's beginnings once: a cool burble of water high up on the moors, where the wind whipped the grass to the hillside and rocks broke through the thin pelt of the land. A lonely place where the only sound was the querulous baaing of sheep. She liked it up there though. It was easier to breathe. But how changeable it was, this coppery water, muscling into the neck of the valley, which fought back at the Stride, the narrowest point of the river, where the water raged and boiled at the constraint, and then plunged on, eating its way through the softer rock and the soil that lay beyond until its fury was finally spent here, in this glassy pool.

'You were still friends?' Alexander glanced up at her.

'Not since school. Hardly then really.' She thought of Danny Masters out front at the sawmill where he'd been apprenticed, a haze of gold rising up around him and settling in soft mounds, the air dry and faintly sweet with wood dust. 'I want to go home now.'

'See the skin on his face. You notice how it's loosened?'

He reached for her hand and pulled her down next to him, an audience with the dead.

Lennie held her breath as he traced the outline of Danny's cheekbone in the air.

'This whole lot's going to slip off like a glove soon. Like a model in reverse really. You can see why the ancient Greeks were fascinated by anatomy. Just a series of layers.'

She jerked her hand back. 'Stop it, Alexander! You can't talk like that when it's real.'

'Another day or two and his own mother wouldn't recognise him.'

A sudden pallor came over him and she wondered if he might be sick.

Someone was coming. She could hear the deep tones of Sam Bracegirdle, the hugely strong farmhand, and other voices too. Lennie slipped her hand from Alexander's and retreated back to the shelter of the wood, where evening was already gathering and the undergrowth rustled with life. Her brother was sure to return with the men and it would be better for him to think her safely back home.

Alexander twisted around from his hunkered position.

'By the way, Helena . . . '

'Ssssh.'

'Did I mention that you look like a dryad in that dress?'

Laughter, sharp like a fox bark.

She had not seen him so happy in days.

CHAPTER 2
Venetia, August 1955

Venetia was on her way from the stables when the men brought the stretcher to the Hall, the procession emerging from the wood and moving flat against the tree line like a panel from a stained-glass window. She saw and smelt the corpse as it arrived at the front of the Hall. The men drew to a juddering halt before her, their purpose fulfilled.

Two pieces of knowledge fixed themselves in her: that the small green car approaching the house was driven by Dr. Harrison—even with her eyes shut she could identify his inability to shift gear at the appropriate speed—the other that Danny Masters' mother must never see her son in this condition. Reverend Jones had been firm on that subject too, so that now, in the cottage that marked the far end of the village, Mrs. Masters could only stand over her son's sealed coffin and worry at the surface, repeatedly pawing the fresh wood as though trying to wear a path through it. It was just as well the lid had been screwed down.

Venetia sat in the best parlour chair beside a window that allowed in a small square of light. She sipped the tea that had been brought to her, thick with milk, and observed the theatre of loss playing out around her. Timid knocks came at the door, as though the dead might yet be disturbed; little collapses were followed by rallying; hot food arrived from a neighbour who did not want to intrude but still was pressed to stay. All these things she had borne witness to before, one version of grief very like another. Her presence constrained the mourners—all female apart from old Samuel Masters, Danny's grandfather, who sat like a wood carving to one side of the coffin—but that wasn't the point. She must fulfil her duties as Lady Richmond, and then leave the Reverend to it.

Her husband would have been better at this sort of thing. Having no particular affinity with women, even of her own class, Venetia had managed as best she could when Angus was away during the war, when bad news was never further away than an opening gate and a few short steps up a garden path. The women of the village would see Venetia and Reverend Jones coming and the screaming would begin before they had even reached the front door. It was as if they could not quite believe the telegram already sitting on their kitchen table until that point. The worst time had been Norah Ward, whose twin sons had been blown to pieces on an Atlantic convoy on the same day. All the tears in the world couldn't put them back together again.

At least Danny Masters could be boxed up properly. The candles at the head and foot of the coffin drooped and stretched on unseen currents. It occurred to Venetia that Danny might have worked on the long, straight planks of the coffin himself—a simple enough project for an apprentice, one supposed.

A thin-faced woman was speaking, a different version of Mrs. Masters, younger by a few years and uncrumpled by a mother's grief. The sister from Malton or somewhere that way.

' . . . what he was doing there in the first place,' she was saying, outrage in her voice. 'That river's always been dangerous . . . '

One or two sets of eyes slid daringly towards Venetia, as if responsibility for all of nature lay in her direction. Mrs. Masters, a midwife who had delivered so many of the village children into the world, stroked the coffin, a stream of silent tears running down her face. But what was the point of crying? Tears came and came and then went away and nothing changed because of them. They served no purpose, thought Venetia, but Mamie Masters would never be pretty again, that was certain. Widowed some years ago and now her only son was gone, loss leaching all the moisture out of her.

Venetia had known Danny better as a small boy, and even then only a little. She pictured him and Alexander on the river-bank, arms slung round one another as they leapt and waved to a Hurricane passing overhead, bare chests puny in the sun-light. She recalled a freckled, open face, smeared scarlet, as he, Thomas and Lennie ate bread and strawberry jam in the kitchens of Richmond Hall; whoops and shrieks coming from the woods on summer evenings; an alliance made possible by that unspoken democracy that exists among children, broken only when Alexander and Thomas had gone off to Prep School.

'It was an accident!'

Venetia jumped at Mrs. Masters' voice. She had missed some exchange, it seemed. 'He would never . . . Don't you *dare* say that in this house. Everyone one ends up in that bloody river. It should have been bloody concreted over years ago, I've *always* said it . . . !' Mamie Masters stared them all down through watery eyes, and then the strength went out of her again and she fell forwards, stretching herself over the coffin. 'Oh God!' Her hands trying to gain a purchase on the smooth wood. 'Christ, not my lovely lad.'

Venetia took the long route home, avoiding the Stride and the river path by cutting around the back of the village on a bridleway. She had no fear of the river—dead men's fingers grasping beneath its surface were childish fancies—but she had no great affection for it either. The horses tended to shy away from the roar of the Stride whenever she rode that way and she did not trouble to insist, allowing them to find their own way through the woods. The water was black and angry and ugly, and she would not seek it out by choice but you could not get rid of it. Energy like that would only find its way to the surface again. You had to find a way to live alongside it.

She crossed the water where the bridle path emerged from the woods, by a humped stone bridge that lay directly below the Hall. Stopping for a moment, her eye ran over the building and its grounds before her, a kind of mental housekeeping she undertook every time she approached this place that had been home to her since she was a young bride.

The sweep of sycamores lining the driveway promised grandeur, yet Richmond Hall was an unremarkable piece of architecture, designed by Vanbrugh but so lacking in baroque audacity that it was clear his patron must have imposed cata-strophic restrictions on his plans. The dark-sand walls of the main house were plainly built, with modest borders at their base and only a blue clock face and a cupola to add interest to the garden wing. Money to build the Hall had come from an ancestor who'd profited from the slave trade, and Angus once remarked that the house looked a little ashamed of itself, hid-den away at the far end of the valley, creeper pulled up over its walls and sills. But the land swelled here, opening out into a plateau, and Venetia, who never felt quite comfortable in the confines of the village, locked in its internecine troubles, always felt a sense of release on returning home.

Glass flashed as one of the French doors opened and Alexander stepped out onto the Great Lawn. Her son home at last, though he'd taken his time about it. *Time.* Time was what Mrs. Masters needed, the Reverend had said, a soothing recita-tion Venetia had heard many times over the years. He'd motioned to where Venetia sat, calmly drinking her tea, as if to demonstrate what time had done for her, Lady Richmond, *widow*, in just a few short months. Time would lessen the agony. Time and God's comfort. Well, Reverend Jones could gesture all he wanted but Venetia did not care for the Reverend's God, nor his comfort.

CHAPTER 3
Lennie, August 1955

How she loved him! Lennie broke off from weeding the vegetable patch at the front of Gatekeeper's Cottage to watch Alexander step out from the shadow of the Richmond Hall and cross the driveway, head bent. Was he thinking about her? Or was his mind fixed on Danny Masters, still caught up by the subject when everyone else had run out of answers? Coming across a body just like that, Alexander had said, cheeks flushing as if he had survived some threat to his person, as if death could rub off on the living. Lennie pushed the hoe beneath a dandelion, slicing through its fibrous roots. Well it couldn't. It mustn't. It had been another accident. A young man with everything to live for. Nearly everyone said so and yet the gossip. It would be better after tomorrow, once the funeral was out of the way.

She would know the shape of him, the particularity of his stride and the set of his shoulders from any distance. She was in love with the straight-limbed golden beauty of him. Like a poet she thought, though he cared more about old ruins than poetry. His name on her tongue: Alexander. Possessing him with her voice.

Something troubled the edge of her perfect picture: Lady Richmond crossing the stone bridge below the Hall, her spare frame elegant even now, as she moved with such purpose, one hand raised to greet her son. Lennie glanced down at herself, brushed her hands against her apron. The clayey soil had wedged beneath her fingernails and drawn the moisture from the backs of her hands, drying them to ploughed ridges. She should content herself with cutting flowers for the parlour, her father said, or tending the herb garden set out by her mother all those years ago. Woman's work. But she *liked* the heft of the spade or the hoe in her hand, the turn of the soil, loamy and pink with worms. There was something straightforward about the lines of vegetables, each plant knowing its purpose, earning its space and time in the earth. Not like her father's marigolds and petunias, buttoning up the earth in garish, useless splodges. They were a child's drawing, a bad attempt at nature, and she liked them only a little more when the wind, which blew constantly across the face of Gatekeeper's Cottage, gave them a straggly, desperate look. Lennie loved only woodland things—ferns unrolling exuberantly in springtime, bluebells, violent on the forest floor—and those plants must be left untouched.

She watched now as Alexander turned back across the driveway, hands deep in his pockets. Would he come to see her today? If only he had come home at the end of his college year when she expected him, as her brother, Thomas, had done. Not sent that tight little note to say he was travelling to Greece. It was still too painful for him here, she had told herself, with the churchyard so close, the spire of its squat tower just visible through the copper beech. Only Easter since his father had been lowered into the hard earth. A few short months to grieve. She waited for him, yes, but unhappiness of her own came bubbling up in that vacuum of time when there had been little to do but hang out the laundry or prepare supper for her father and Thomas.

Lennie pushed the hoe deep into the ground, so that it stood of its own accord, and then felt inside the collar of her dress for the ring: a silver band etched with an acanthus design.

'It's a traditional Greek pattern,' Alexander said, a few days after he'd arrived home. From the *continent*, her father said, speaking carefully as though such a word—such a place and all its inhabitants—was not to be trusted. 'Remarkably cheap,' Alexander teased. 'I bartered, of course.' She had strung it on a chain that once belonged to her mother, her fingers seeking its cold surface whenever she was alone, feeling the way it had been worked, trying to read it. Like a picture she'd once seen of a girl, upright at a desk and dressed in Victorian clothing, all ringlets and unseeing eyes, and fingers moving across a Braille pattern. She liked the way the design turned back in upon itself, like a secret or a lie.

Alexander must not have noticed his mother approaching. Just as Lady Richmond drew close, he turned towards the house and a moment later there was the glint of glass as a door closed behind him.

Home. He was home at last and the ring around her neck proved that she was his again. Such a good girl, everyone said. Kind, loyal, gentle Lennie. She was a good girl and his, and tomorrow Danny Masters would be lying in the quiet earth.

CHAPTER 4
Danny

He loved her alright though he couldn't say when it'd begun. They'd been kids together once, running wild in the woods and making up stories about the wounded soldiers who were taken up to Richmond Hall in ambulances, and he'd not paid her any attention, except to think Thomas Fairweather short-tempered with his little sister. He'd not cared much for Thomas back then, you never knew where you were with him, but Alexander had been a fine friend with his plays and his plans and his laughter.

Later it was that he noticed her, in the village schoolroom, high and echoey, after all the evacuees had gone home again, taking their accents and their Mickey Mouse gas masks with them and nobody all crammed in anymore. When Miss Price called 'Helena! Helena Fairweather?' Lennie would start, only then remembering who she was. Bridie Martin sat directly behind her and sometimes she would lean forward to make a braid of Lennie's hair, hands made deft and strong from milking her father's dairy cows each morning. The two girls must have been about ten years old then and not special friends as far as Danny could tell because Lennie never seemed to have friends in that way. He found himself drawn in by the sight of that pale fall of hair which seemed to shiver in Bridie's hands with a strange life of its own. He was in awe of the casual way that Bridie gathered it up without even asking and Lennie allowing it to happen, not even turning to see. A small white statue, shining in the cold light of the schoolroom.

CHAPTER 5
Venetia, August 1955

C an't see much point in opening to the public,' he said. 'Well, you won't be able to stop Fairweather giving his tours, so we might as well charge for them. And the rose garden, definitely. We might think about a farm shop too.'

Venetia had asked James, her brother-in-law, up to the office. It was the morning of her birthday and the household was busy with preparations for the party, which was to be held on Saturday. Venetia had been struck by a sudden anxiety to get other things settled too. James had come directly from the market in Malton, bringing with him an awful bouquet: stiff, hot-coloured blooms of the kind she despised. Thanking him, Venetia had jammed them into a vase and put them out of the way on the mantelpiece, but still they were there, insistent at the edge of her vision.

Both of them remained standing, neither willing to sit in Angus's old place behind the desk, or to take up his fountain pen which lay beside its wooden holder where he'd left it—like most things—almost put away. *My husband is dead.* It was hard to believe in the truth of that statement. The words might reach her lips, but they had no meaning.

'The rose garden's only worth seeing for a month or so in summer. And the farm looks after itself. Always has done.'

She felt the accusation. James had kept his side of the bargain. Why hadn't his brother done the same? Now was the not the time to point out the disparity in the weight of their responsibilities. The biggest problem James had faced since the war was holding onto the labourers on the estate's farm. So many of the men had come back to find they could not fit themselves back into their old lives. The brutal twist of war had severed their connection to the past.

But James knew about death duties well enough. Both he and Angus were long home from the war when their father, Laurence, or Sir Laurie as everyone called him, had died. The war years had seen the old man in his element, overseeing the transformation of the garden wing into a hospital, cheering up the wounded with tales of the Somme. The worst winter on record couldn't finish him off, by then he spent most of his time in his own quarters, but Venetia remembered him rallying sufficiently to get himself trussed up in a greatcoat and galoshes, and careering down a snow slide that the children had built at the edge of the lawn like some tremendous snow-plough, the children shrieking in terror and delight at the bottom. It was a news report about government plans for higher taxation that killed him. In a fit of rage he'd leapt up to turn off the television set and his great, bear-like heart had clapped to a halt. The thaw arrived in time to bury him three days later.

Things were so much worse now that her own husband was gone, thought Venetia: higher taxes and death duties on top of death duties. Did one have a duty to the dead? Surely it was enough to have fulfilled one's duty while they lived.

'But if it brings people here. We could build a nursery in the old barn and we might sell other things besides plants. The chickens produce more than we could ever need and not everyone keeps them these days.'

Strange that she cared about those creatures. Alexander had been terrified of the hens as a small boy, running from their red devil's eyes. But during Angus's last days they had taken her from a room, darkened, death sealed in, out into the blustery days of a too early spring. And she had looked forward to that walk to the pen each morning—nibs of green pushing relentlessly through the cold earth in the fields—waiting for the rush of clucking at her approach. Creatures depending on her to be alive. Life needing to go on.

If only she understood more. But Angus had gathered all their financial troubles to himself, and she was aware now, more than ever, of her shocking ignorance, her failure to address her lack of knowledge over the years. She would have to learn, though she was in the middle of her life and learning was for the young. If there had been a daughter she would have made sure that she was schooled, just like a boy. An education gave one armour and weapons against the world, the confidence to take a stand. To earn a living. Without it, a girl was always just that, no matter how old she grew, entirely dependent on others, vulnerable.

'We'll have to sell another piece of land.' She rose from the desk and crossed to the window, looked towards the woods. On the far side of the trees, where the village lay, was a semi-circle of land, like a bite mark. From where Venetia stood, it was just possible to see the rows of neat, new roofs that filled the space.

'The village has enough houses, I would have thought,' said James. 'It's not as though we had proper bombing.'

Once had been enough to leave its mark on little Starome. The villagers had thought themselves safe, tucked away beneath the lip of the North York Moors, well away from the coast, or any kind of industry, and the Canadian airbase a good few miles distant. That was until young Francis Pearson, a delivery boy, earned himself a special place in history by drinking six pints in Pickering one night and then driving home with his van lights on, leading a German bomber, bound for Middlesbrough, all the way to the little row of cottages that made up Starome High Street.

Maisie Pearson, Francis' eighty-seven-year-old grandmother, died of a heart attack when the bomb dropped, and the thatched roofs of the cottages generously shared the flames amongst themselves until one side of the High Street was ablaze, with only the unthatched schoolhouse remaining intact. The High Street had been rebuilt for the most part, the inn even rethatched, but people seemed to need more space after the war, bigger gardens too, and the new houses, built where the trees had been, formed a crescent behind the High Street and had been filled with young families.

Venetia could understand James' reluctance to add more. She had ridden every one of the bridle paths that threaded through the trees, had heard the crump of snow falling from boughs each winter and been caught in the carousel of leaves in autumn when the whole wood seemed to snap into life after the languid days of summer. And James was a farmer; everything was measured in land. But the woods belonged to everybody—the land on that side of the river had always been seen as common ground by the villagers. It was where their children learned to climb trees and build dens and the older boys took their girls when the time came, and neither Angus nor his father had ever shown an inclination to prove it otherwise until money became short

'People always need houses, James,' she said.

I sound like Marina, she thought, and she had to steady herself against the window pane.

That name from nowhere. Eyes, amphibious, watchful.

She waited for the old threat, twisting in the pit of her stomach.

But no. Marina was long gone, and she, Venetia, remained. Richmond Hall remained. Energy cannot be created or destroyed, she remembered. That was what Freddie, her eldest brother once told her, trying to lift her from the mire of her own ignorance. Energy just was. Her birthday party would take place, as always, and in the woods the ground would still spring beneath one's feet, years upon years of leaf fall, forever breaking down and renewing.

'Alexander ought to be here.' James frowned. 'These are his problems too now.'

'We've discussed that, I thought.' She started again, less brusquely. 'He's terribly young.'

'There were plenty younger during the war.'

Had he absorbed this northern bluntness over time? She did not remember James speaking in that way when they had first met, among the cool, palmate foliage of a conservatory, both of them catching breath from the crush of a country ball-room. She wondered when that boy with the dark, uncertain eyes, the sweet manner, had become this hard, fully grown, sat-urnine man. Too many years of working the land with sparse company, she thought. Or all those months in the deserts of North Africa where the light was too harsh for subtleties.

Well, she hated that kind of talk. As if young people now were to blame for the timing of their births. Venetia was just glad it was over, thinking of the ploughed-up lawn where the army vehicles had come, bringing all those poor, wounded boys to the makeshift hospital. She had helped the nurses all she could, learning as she went, and then filled the house with flowers after they had gone, ignoring the extravagance, driving that smell from the house. *Imagine it's your own husband,* one of the nurses had advised her in the early days, a strategy that was meant to make the most appalling tasks bearable, but Venetia did not hold with imagining. Besides, Angus had been very much alive, somewhere in the Arctic, where the waves froze as they crashed over the deck of his destroyer and the men grew shaggy beards for warmth.

'And once college finishes, he might be called up at any time, you know that. I don't imagine they'll do away with National Service before then.'

'Well, let's just hope he doesn't go mooching around the globe all over again. Especially if you reckon he and Lennie are courting.' James said. 'Everyone wanders off these days instead of staying where they belong.'

'He's just lost his father. What on earth do you expect?'

Her voice was sharper than she'd intended and James looked away. He was pale today and Venetia wondered if his leg was bothering him: that more tangible wound where white-hot shrapnel had seared sinew and bone. She must try to be kinder.

'We must let him work things out for himself,' she said, more gently.

'Yes. Sorry, my love.'

Love.

The word had been sitting in his mouth like a quiet stone. Years. It had taken his brother's death for him to dare speak it. Venetia had no taste for endearments and they certainly did not suit James. She could only guess what it meant to him to give voice to his feelings in such a way. How ridiculous that a man could wait half a lifetime to speak. The words no longer fitted him. She glanced down to the accounts books opened on the desk. 'What else is there?'

All week they'd been working, the older girls stitching headbands out of elastic covered with cotton and cutting eye masks from black card, with custard-yellow cardboard beaks stapled on. Yesterday, Miss Price mixed a tub of black dye, dipping old sheets into it and swooshing them around with the end of an old broom handle. The sheets were rinsed in a separate tub and draped out in the sun to dry. Miss Price took up her shears and cut each sheet into smaller squares with a hole at the centre, and then she popped a square over the heads of the littlest pupils. It was then the job of Bridie Martin, who was good with her hands, to cut the sheet again, this time into the shape of ragged wings. Up and down the schoolroom the little ones ran, flapping their arms and practising their best caws, while outside the older boys helped Jim Madgwick, Miss Price's fiancé, to stretch thick white canvas over the metal framework he'd built on the back of his truck, fixing it down at the bottom edges through loopholes that he'd punched through the fabric. The boys then strung Union Jack bunting all around the perimeter of the truck, which was more usually used for taking mangelwurzels to the livestock.

Now everything was ready. The truck stood outside the schoolhouse with the canvas rolled up on one side, and Miss Price and several of the older girls were passing up oval plates covered with tea towels, a stack of tablecloths, a basket of rattling crockery, a teapot and, last of all, an enormous kettle.

'Right towards the front please, Jim. So they don't get squashed. Has everyone their flags? Remember, we can't go back once we've set off!'

The small children were helped up and then the rest of the class clambered up and jostled for position. Miss Price counted heads, and put Mary Stockton in charge of the girls, Jackie Bracegirdle in charge of the boys, and climbed into the front seat of the truck, alongside Jim. The smell of petrol filled the fresh morning air as the engine started and they were on their way, waving to mothers and younger siblings who stood on doorsteps to see them off.

Lennie was in charge of little Dennis Dewsnap, who could be relied upon to turn bilious at the least motion, even on his Dad's tractor. The truck entered a tunnel of trees woven together over the lane and Danny, seated on the opposite side from Lennie—sick bag ready on her lap—turned his face up to the cool green leaves, the splintering light, and wondered if he would have a chance to talk to her today.

Not that long ago it was easy enough to speak to a girl without drawing attention to himself. Only last year, girls of his own age had been straightforward creatures—hopscotch and skipping at break times, chants rising and falling with the thwump of the rope: high, low, Dol-ly Pepper, white ankle-socks flying through the air. But now they turned fif-teen and had given up on playing and they stood around in huddles, shoulders slumped or pushed too far back, angry or friendly, eyes sliding towards the patch of field where the boys had played football or wrestled until their shirts hung open and their faces turned red, the mud baked to a crust, cracking open. How deep did the cracks go, Danny used to wonder, you might disappear down one until you reached the centre of the earth which was on the map on the class-room wall, a great orange yolk made of lava, boiling and pulsing, like the molten glass up at the glazier's where his uncle worked.

So girls were no longer to be counted on and he did not know where Lennie belonged in this new mystery, only that he was aware of her all the time, could feel her presence even when she wasn't in direct sight, a kind of heat spreading over his skin. There was nothing he could do about it, he had decided that some time ago, and yet there was a strange, jangled-up feeling about today, all of them crammed together like this in the back of the truck, the small ones frantically flapping their flags in one another's faces, the boys trying to get a rude song going, as if something out of the ordinary might be possible.

He'd have to be careful and not just for his own sake. Everyone knew that Lennie didn't quite belong to the village and that sort of thing mattered now that the evacuees were long gone and there were no POWs to throw stones at on the way home from school. The other girls were nice enough to her most of the time, but they could change their minds, especially the popular ones like Bridie and her gang, and there was no reason you could see or anything you could do about it. Even a lad could tell that. He watched Lennie even more closely on those days, for signs of sadness or anger, but she took the cold-shouldering for as long as it lasted and went her own way, wandering amongst the trees where the woods edged the playing field. Once he had thought she was crying, but when he came closer, she was singing to herself in the low and lovely voice he could always hear among the others when they were made to sing in class. Now, it wasn't just the girls he had to worry about. Lennie had something that made you look at her these days, whether you wanted to or not—but it was a strange kind of beauty she had, uncomfortable in a way that meant you could be mean about it if you had a mind to be.

In Helmsley, the church hall was packed. Even with the magnifier in place over the television set screen, it was hard to see what was happening. The little ones were restless, wanting their party food before it was time, and Miss Price had her work cut out, making sure they didn't embarrass themselves in front of the host school. Danny hadn't been much interested in the whole proceedings before, except as a distraction from lessons for the day. Miss Price had spent the last few weeks trying to cram their heads with facts about what was to happen and its place in history and although he knew that it was supposed to be big and important, it didn't seem to have much to do with his world. He'd been far more excited to hear the news announced that morning that Hillary and Sherpa Tenzing had reached the summit of Mount Everest. The school kids on the television screen were shouting and waving on either side of a street that was as wide as a field, but he couldn't share their excitement. He knew they weren't really grey, it was just the television that made them look like that, but it was how he imagined London to be and, come to think of it, there had definitely been a kind of grey look about the ones that'd turned up here in the war, as if the dirt and the bomb dust had been ground into their skins.

But the grandeur of it all got to him in the end. Once they showed you inside the Abbey with its great aisles and all those people processing. He'd never seen a building so enormous, though he'd been to York Minster on another school trip, felt he might fall backwards when he craned his head and stared up into the space of its central tower. There was something too about the young woman in the middle of everything today, that solitary figure, with her Snow White skin and her eyes all dark and serious. She had a steadfast look upon her face but Danny felt something swell in his chest. He wanted to protect her. He could not explain why, only that she looked alone and brave. Then the choir sang out:

'Zadok the Priest!

And Nathan the Prophet!'

And he felt his heart soar with pride and great hope for the new Queen.

The man on the television said: 'Then shall the orb and the cross be brought from the altar by the Dean of Westminster . . . ' and Danny thought it an odd way of speaking, the words as jumbled as the day itself. The room was overheating from too many bodies crammed in together and his attention began to drift again.

'How heavy it must feel,' said a voice next to him, and he saw that the crown was being lowered onto the Queen's head, and also that Lennie was right beside him. 'Imagine having no choice like that.'

He couldn't think of a sensible thing to say, but it didn't seem to matter. Lennie continued, staring intently at the screen. 'Everyone expecting so much and you didn't ask for any of it.'

'Maybe she should have stayed in Kenya.'

The King's death had been broken to Princess Elizabeth while she was in Africa, staying at a place called Treetops Hotel. None of them would forget because Miss Price had sent them home from school that day and the newspapers had been edged with black.

'With the elephants and leopards, you mean?' said Lennie, smiling in that slow, gentle way of hers. 'How lovely.'

The room was hotter than ever.

'She can do anything after this,' Danny said. 'Go wherever she wants, being Queen.'

'Yes, but they'll always find her now, won't they?'

The trestle tables were cleared away, plates washed, tablecloths folded, and then it was time to get the children into their costumes. In the adjacent street, someone had plugged a radiogram into the lamppost and dancing had already started. Bunting fluttered and flapped at every window as the wind picked up.

How gentle Lennie was with the little ones, never pulling or tugging at them or pinching at them to hurry as they put on their wings and beaks and patiently helping them back up onto the truck again. When everyone was in, Danny and Jackie Bracegirdle unfurled the cream canvas and spread it over the domed metal framework above their heads, while Jim Madgwick drew back the central section and tied it with several lengths of rope.

'Well, there may not be not four-and-twenty of 'em,' he said, jumping down beside Miss Price when he was done. 'But that's not a half-bad pie.'

'Quiet for now please, blackbirds! Smooth it down at the bottom!' said Miss Price who was, everyone could sense, becoming increasingly worked up. Robin Hood and his Merry Men, complete with an overstuffed Friar Tuck, had just passed the top of the street, and the rumour in the church hall had been that Hartsby school had got up a tremendous The-Old-Woman-Who-Lived-In-A-Shoe float. 'And can you roll the edges back a bit more too, so it looks more PASTRY-like? Watch out for the bunting though. Does everyone have their FLAGS?'

At last the little ones were all in their correct positions beneath the pie crust, and older ones took their places behind the float. A brass band passed the end of the road and then the truck thrummed into life, cloaking the older pupils in a bluish petrol haze, and set off towards the High Street, where they would join the coronation parade.

'This whole thing looks a mess before we've even started!' cried Miss Price, coming to an abrupt halt at the head of the procession. She was, Danny noticed, bright pink in the face now, the colour travelling all the way down her neck, to the V of her bosom. Damp semi-circles were spreading beneath the armpits of her blue, shirtwaister dress. 'All of you find someone to hold hands with please!'

The older classmates looked at one another in horror but their teacher was already moving along the procession and forcibly pairing them up.

Before she could reach him, Danny found his way to Lennie. She looked down at her hand in his, as if surprised to find it there, but made no attempt to withdraw it or to find an alternative partner.

'Thank you!' said Miss Price, approving the new tidier arrangements. 'Now blackbirds, TWEET!!'

The truck turned onto the High Street, slotting into a row of other floats and the fifteen or so Starome blackbirds poked their heads out of the rolled-back canvas and shrieked and cawed and flapped their sheeted wings at one another for all they were worth. In the chaos, Dennis Dewsnap's beak was broken in two and Milly Marwood was poked in the eye and promptly burst into tears. Just then the storm that had been threatening all morning broke with a great clap of thunder overhead, and a light but determined downpour began.

'Keep marching! Straight on,' said Miss Price. She had spotted the towering cardboard roof of the Hartsby school float up ahead, heard the cheering of the crowds. They marched and the rain began to thrum on the canvas pie-crust, as if some heavenly tap had been turned on. Onlookers lining the streets began to retreat into doorways, beneath shop awnings. Miss Price ran ahead of the procession and clambered up onto the truck, trying to do something about the poor show of soggy beaks and wailing, flapping wings going on inside. Just for a second, Danny thought he felt a pressure from Lennie's hand, a tightening against his. Another clap of thunder; another turn of the tap.

'Back beneath the canvas! Quickly now!' Miss Price said,

making herself heard above the rain, and the crying and the sullen rumble of the truck's engine. 'Everyone!'

The little ones did as they were told, just as a great tumble of rainwater freed itself from a fold at the top of the pie, slid down the canvas pastry and onto the heads of Miss Price and all the screeching little blackbirds within.

Danny was about to help but there was pressure on his hand again. No doubt about it now, and then Lennie was tugging at his arm, pulling him from the procession and into the straggle of stalwarts at the roadside sheltering themselves as best they could under a rag-tag sky of leaking umbrellas and dripping oilskins.

'Are you ill or something?' They had found their way to a clearer space at the back of the thinning crowd. Her hair was soaked to her scalp, dripping over her shoulders and down her back, like some lovely river creature. She shook her head. There was something in her eyes he didn't understand. She smiled and then she was gone, breaking into a run down a side street. He had to sprint to keep up with her.

There was a moment, sheltering under the trees by the bus stop, when he might have kissed her.

'Why did you leave?'

She shook her head. 'The noise and everyone marching together like that for no reason. Like some terrible rally.'

The bus rattled as it sped along the back roads to Starome. Sunlight had broken through the rainclouds and ahead of them the tarmac steamed. Lennie looked pale and worried.

'They'll be awful trouble, I expect.'

'We'll say that you twisted your ankle or something. That we lost everyone in the crowds. Don't worry.'

In bed that night, beneath the eaves, Danny told himself that it could have been anyone. She might have taken anyone's hand for the procession. But all he could think of was the pounding of their feet on the cobblestones, puddles that brimmed and bubbled like shallow cauldrons, and Lennie's laughter echoing down the narrow street like the call of a bird, high and wild. He pictured Hillary and Tenzing high above the rest of the world. They stood either side of a summit sharp as a pencil and topped with snow, its point so delicate that it could snap off at any moment, their footing so precarious that with one wrong move they might fall into thin air.

CHAPTER 7
Lennie, August 1955

I'm taking you out.' Alexander stood at the door of
Gatekeeper's Cottage. The car engine was still running
on the driveway behind him. 'Come on,' he urged,
'your father's up to his eyes in table plans up at the house with
mother. I've rarely seen him so ecstatic.'

Lennie looked down at herself. 'I'll need to change first.'

'Well do hurry. I'm starting to suffocate around here, what
with all the fuss about mother's party.'

Lennie thought she'd never seen anyone less in danger of
suffocating than Alexander, in his freshly-ironed clothing, a
cigarette resting between his lips and a sweater slung over his
shoulders, but she hurried upstairs anyway.

'I've champagne from the cellar!' he called after her. 'Half
the county'll be guzzling it on Saturday so we must be sure to
drink as much as we can.'

He drove them out of the village, turning north as they
reached the main road, and soon they were heading towards
the foot of the North York moors which swelled to a green
crest ahead of them, as though a great hand had ruffled the
earth's surface.

As well as the champagne, Alexander had charmed cold
chicken and a basket of apricots from the girls in the kitchen.
Sheltered by the heather that spread across the moors from
horizon to horizon, vibrating with the hum of bees, the two of
them stretched out on the bank of an icy stream. They ate and
then Alexander sunbathed with his eyes half-closed against the

high summer sun, while Lennie wriggled down the bank a little so that she might dabble her toes against the cold, round
pebbles on the bed of the stream.

It had been last Easter when it had begun, only a few short
months ago. Lennie had run up to the Hall in search of her
father in his workplace and come face-to-face with Alexander
instead. He was standing by the vestibule of the chapel at the
far end of the Hall, a gloomy corner even on the brightest of
days. He looked so sad and she wondered whether he had
been praying for his father, so recently buried, and how that
word sounded like itself, *buried,* all heaped-up darkness. But
Alexander did not believe in souls, he'd once told her, and she
felt embarrassed for him then, as if she had caught him in the
act of something dishonest. She turned to leave but he seized
her by the hand. She stood quite still while he lifted a lock of
her hair, gazing at it as though it were some entity altogether
separate from her.

'It's almost unreal in this light, Helena, this colour. You
must have Nordic blood in you.'

How he loved to look at her that springtime when honey-
dew dropped from the limes and the goslings were sulphurous
balls of new down, slithering down the river bank for the first
time, instinctively drawn to the great rush of water. She was a
Viking child, he said, a changeling, Artemis of the moon, a
fairy creature that had strayed from the woods. He invented
ever more ludicrous descriptions just to make her laugh, but
when, at last, he had kissed her, beneath a horse chestnut can-
dled with snowy blossom, its soft umbrellaed leaves sheltering
them, she had barely been able to breathe.

And then he returned to college and she didn't hear from
him until halfway through term. 'I need to see you.' His voice
echoing on the telephone line at the Hall, where she'd been
summoned to take the call. 'Your father's visiting Thomas and
you must come too.'

Her father fussed over train tickets and connections and room bookings, while Lennie, who had never travelled further than Leeds, gazed out of the window as the Cambridgeshire skies broke open above her, vast and blue. She felt herself becoming more and more insubstantial, as if she might dissolve into the wide air. Had she made a mistake, she wondered, leaving the safety of home where her pretty new dress had made her brave and real enough for anyone?

Thomas and Alexander met them at the station and Lennie's father was sent ahead to the little hotel on Parker's Piece where they were to stay. It was awkward at first—questions of bags and taxi fares—in a way that it had never been between the three of them before now. How much did Thomas know? She could not be sure, started to think she should not have come. Soon though, her brother had to go to his college to meet his tutor and Alexander grasped her by the hand and remade everything just for her. He took her for tea, and they walked along Trinity Street and King's Parade, stopping only briefly to talk to acquaintances of Alexander's who were, on the whole, perfectly ordinary young men, with only the occasional earnest, non-intimidating kind of girl wearing nothing as pretty as a cornflower-blue dress. On this rare warm day of early summer, Cambridge became his gift to her, a magical place of sunlit alleyways and enclosed worlds behind doorways, of secret gardens and the plash of green water beyond the meadows. A place, Lennie felt, where it was splendid to be young and lovely.

'It's different in winter,' said Alexander as they crossed Clare Bridge. 'The wind comes off the North Sea and straight over the Fens and you're never quite warm enough, even with the fire going all day long. It's still beautiful, of course, only more austere.' He sniffed. 'If you want pretty you go to Oxford.' They stopped on the apex of the bridge, looking down at the water, mild and green beneath them. 'I suppose I should take you punting. Everyone does at some point.' She merely nodded, not wanting to appear straightforward like other people but secretly longing to be taken. And it had been perfect, that hour they'd had upon the river, her head resting upon a cushion and Alexander standing above her, the sunlight behind him and the slender punt sliding forwards, noiseless in the quick shadows of the bridges. Fingers touched peeling varnish, the leaves of the weeping willows that grew along the river bank above; sun-dazzle, eyelashes, supple branches.

They moored near an inn and Alexander brought them beer to drink and lay beside her with his arm resting around her shoulders, his cigarette smoke drifting lazily in the sunshine. She smoked some of the cigarette too. When he kissed her they tasted of illicit things.

Only an irate porter could have marred that day, insisting on their return that Alexander had not signed out the craft in the correct manner.

'As far as I'm concerned, the punt's been stolen,' he said, jabbing at the log book and looking around the Porter's Lodge as if seeking witnesses to the crime. Lennie's instinct was to placate—the porter reminded her of her father, wanting everything to be in its right place—but Alexander was proud and she dreaded a row. To her relief, he spread his palms in mock-submission and walked away.

Later, he took her to the hotel. 'You're my girl now, Helena,' he said, kissing her fiercely. 'My good girl.'

CHAPTER 8
Venetia, 1932

'Escaping?'

The voice came from a window ledge behind a trio of palms, belonged, she saw, to a dark-haired boy she'd noticed earlier in the evening. Venetia smiled as if in agreement, though it was more that the ballroom was small and a little too crowded. Seeing glass and cool greenery on the far side of the hallway, she'd stepped out in this conservatory for a little air.

'It's like a big, hot coffin in there, isn't it? All that wood-panelling, I mean.' The boy stood, confirming what she'd spotted before: he was one of few there who could match her for height. 'James Richmond,' he said, offering his hand. 'I've been wanting to talk to you all evening—to tell you how elegant you look in that dress.'

He was neatly-built despite his height, and with a delicate edge to his features. Venetia had spent half the evening in the company of boys she'd known for years—nice enough in any other setting, but red-faced and boisterous tonight. She could hear shouting from the ballroom and it emphasised some gentle quality in her companion.

'My mother chose it.' Venetia pushed aside the fibrous palms and took a seat on the window ledge. 'I didn't particularly want to come.'

It wasn't quite a lie and it felt like a friendly thing to say, something that this James with the uncertain look in his eyes would like to hear. She had been riding all afternoon and it certainly had seemed a bother to bathe and change and have one's hair smoothed down and waved, but she liked the look of herself in the mirror once she was done, her brother Freddie clowning around beside her pretending to be an awestruck beau, and her other brothers coming in, curious to see how she had turned out. It was later, arriving at the McAndrews' hunting lodge which was lit up like a theatre, that she started to think she might have been better off staying at home.

In the ballroom, it was as if a script had been distributed to everyone but her; that some pre-rehearsed performance was underway. Girls she knew and secretly considered less attractive seemed to have transformed themselves in some way that wasn't just to do with their appearance. Something about this evening seemed to prevent even the perfectly sensible ones from holding a sustained thought in their heads, so caught up were they in being petite, appealing creatures, waiting to be swept around the ballroom like little dolls or adorable puppets. Venetia, even at seventeen tall and rangy, felt out of place. She did not want to be a giggling nothingness, she was almost certain of that, and so she held herself upright as her mother had taught her—it was no good slumping and slouching to make yourself appear smaller—and carried on in the normal way, but even the boys she knew seemed to have become over-excited by it all, too unfocused for any sensible exchange to occur.

'I hate parties too,' said James. 'I only came for the shoot. We're up from Yorkshire for the weekend.' He nodded toward the ballroom where the whooping had just increased as the music struck up again. Venetia had been less disappointed than puzzled by it all; she'd been asked to dance a respectable number of times, had done so graciously, yet being swung round the room by one of Freddie's schoolfriends a good five inches shorter than her, she had felt like a horse let loose in a field of sweetly-trotting Shetland ponies.

'Anyway, as I said, you look so elegant in that dress that I thought you deserved to have a wonderful evening. I hope you don't mind me saying. Do you read much? You look like the kind of girl who might.'

'A little', said Venetia, stretching her legs out in front of her. It felt rather nice, the cold wash of the moon on her skin, upon the white satin of her dress, knowing herself to be both elegant and bookish in appearance. 'I'm halfway through *Great Expectations* at the moment.'

Halfway was an exaggeration though she was definitely enjoying the story more than she'd expected to. She had taken the gold-embossed, hard-backed book from her mother's special collection with trepidation, begun turning the tissue-thin pages without enjoyment in the beginning, so afraid was she of damaging them or marking them in some way, or snapping the spine of that precious book, but the story began to absorb her. Between the pages she had found a pressed flower—perhaps a peony—that must have been there for years, though her mother when asked could not remember having placed it there nor what, if anything, it signified.

'Dickens is always fun,' nodded James. 'I've been trying some of the Modernists recently. They're turning everything that came before on its head.'

She chose not to admit her ignorance, though she didn't imagine he'd mind or try to lecture her in some tedious way. Modernists. She did not know that writers gathered themselves up like that, into named groups. She had thought that a writer sat at his own desk getting on with it.

'Would you fetch me something to drink perhaps?' she asked him. 'I think there was punch in the hallway. Oh!'

A little dachshund, barely more than a puppy, had been making its way around the ballroom all evening, getting perilously under people's feet during the dancing. Now it had found Venetia and was snuffling against her ankle. She lifted it up and onto her lap. It had toffee-coloured and black fur, and someone had tied a neat tartan bow around its neck.

She stroked the dachshund's velvety ears and he gazed up with at her with eyes like glossy pebbles.

'Of course, I should have—'

The palms parted for a young man carrying a bottle of champagne in one hand and a bouquet of glasses in the other. He set the glasses down on the window ledge. 'There you are,' he said to Venetia.

With James standing beside him, it was impossible to miss the family resemblance, though the elder boy was marginally plainer and had different colouring, hair goldish-brown. He had an open, good-humoured aspect, as if he found the world delightfully entertaining and it had responded thus far by returning the favour. He was, she noticed, an inch or so taller than James.

'This is Angus,' said James. 'My brother.' James seemed caught between staying and leaving. The delicacy she had noted in him seemed exacerbated by the arrival of his brother. 'I was about to fetch some punch for Venetia.'

'She's not to drink that filth.' The champagne bottle swung easily in Angus's hand, the cold breath of its contents unfurling like some lovely genie from the neck of the bottle.

'Look,' she said, scooping up the little dachshund from her lap and proffering it to Angus. 'Isn't he sweet?'

'It's a fucking runt,' said Angus, with a grimace.

Alexander said I was to come.'

Lennie held her father's gaze as she spoke, though she could see his agitation already rising.

'The invitations went out at the end of July,' said Peter Fairweather. 'That was late as it was.'

Of all the objections Lennie had countered in her mind—*too young, what would she wear*—this one had failed to occur to her. Alexander wanted her at his mother's birthday party. It would never have crossed his mind that she would need to be invited formally.

'Should I ask him to speak to Lady Richmond?'

Her father shook his head in confusion, this suggestion not fitting any code of behaviour that he understood.

'Thomas is going.' Lennie looked in despair to her brother who sat over his newspaper at the kitchen table, head resting on one hand. 'He goes every year.'

'Exactly.' Peter Fairweather was not an unkind man, but any sympathy he might have felt for his daughter's distress was overridden by certainty on this point of etiquette. 'Thomas is expected. It was very kind of Alexander to think of asking you but you can't simply invite yourself.'

'That's not—'

'People would wonder what you were doing there, you see.'

'Why should anyone care?'

'Apart from anything else, I've just finalised the table plans. Johanna was supposed to be seeing to them, but I gave up on

that when she couldn't grasp the idea that the Wagstaffs mustn't
be seated anywhere near the Marshall-Joneses . . . '

When Alexander had first mentioned the party, Lennie
panicked, not daring to ask what she was to wear and must she
dance, what she should say to all those strangers. Only now it
was not to be and her fear changed shape into something dull
and heavy in the pit of her stomach. The world was suddenly
grey with nothing in it to make the blood pound in her young
heart. She watched her father as he combed back his hair in
neat military style, then stooped to rub a spot from the tip of
his shoe. How silly of her to question him when he was about
to leave for work at the Hall and at his most correct.

'Please father,' she tried again. 'I don't want to cause any
bother to Lady Richmond or you . . . '

'Oh for Christ's sake, Lennie!' Her brother flung his newspaper across the table and pushed his fingers into the dark mess
of his hair. 'I'm trying to read! Look, you can't turn up without
an invitation. It's bad form. Alexander jolly well knows.'

'Don't upset your brother,' their father would say, even
when Thomas was small and raging at some minor injustice—
a broken toy, the last of his sweet ration—and Lennie, smaller
still, would try by turns to placate him or to make herself invisible because Thomas's feelings were bigger and more important than anyone else's. It was the Italian in him, people said;
on his mother's side. Made you wild and volatile, apparently, a
volcano that might explode at any moment. Lennie did not
understand this. There were Italian POWs on the estate farm,
small and wiry with voices that rose and fell like gentle songs.
They waved and smiled as she passed them on her way home
from school. Still she lived in thrall to her brother's moods.
You never knew which Thomas you might get, one moment
tripping up the stairs full of sunshine, only to return with a
devil on his shoulder, spreading his displeasure into every corner of their tiny cottage.

Their father long ago gave up power to his son, could only sue for peace.

'Please, Thomas, you'll make yourself ill,' though it was he who turned white and sick-looking at every explosion. Lennie would try to reassure their father, pat his arm or clear away the tea things as tidily as possible.

Once when they were small, Thomas was screaming at their father, tugging at his arm while they stood in line at the green-grocer's stall at Helmsley market. Lennie remembered it because the other ladies in the queue looked cross and she did not like the feeling it gave her.

'Lost his mother, poor little lad,' said a voice behind them. She turned to look. The lady who had spoken had a nice, tired-looking face. She smiled down at Lennie in a kind way. Lennie felt an understanding passing between them, knew then that it was her job to make Thomas feel better about everything.

Occasionally her brother co-opted her as an ally. On his seventh birthday Thomas decided to leave home and Lennie was summoned to his room to pack his case. She promised to bring him food each day, to the woods where he intended to build a house of his own to live. For the most part though, he thought her young and silly and only barely to be tolerated. She would tag along anyway, following him and Alexander when they went to sail their toy boats on the river.

'Take you straight down to the bottom,' Thomas teased, pretending to teeter on the edge of the forbidden Stride, that point on the river where the water was most dangerous, though the distance he kept was safe enough. 'And then the crabs eat your eyes out.'

'Crabs live in the sea,' she said, though she'd never been.

'Don't be so stupid, Len. There are freshwater crabs.'

'Not in this country though.' Danny Masters said that, joining them with his own boat to sail, a fine vessel that his dead father had made him.

Sir Angus insisted on paying for Thomas's education and he went off to prep school without thanks or complaint, seeming only a little subdued on his first trip home. There had been that incident with a boy in the year above him, a bully and a frightful snob according to Alexander. The elder boy had only got what was coming to him. Nevertheless, there was trouble with the boy's parents because Thomas had beaten him badly, breaking his nose and knocking out a front tooth.

Thankfully, it proved to be an isolated incident. Thomas excelled on the sports field and his clever, restless mind impressed his teachers, later gaining him a place at Cambridge.

Lennie remembered his first Christmas home from university. Thomas came across their father helping Sir Angus to remove his riding boots after the Boxing Day hunt.

'Down on his knees in the mud and happy with it!' he shouted, bursting into the cottage.

Lennie tried to soothe him. Father thought the world of Sir Angus. They all did. She begged him not to cause a row. He just glared at her in pity and anger.

'It's a different world now, Lennie. People should question things.'

The universe was made up of two types of people, Lennie thought: those who wanted to smash things to pieces and those who wanted to keep the world just as it was. Implacable, opposed forces, like the rocky banks at the Stride, the twisting iron-dark water trying to find a path between.

A lexander was sitting at the very edge of the salon in a posture of solitude. Venetia had a sudden urge to slap him. The thought of how scandalised everyone would be amused her. Alexander had never been punished, even as a child—Angus had insisted that he had seen too much violence in his lifetime to inflict any on his only son. Yet Venetia's own father had administered regular beatings to her four brothers, who had seemingly borne the punishments equally enough. Sometimes she wondered whether Angus's way had been a mistake. Perhaps it didn't always do to be so sensitive. Her son had always abhorred physical engagement, loathing the cheerful brutality of the rugby field and absenting himself as often as possible. Lucky then that he'd had charm, and a gift for mimicry that edged close enough to cruelty to satisfy the impulses of the most barbarous of schoolboys, gifts that had earned him popularity and the leading role in practically every school play. How very talented, other mothers would say, voices a little shrill with envy. *So funny.*

There were no signs of any such antic behaviour tonight.

Venetia allowed her glass to be refilled a little and readied herself for the next tranche of guests, observing first the Middlethorpe sisters and then Annie Faversham, the most handsome girl in the room, trying to engage Alexander. When even Annie's face lost its customary animation, Venetia gave up watching. Sometimes it was difficult to know the difference between sensitivity and self-absorption.

'Everything all right?' James asked, appearing suddenly beside her. Her brother-in-law was fiddling with his collar and she knew he was worrying that people would think there was something unseemly in this year's celebration when Angus's wake had taken place in this very room only months ago. Continuity had to mean something though. There *was* nothing else. Besides, James always looked uncomfortable in a formal setting, even here in his childhood home. He'd have been happier, she imagined, down at the Black Swan, discussing grain prices or debating the merits of some new farming practice.

The Markhams, nearest neighbours to Richmond Hall, descended upon her.

'So brave,' Caroline Markham said, or something like that, and Venetia bent her head in thanks and to hide a moment of confusion. For a second she'd imagined Lady Markham was referring to the death of Danny Masters, not to that of her late husband. The poor boy's death had upset everything again, just as Venetia was beginning to feel steady. All the more reason to follow the ways she knew, the old routine that gave her a sense of purpose and comfort. For the next hour or so, Venetia focussed on her guests, joining and then extricating herself from the various groupings around the salon. Everything was as it should be, separate voices swelling and homogenising into a pleasant rumble of humanity, the chandeliers swaying and glittering in the rising heat.

She could tell by the way he moved, stiffly upright as he made his way to the drinks table, that Alexander was drinking heavily. It would have been better if Lennie had been here beside him, but Fairweather's silly pedantry had put paid to that.

'What does he want, something in copperplate?' Alexander had snapped. She'd promised to intervene, but he rejected the offer: 'Oh what's it matter? It'll be hellishly dull anyway. I don't know why we're even bothering this year.' And after that he seemed to lose all interest in the idea.

Venetia wondered where Peter Fairweather thought his daughter belonged, when the villagers were beneath her but he deemed her too unformed, too naive for smart company. At home in the cottage, making soup for him, she suspected. If only Fairweather would allow the girl some kind of life.

Last year there had been talk about a typing course. Fairweather had at first resisted, only relenting because another girl from the village was thinking of going. But then Lennie had fallen ill at the wrong time and that, it appeared, was that. Venetia's own father hadn't seen the point of educating girls either, but something—perhaps it was Scottish winters and the harsh certainties of farm life—had hardened her for adulthood. Lennie, who'd lived all her life in the clutch of the valley, was still an innocent.

'Venetia, should I say something?' James was by her side again, the faint warmth of farmyard still on him despite his newly-washed and combed hair. He was still nervous and evening dress sat oddly on his frame, as if it knew it didn't belong there. 'Most people are here now and I'd rather not wait longer.'

'Angus always spoke just before dinner was called,' she said. 'That's what we'll do.'

Annie Faversham was persistent. She had hold of Alexander's arm now, preventing him from leaving her side. Venetia half-pitied her, knowing her son as she did. Alexander could be charming when he chose to be, might appear to give you all his attention, until something else distracted him and the next moment he'd be gone. But then Lennie had grown so luminous and Venetia had become easy in herself. For all her ethereal appearance, Lennie was rooted here. She had been exactly what Alexander needed to help him through those first raw weeks after Angus had died. The thought of the two of them gave her comfort: a pathway into the future, more important than grief or loss or all those tedious intricacies of self. The girl would have to learn a great deal, as she herself had done when she'd first arrived at Richmond Hall, barely a few years older than Lennie now. By observing, and pretending courage until it became real. Venetia remembered what it was like to have awkward teenage limbs and a tremor in one's voice and yet earn a reputation for poise, coolness even. And it had served her well. She had restored this salon meticulously: duck-egg walls, graceful swags of plasterwork, the great fireplaces at either flank, the gorgeous soft colours of the ceiling, painted like so many Chinese parasols, the frieze with Dido and Aeneas and all the other paintings of antiquity glowing in the lamplight. It was hers for now; she had made it so, and yet if Lennie and Alexander were to marry, how content she would be to slip into the background.

The sound of a glass being struck. James, standing by the lower fireplace, had called for silence. A speech. Happy birthday. Difficult times. Also time to celebrate: welcome home to Alexander, the future, new plans.

She didn't care for the beard. Like an apology. Something to hide behind. Better without it, especially since his handsomeness was of the subtle type. Poor James. Always in the shadows.

'Congratulations, mother.'

Alexander had steered his way towards her during the speech. He stumbled now, causing elderly Lord Markham to spill his wine.

'Careful.' She reached for him but he stepped back, pulling himself up with the dignity of the very drunk. She sensed the attention of those standing nearby.

He spread his palms in mock dismay.

'I'm awfully sorry Lennie couldn't come,' she said. 'It simply didn't occur to me when we were writing—'

'Just as well. Wouldn't have wanted this lot pawing at her.'

She tried for a neutral topic.

'I've heard next to nothing about your Greek trip since you've been home.'

'What's to tell? Just different piles of rubble left by different people. Nothing that would interest you.'

'I rather thought that was the point of Greece. Ancient history.' She smiled. 'Have you thanked your uncle? He organised all this when everything was still so . . . ' She gestured to the room, to James still hot in the face from his speech. She ought to have asked Alexander first. She saw that now. But Angus dying had shaken everything up and even now she had to concentrate hard to work out how the pieces had fallen. Alexander would not have wanted to play host, she was almost sure of it, yet she realised that she had made an error of judgement.

'*Thanked* him?'

'These parties don't just happen, though of course Fairweather did a great deal . . . ' The look in his eye at the mention of Lennie's father stopped her. She didn't want that conversation right now. 'Let's go into dinner and do try to be cheerful. We have to carry on, Alexander. Somehow.'

'We do?' Behind the defiance, she saw uncertainty in his eyes. Give *me* your suffering, she wanted to say. I am capable of anything now.

'Your father would have expected it. You know that.'

Laughter, spiritless.

'Not sure he has an opinion on the matter, mother. Poor bastard'll be spitting maggots right now.'

CHAPTER 11
Lennie, August 1955

Music drifted through the kitchen window as Lennie cleared away the dishes and her eye was inevitably drawn up to the Hall. It was a still and humid night, the afternoon breeze having sunk like a stone as the sun slid towards the ridge. She imagined the doors of the salon would be opened out onto the Great Lawn in order to let in the evening air. She went to the dresser and took out her sewing basket, remembering a sheet that needed re-hemming. It was dull work for a dull evening and she welcomed it, anything to stop her thinking of the cars that had been passing by the cottage since early evening, snapshots of lace and satin, of expectant faces.

'That was the Terrington girls,' her father said from the doorway, about to leave. 'Their father's a general, you know.'

Every Friday night after supper, Peter Fairweather polished his shoes to a mirror shine, combed back his hair, and walked along the river path to the village inn, the Black Swan, where he would drink three pints of beer spread out over a space of three hours, before returning home.

'It goes down well with the chaps,' he would say, thinking of a war hero he'd read about, whose habit of hunkering down with his men in all circumstances had made him popular. Such nods towards egalitarianism were in vain: Sir Angus had been welcome at the inn any time he chose to drop by, with his affable manner and easy humour, but the men who laboured around the Hall resented the intrusion of one who felt his marginal superiority so keenly. Her father's presence made them uneasy, as if they were still being watched, judged, during the few hours of the day when they were not in thrall to the estate.

'You won't be missing anything, Len,' said Thomas, wrists held out so that she could fasten the cuffs of his dress-shirt. He sounded weary, as if she had insisted otherwise. 'The place'll be full of the usual set, quite sure of their own importance and not an interesting thought between them. I won't be staying for any longer than I have to.' Thomas glanced down at the sewing basket which she'd set on the table in readiness. 'At least persuade Father to buy a television set.'

His voice was gruff but it felt like an apology for something.

'You'll be home soon then?'

She was often alone in the cottage, but tonight there was some uneasiness inside her, wanting to come to the surface. She could feel it prickling beneath her skin.

Thomas shook his head.

'Jamie Markham's a poker night set up at his, so I'm heading over. Hopefully I'll grab a lift home with Alexander, if I can persuade him to escape too. Otherwise I'll be back in the morning.' He looked at her. 'I gather father's still in the dark about you two. I must say I was surprised you didn't speak up when he was blathering on about Annie Faversham. You're going to have to get a bit of backbone about it at some point, you know.' He drew together his dark brows. 'It'll send him into a panic, of course—one more thing to fret about. It *is* still going on, I presume . . . ?' said Thomas.

Lennie's instinct was for secrecy, not wanting to sully a thing so delicate by clumsy words or by exposing it to the commonplace. At the outset, she had liked the separateness of it all, but now she felt less sure of herself. 'You're my girl,' Alexander said, and yet how quickly he had forgotten about wanting her by his side at tonight's party, the Salon a whole world that barely knew of her existence. Everything had become complicated, turning back in upon itself like the pattern on the ring he'd bought her. She wished it was still springtime, when the cow parsley swayed in the hedgerows and everything was new.

'Yes.'

Her brother had grown taller since Easter, she'd noticed, so much so that he must duck his head to prevent it grazing the door jamb when he entered the cottage. With his height and the explosion of dark curls inherited from their mother, it was hard to believe the two of them were related.

Thomas gave a sigh of exasperation. 'Well, he really ought to have sorted a bloody invitation for you then. If nothing else, to shut father up.'

His words seemed to acknowledge and negate something in the same instance. Lennie felt the situation had provided him with a useful yet minor point in some greater argument.

'Anyone would think you and Alexander weren't friends.' she said.

It was a ridiculous thought, after all these years of the three of them growing up side by side, but something was out of kilter.

He frowned in the way he did when working through some philosophical problem.

'That's not what I'm talking about. Look Len, I know he's lost his father but I just reckon Alexander's been odd recently. All that stuff about Danny Masters, for instance. And yet they were thick as thieves as kids.' Thomas hesitated, as though deciding whether to continue. 'I don't much like the way he behaves around girls.'

'What do you mean?' She tensed.

'Oh, I don't know, Len.' Thomas said, as if aggravated by her failure to grasp by instinct what he meant. 'He's very charming when he wants to be but somehow people end up unhappy and he's quite untouched by any of it. At college, I mean.'

Because he loves me!

She forgave her brother for his stupid cleverness; he was only trying to protect her. She had sometimes wondered about Thomas himself when it came to girls: there was never any mention of anyone at Cambridge. It was clearer now though: either he didn't yet understand about love, or he was jealous of Alexander's easy charm.

'I should speak to him,' Thomas said. 'Make sure he's serious.'

'No, I don't want that!' The bulk of her brother suddenly seemed to fill the small room, leaving no space to breathe. 'Tom, you must promise not to.'

Thomas had already moved on. 'Well, it'd be a fine thing for Annie Faversham and the county lot if you *were* to end up marrying. They wouldn't be quite so pleased with themselves then.'

He grinned at his own joke, while Lennie wondered if it was quite right to mock the local gentry when he planned to enjoy the hospitality at Markham House that very evening. Thomas brushed down his jacket with a last irritated flick of the wrists. 'Anyway, you don't want to go making a fool of yourself, Len, that's all.'

The light was beginning to fade. She would have to move to the armchair and switch on the lamp to continue her work. She went to the door, telling herself it was only to breathe the evening air. Light spilled from the entrance to the Hall until it was absorbed by the black-green shadows, while the house itself was almost in silhouette against a violent child's scrawl of a sunset, the trees paper cut-outs strung across the ridge. Laughter from somewhere. She reached inside her collar but the ring was just cold metal patterned in a way she did not understand. *I'll take you there*, Alexander had said, to places where the villagers would marvel at her pale hair, clutch at talismans to ward off the evil eye. A land of temples and vases and sails, and she could almost imagine herself there, bare rock, tense blue light and the sea echoing in hollow chambers beneath her feet. How real everything would feel with her beside him, he had said, yet tonight the world seemed to deny her existence. The rooms of Gatekeeper's Cottage were quaint and beautifully appointed—Lady Richmond herself had overseen the refurbishment when Lennie's parents had moved down from the Hall—but she had come to hate the way they closed in on her when she was alone.

The Favershams' eldest has her eye on him, her father had said. It couldn't be true. Or it was, but Alexander wouldn't care about it. Besides, most of those girls weren't that pretty if you took away the tulle and lipstick. Lennie had never been admired beneath glittering chandeliers, but she knew. The young men in the village stared now, even those who'd known her all her life, and there were crude words whispered between them that excited and repelled her all at the same time.

Girls like the Favershams possessed a confidence that came from knowing where they belonged and what they were for. Since she'd left school the previous summer, Lennie had felt less tethered to the world, just the empty space of each day to fill with domestic chores. Sometimes she felt as if she'd been cast adrift and might float away altogether. Often, she thought that everything would have been better had she been able to start the typing course last September. She hadn't the least interest in secretarial work, but she'd liked the idea of travelling to York on the train each day. She would have worn her smartest clothes and, though she was only going to the college and not to an office, people would have thought her a woman of purpose, expected somewhere. Miss Price said the course would 'open doors.' Lennie had no notion of what might lie beyond those doors—anything was better than long, blank days at home in the cottage.

Joan Nicholson, who was taking the course, was going to look for a room to rent in York, or even Leeds. There were big offices in those cities where you could start at the bottom and make yourself useful and in time you would 'progress.' Progress had no shape in Lennie's mind but she liked the sound of it, the way it stretched itself into the future.

'It's just a typing course,' Thomas said, wondering at her excitement, but Lennie, imagining the possibilities, felt as if she'd just awoken after months of sleep, her body and mind alert in a startling way, feeling herself more capable before she'd even started.

Such new skills could be put to use up at the Hall, her father supposed. Lennie could help him with correspondence from time to time, releasing him from the task of writing everything longhand. That, at least, would be fitting and it was the best outcome he could hope for, though truthfully he would have preferred her not to work at all. Peter Fairweather was proud that his living provided for them, saw no need for his daughter to have to sit in some dreary typing pool from dawn till dusk. She was not a city girl like her mother had been, more than capable of seeing off any difficulties or unwanted attention to which a girl in such a situation might be exposed. Lennie was an innocent.

None of it mattered in the end—the day before enrolment she came down with scarlet fever and Joan disappeared into a new life without her. It took Lennie longer to recover than expected, some kind of fatigue setting in afterwards which Dr. Harrison thought viral, and by the time Christmas came and went and they saw in 1955, her father decided against the plan, thinking her too weak to travel on a train full of strangers. With spring approaching, Lennie wandered restlessly through the woods in the long hours after her chores were done, wondering if she might pluck up the courage to ask Lady Richmond for support, but Sir Angus was ill by then and soon that was taking up everyone's time. Sir Angus had passed away at Easter. In the midst of that another door opened. The empty days were delightful to her then, full of Alexander's voice, the touch of his arm against hers as they walked by the river.

It was pointless to think any more about that time. Thomas had made her see the obvious: she could never compete with those girls who travelled to London to buy their clothes each season, not now or in the future, and everyone would despise her for thinking otherwise. A different tune on the breeze, a lighter tempo. Lennie came away from the door with a choke of despair in her young throat. Her father was right—Alexander would marry the hateful girl with the vulgar red mouth who had seemed to be laughing right at her from the window of the Favershams' car as it had passed through the gate earlier that evening.

Another car passed by, the occupants oblivious to her existence. None of it mattered but she would put on her cornflower frock anyway in case, by some chance, Alexander tired of the party and came looking for her. It wouldn't do for him to find her looking dowdy and crushed by his absence. Leaving the lamp unlit, Lennie put away her mending and climbed the narrow wooden stairs that bisected the cottage. At the head of the stairs, where the boards creaked once, and then again, she paused for a moment. Just there, on the threshold of the little room that had been hers since childhood, Lennie changed her mind.

CHAPTER 12
Danny, June 1954

Everything was different now that school was coming to an end.

It was a spring day that felt more like summer and the whole class was fidgety—something to do with being alive and young when other folk weren't. A breeze came in through the high windows of the schoolroom and played with the edges of exercise books, the pile of paintings from the lower school that Miss Price had stacked upon her desk, while outside, bees fumbled against the glass, all heavy with pollen, and young birds shrieked from their nests, raw mouths turned to a sky that was cloudless and high and made you restless in your skin. The scratch of chalk on blackboard seemed drier and more pointless than ever to those of them who were almost ready to escape the classroom. All that morning Jackie Bracegirdle and Mary Stockton had whispered in the back row, passing notes back and forth. The two of them were courting and then some if the rumours were right, though neither of them would admit the other stuff. But you could tell, and they'd been seen going off to the woods together and coming back with that look about them. Jackie was almost six foot tall and barrel-chested now, just like his brothers and his father, and looked a sight, all limbs exploding from behind his child-sized desk. Mary had heavy breasts and pink skin and everyone said she was pretty, but Danny always thought her more animal than girl, all healthful and burgeoning, like the sows on her father's farm. Last week, Miss Price had caned Jack for carrying on in class with Mary and the class had said how Miss Price had enjoyed it, Jack towering over her as she brought down the cane upon his great hand with such force that she was breathless and all flushed around the neck by the time she'd finished.

This was the last ever term of school for Danny. He'd already been the eldest in the school when he persuaded his baffled mam to let him carry on another year, instead of leaving at fifteen as you could. That was just because Lennie was staying on too. The lads all were keen to be out the door, to the fields or the forge or the baker's yard, anywhere there was proper work, man's work, instead of soft book learning that was no use to them. And anyone could see it was time, with their hands too big to hold a pencil properly, knees hitting desks and legs and arms sprawled. Before they knew it, they'd be called up for their National Service, and though they complained about it, that proved that they were almost men. By the end of each day the schoolroom was thick with the smell of them, all crammed in.

Most of the girls were to stay in the village, though a couple of them were off to the Rowntrees factory in York, where you could work inside all day long and still earn a decent wage, while Joan Nicholson, the cleverest girl in the class, was to train as a shorthand typist and then try for work at a bank or a law firm. Lennie seemed to have no plans at all. She just shook her head on the one occasion anyone enquired, though Danny did overhear her telling Joan that her father didn't like the idea of her working outside of the house.

Danny was to be apprenticed to the sawmill, just like his Dad had been. His mam had fixed it with the new foreman without even asking, and there wasn't any point in arguing when it was as good a way to earn a living as any, but he dreaded the day when school would finish because that would be that. Lennie would be expected to do something up at the Hall, where her old man worked for the family, and he'd not see her after that, not properly and, being the oldest boy in the year, he would likely get his call-up before anyone else and then he'd be away for months at a time.

A poem, Miss Price had said to the upper year. Anything at all, and everyone had groaned because poetry was daft and for girls and anyone would feel stupid, having to stand up and read something out in front of the whole class. Danny had been away from school the day the homework was set, helping with the lambing on his cousin's farm in Hartsby, so had escaped the task itself. It was bad enough though, watching his classmates file up one by one to stumble through some limerick or other, trying to get their words finished before they'd even started them, and Mary Stockton turning scarlet as she began: 'My love is like a red, red rose,' and everyone looking at Jack and smirking.

'Thank you, Mary,' said Miss Price. 'Lennie? Do you have something for us?

Danny swivelled in his chair and stared around the classroom, daring anyone to say a word. There was no sniggering as Lennie walked to the front, though. Lennie was calm and pale and not the sort a lad could tease even if they wanted to. She was too queenly for that. Either she wouldn't notice you doing it, or it would not matter to her.

'The Lady of Shalott,' she said, when she reached the front of the classroom.

Miss Price nodded her approval, explaining to the rest of the class: 'Alfred, Lord Tennyson,' as if that meant anything.

Lennie set down a book on the desk in front of her. Danny could see, from its shiny plastic cover and the label on its spine, that it was from the school library, which consisted of a bookcase with five shelves in the entrance to the school building. Lennie folded her hands together, long and white like a saint's, and began:

'On either side the river lie

Long fields of barley and of rye,
That clothe the wold and meet the sky;
And thro' the field the road runs by
 To many-tower'd Camelot';

Her voice was low and clear, and there was no other sound in the schoolroom.

'Willows whiten, aspens shiver.
The sunbeam showers break and quiver
In the stream that runneth ever
By the island in the river
 Flowing down to Camelot.
Four gray walls, and four gray towers
Overlook a space of flowers,
And the silent isle imbowers
 The Lady of Shalott.'

Danny felt his chest swelling with something like pride, though that made no sense. For one awful moment he thought he might cry.

Beneath the moon, the reaper weary
Listening whispers, ' 'Tis the fairy,
 Lady of Shalott.'

He would have placed bets on someone laughing at the word 'fairy' when it was bad enough having to listen to poetry in the first place, but the room remained still.

No time hath she to sport and play:
A charmed web she weaves alway.
A curse is on her, if she stay

Her weaving, either night or day,
*   To look down to Camelot.*
She knows not what the curse may be;
Therefore she weaveth steadily,
Therefore no other care hath she,
*   The Lady of Shalott.*

Her gaze was fixed over his head as she told the tale of an imprisonment, of an empty life and it seemed to Danny's youthful soul that she must be telling the story of her own future.

I'm half sick of shadows!

Lennie pronounced these words with a sudden vehemence that made Danny jump, and in that moment he knew that he must find a way to rescue Lennie Fairweather from the life which others had mapped out for her.

T he door unlocked with a singular jiggle and a grate of metal. No workaday clothes here. Had her father got rid of them or put them away in some corner of the attic? Here were fabrics that shone and slipped over your fingers; a fox stole curled in upon its hanger as if asleep; a little lace jacket, pale green and delicate as a web. She had come here often as a young girl, not in search of the shape of a mother she could not remember, but in play, the wardrobe as dressing-up box.

The last time she had taken that particular dress from its place in the wardrobe—it must have been at least a year ago—it had been wide of her frame by several inches and the precise cut of its lines had hung off her body in an unstructured mess. How young she'd looked. It had made her cross with herself: a silly, Russian doll version of a woman. The other dresses were pretty but made of flimsy, flyaway fabrics that clung to her skin. The silver gown was different. As she stepped into it, feeling the cool material against her bare skin, Lennie wondered again how her mother could have afforded such a dress, a long, heavy, sweeping skirt and a halter neck. Desperately old-fashioned, she feared. Today everyone was wearing short dresses with starched petticoats beneath the skirts, and tight bodices. This dress must have been bought or made well before the war, in imitation of some Hollywood movie star's perhaps.

It was beautiful. She knew that much even before she checked her reflection. She had grown and the dress now fitted her perfectly, dipping between her small breasts and clinging to her torso and hipbones, before it fell in fluted lines to the floor. Like a column from a temple, she thought, lifting her hair from her shoulders and standing on tiptoe to look at herself in the octagonal mirror on the inside of the wardrobe door. A strange new self—poised, defiant—stared right back.

The sky was clear and high, exposing her. The satin dress slid on her skin in an unfamiliar way. Gravel shifted beneath her heels as she made her way onto the driveway leading up to the Hall. Small, sharp stones kept slipping inside the open toes of her sandals, as if punishment for her temerity. A car hurtled up the driveway towards her, and she stumbled, turning her ankle as she drew herself into the shadow of the trees. Safety beneath that dark canopy. She should have worn ordinary shoes and carried the sandals with her. Above her, the stars signalled a message Lennie could not understand. The moon pressed down upon the branches of the sycamores that lined the driveway. Almost certainly her father would hear about this: there were servants at the house who had earned their positions by reporting everything they knew to Peter Fairweather. Thomas had warned her not to make a fool of herself, and yet here she was in their mother's dress on her way to the party. Even if Thomas had left for Jamie Markham's poker night, he would find out what she had done and be furious. She should go back to the cottage right now, before it was too late.

Her father liked to begin with these sycamores, on the odd occasion when a tourist party from York ran out of rainy-day distractions and happened upon the Hall. How they had been planted out before the Hall itself was complete, over two hundred years since. See how they form a green tunnel over the driveway, and would the ladies and gentlemen care to view the plans drawn up all those years ago? Lennie did not care about landscapes and dead people's drawings, but she felt at home here, beneath a sycamore that had planted itself firmly in the ground, like the leg of some ancient giant, swollen and knotted. Trees were something true. She pressed her cheek against the rough mosaic of bark and, breathing its breath, sharp and woody, quietened.

The lights of the car had died, its occupants swallowed up by the Hall. She must find Alexander before the Faversham girl who had her eye on him could seek him out; before Alexander could disappear to another country, or within himself. You couldn't get past the surface of him when he did that, a kind of the flatness entered his voice. She couldn't remember losing him in that way when they were small and just playmates. This was something new.

The Hall loomed larger as she approached, sounds of laughter and music on the air. She could not go to the main entrance in her slipshod sandals and a dead woman's dress, just announce her own arrival. Why was nothing as simple as it needed to be? The lamps on either side of the portal glared out of the dark like lighthouses. It was no good. She was not a hard, polished girl in a car full of laughter. She did not know anything.

Lennie glanced over her shoulder. She could not see the river from here, only the break in the woods above it, but she could still feel it and hear the call of it, cold and black and alive, forever altering. An odd sensation rose up in her, like something tearing free of its moorings. She pushed it down, made her way towards a small wooden door in the garden wing that would, she knew, allow her quickest access to the back of the house. It was unlocked.

She saw him from the pathway: an outline against the hot, glassy light of the salon. She could smell the foreign cigarettes, knew him by the angles of his body. She would need to hurry, before anyone could draw him back in and put him beyond her. She could not run in sandals, nor must she ruin them, these shoes with the imprint of her mother's feet on them. She bent down and with hurried fingers unbuckled the thin, worn straps. Her feet free, she stepped off the gravel path. The ground sprung softly beneath her weight, her feet, long and pale and alien in the dark grass, beating down the distance between him and her.

Annie Faversham pranced into view behind the glass like a glossy show pony, red mouth opening and closing on empti- ness, she and Alexander standing side by side. Lennie approached more slowly now, eyes fixed on those confident teeth that gleamed squarely, as if they might take a bite right out of Alexander. She had heard that Annie was striking, and it was the right word; not pretty, but handsome in a vulgar, vital way, all movement and feigned impatience, tossing her head, and turning here and there, so that everyone could admire her small, muscular figure. Out in the darkness, Lennie was transparent, insubstantial, a moth beating at the glass with silent wings.

'Helena?' Alexander's voice.

Had he seen her or sensed her?

Lennie turned from the opening door and stood very still. She saw herself as she hoped he might, back, bare and white in the moonlight, the curve of her breasts.

'You must have hurt yourself,' Alexander said. His hand went to his pocket, reaching for his cigarettes.

'What?'

'Your hands,' he said.

'I wanted to see you,' she said; her voice rang out as if it belonged to someone powerful. She had summoned him and he had come.

Alexander was moving towards her, his expression chang- ing from puzzlement to something else as his vision adjusted to the darkness beyond the salon. A breeze carried the scent of damask roses across the Lawn. Lennie had painted her lips crimson. Would he suppose her a mermaid in the silver dress, or perhaps some strange perfumed goddess?

'Why are you dressed like a whore?'

A ngus came to collect her in a shiny green Sunbeam sports car, which brought her younger brothers tearing out to the yard to admire it. There was a lengthy drive ahead and so she had worn her long coat and a headscarf. Her mother insisted on extra blankets to warm her knees, though Angus promised her they would stop off along the way. They drove down the Northumbrian coast, all empty beaches and castles rising out of the sea mist. Venetia thought that if one were a romantic type—she'd decided some time ago that she was not—one might almost expect King Arthur and his knights to come galloping across the sands.

Angus drove fast but Venetia was pleased to see that he slowed down almost to a crawl when they passed two riders on a narrow country lane. When they stopped to buy petrol from a small garage, he let the owner's young son clamber all over the car, lifting the bonnet so that the boy could look at the Sunbeam's 3-litre engine. They discussed something called dry-sump lubrication in earnest, man-to-man fashion.

Later, they stopped for lunch at The Welcome Inn, a deserted roadside pub so inhospitable it made them slightly hysterical. Angus began to tell her about his family. 'You mustn't mind them,' he said. 'Father lives like a bachelor really.' He pushed his chair back and leaned in towards the fireplace, holding his hands over the miserly molehill of coal the landlady had reluctantly lit on their arrival. He didn't look unduly worried at the prospect of the meeting. 'Mother died years ago, you see, when she was having James.'

'Who else is there? Apart from James, I mean?' Venetia gave up on the gristle pie they'd been served and helped herself to one of Angus's cigarettes instead.

'Just my grandmother, Thomasina. Now she really is bats. She's about a hundred and eighty and mostly keeps to her rooms, but don't be too alarmed if you happen to see some spectral creature wandering about. Her husband Teddy died years ago, just at the end of the war, and she likes to go to the chapel sometimes to pray for him.' He sat back while the landlady's daughter removed their barely-touched plates with a sniff.

'You have your own chapel?'

'Just a small one. It was built by the Knights Templar, so it's the most ancient bit of the house. Dates back to 1200 and something. The Hall's on the site of the old preceptory, though there's nothing else left of that now. The chapel's rather sweet but it only gets used properly a few times a year, when the Reverend turns up for Evensong.'

It was evening by the time she saw it for herself. They drove through a gateway, with a small cottage to one side, and onto the tree-lined driveway. Richmond Hall came into view, the little chapel looking as though it had been tacked onto one end as an afterthought.

'It's been perfect weather for riding,' said James, jogging down the steps to take Venetia's bags from the car as they pulled up. 'You'll be exhausted now, of course, but maybe tomorrow . . . .'

'Venetia's tougher than you imagine,' said Angus, clapping his younger brother on the back. 'You should see what she ate for lunch.'

Richmond Hall's grandeur was all in its breadth. The

interior of the house mirrored this first impression, its tiled entrance hallway leading through to a long, widthways corridor with curving staircases at either end. Lying directly behind the corridor, and running parallel to it, were the main rooms, linked to one another like a paperchain, so that the footprint of the house was a long, narrow rectangle, with a garden wing at one end of it—a later addition, Angus told her, in the style of Palladio—and the chapel at the other. From the driveway the house had looked splendid but as the Sunbeam drew closer, Venetia saw that parts of the building were in poor repair. Inside, the house was an odd combination of luxury and dereliction, the bedrooms icily cold with windows that rattled in the wind while the public rooms were gracious, with sumptuous, jewel-coloured hangings and oil paintings of vast battlefields or hunting scenes, yet furnished with an odd jumble of utilitarian bits and pieces, lamps that didn't match, ornaments that looked as if they'd been swept up from various places and hurriedly bundled together, and the odd piece of once-exquisite furniture, now with a leg missing, or a cover faded or ripped at the seams. The salon, which lay at the central point of the house, was magnificent when you first entered it, with its view out over a great expanse of lawn, the glowing wood of the grand piano, elaborate cornicing and its painted ceiling, but the plasterwork was rotting and the carpet so badly frayed you had to be careful not to trip. At least it was warm in there—Sir Laurie, the boys' father, insisted the two vast fireplaces at either end of the room were lit at this time of year, masking the damp in the air.

She was relieved to be introduced to Thomasina instead of chancing upon her by accident in the draughty corridors of the Hall. Angus and James took her up to their grandmother's rooms on the first floor—'She's fairly sane today,' Angus assured her—where she was dozing beside the fireplace in a small sitting room, surrounded by miniature figurines of her beloved Beatrix Potter characters. The room was cluttered with family photographs. Thomasina pointed out those of her two grandsons, as well as one of Sir Laurie as a young man, beside a small girl with serious eyes and a direct gaze.

'That's my younger child, Violet,' said Thomasina, picking up the photograph with trembling hands. 'She went off to be a suffragette. Ridiculous.'

'Did she come back?' Venetia asked.

'No no. Silly creature wore herself out with all that protesting. People should stay where they belong.' Thomasina herself was so small and dried up that Venetia feared she might rattle like a seed pod and blow away if the wind were ever to catch her. 'Grinling Gibbons!' Venetia jumped as Thomasina banged her stick on the floor. 'The fireplace. I saw you notice it.'

'Oh yes.' She had no idea who or what Grinling Gibbons might be but in a room that was plain and small in proportions, she had not been able to miss the huge wood carving over the fireplace: a twisting garland of nut-brown leaves, seed pods and flora that looked as though they had been swept up from a forest floor. This wooden garland framed a panel above the mantelpiece, with a swag at its centre point, from which hung a tangle of carved birds—pheasants from a shoot, she thought—their feathers, beaks and claws intertwined and all fashioned in intricate detail.

'And whose friend are you?' said Thomasina, her small blue eyes suddenly sharp. She looked at Venetia and then at each of her grandsons. Her bones sat close beneath her skin and, just for a moment, Venetia could see how striking she must once have been.

'We met at a ball recently, Grandmother,' said James. 'We know Venetia's brother too.'

Thomasina had already lost interest, addressing Angus now. 'Have you spoken to your father about Dido and Aeneas, my boy?'

'I shall remind him,' said Angus. 'Would you like some tea brought up for you, grandmother?'

'No, you can all go now.' Thomasina sat back in her chair and pushed her twiggy legs towards the fire. 'Visitors are dreadfully hard work.'

'Are Dido and Aeneas the dogs?' Venetia asked as they went downstairs. Two Labradors—'Proper dogs' Angus said—had been bouncing up and down the steps when they arrived.

'No.' said Angus. 'It's one of the bloody paintings in the salon. Grandmother is obsessed about getting the lot cleaned up. The ceiling too, but especially the paintings because it was her grandfather who had them done. He had some fellow from Rome brought over especially.'

'Does your father dislike them?'

'I've never asked him. It's just that it will cost an arm and leg getting electricity in everywhere and there's always something or other that needs doing first.'

'It *is* a beautiful room,' said Venetia, thinking of the gilded mouldings around the doorways, the light flooding in through the windows. 'I rather love it.'

'All in the proportions, apparently.'

With Freddie and the rest of the houseguests yet to arrive there was time for riding the next morning. James and Angus met her in the hallway after breakfast, where Venetia was looking at the many portraits that adorned its walls.

'That's Thomasina and Teddy when they were young,' said Angus, pointing to a fading formal portrait of his grandparents, with a just recognisable Sir Laurie at their side, all knickerbockers and scraped down hair, his baby sister in their mother's arms.

How solemnly his grandparents stared into the camera, yet they'd been renowned for their extravagant parties, Angus said, throwing open Richmond Hall to all comers before the century had turned and that kind of life had been destroyed forever. There were photographs of Angus and James as children too; of their parents' wedding day. Venetia would have liked to stay longer but the boys were keen to make the most of the day.

James was a far better rider than his elder brother, who rode the way he drove, slightly too fast for anyone's comfort. Angus was turned out rather more carelessly too, yet it was hard to take your eyes off him. There was something mesmerising about the way he went at things with no half-measures, taking a kind of joy in imperfection.

There was a joyousness to that whole weekend in fact; something to do with the chaos of Richmond Hall, where extravagant meals were served but no-one minded if you arrived late or did not feel like eating—Sir Laurie at the table roaring for more wine—or whether you turned up at all, and where everyone seemed to do precisely as they wished at any hour of the day or night, whether it was playing the gramophone in the early hours of the morning or making raids on the wine cellar for some rare vintage. Groups of guests and near-neighbours drifted in and out over the course of the next few days. Some of them seemed to have been invited and others not, and Venetia, who knew only the comfort and order of home, a mother who ran the household with a firm, parsimonious hand, found everything delightful—modern and at the same time immersed in some glamorous past.

Angus was to drive Venetia home at the end of the weekend. She was waiting in the hallway with her bags when she heard hurried footsteps and then James came out. He stood by the doorway with his back to her.

'We've hardly had a chance to talk,' he said. 'And now you're leaving.'

'It's been wonderful,' she said again, having already said goodbye earlier, at breakfast.

He shook his head, as if in disagreement, turned around. 'I thought you might like something new to read,' he said. In his right hand, she saw, was a slim, cream-coloured book.

'Thank you.' The title of the book was *Prufrock and Other Observations* by T.S. Eliot. It looked serious and rather terrifying.

'Modernism, you know,' said James. 'We talked about it the ball. You might not like it but . . . '

Venetia thanked him again. There was the roar of the car engine outside.

It was too noisy to talk during the journey and though lunch was perfectly edible this time when they stopped, both she and Angus were quiet. When they got back in the car, he turned to her, took her by the shoulders and kissed her. It was not as she had been kissed before, by boys who weren't sure what they were doing or why. It was only when she reached home that she realised that she had left James's book behind on the hall table.

The following year Venetia turned eighteen and she and Angus Richmond were married.

CHAPTER 15
Danny, September 1954

One Saturday afternoon he took the train to York. He went to Coney Street first but the shop there couldn't help him.

'Try Ebor Books,' said the assistant. 'On Fossgate.'

It was just off Fossgate as it happened, and Danny would never have found it if it hadn't been for the sign pointing down the narrow alleyway.

EBOR BOOKS: NEW AND SECOND-HAND BOOKS COLLECTORS' ITEMS

'Alfred, Lord Tennyson,' he said to the girl behind the counter. His voice was too loud and he waited for her to give him a look, wondering what someone like him would want with a book of poetry, but if she was surprised she didn't show it. He was still doubting himself—shouldn't it be Lord Alfred Tennyson and maybe he'd got it all the wrong way round—when she handed him a copy, second-hand and the spine all broken. And yet still it was half his apprentice's wage. He'd worry later about how he would explain it to his mother, who wanted money for board now that he was earning.

With an hour or so to spare before his train home, Danny walked back along Coney Street, stopping to look at the ruins of St. Martin's, demolished in the Baedeker raid, and the Guildhall still covered in scaffolding from the damage. He drank a pint in the first pub he came to, the weight of the book like a stone in his pocket as if he'd not bought it with his own good money but stolen it when the shop girl's back was turned.

On High Petergate, dusk was drawing down between the narrow streets and settling over the Minster like a hood, shadows gathering in its great folds. A couple hurried by, dressed up for a dance and laughing together, as if they lived in a secret world of their own. Lights came on in a hotel over the road, where tables were already set for dinner. Between the waiters dressed in black and white, Danny could see white tablecloths; glowing cutlery; complicated glassware that caught the light.

The big window at this end of the Minster was empty, a gaping mouth with boards for teeth, elongated like an old person's, but he knew the East Window had been put back in last year—there'd been an article about it in the paper. He took a wide loop round to the other side of the cathedral, passing by a sign for the glazier's workshop on his way. Outside the workshop door stood a man in dog collar and an odd-looking black hat, talking to an older fellow in a flat cap who wore an apron over his clothing. Danny wondered if this clergyman was the Dean himself, the one in the paper. The Minster's windows had been scattered across the county during the war, the article had said, locked away for safekeeping in the cellars of the big country houses. The Dean was determined to get them all back again. The story had caught Danny's attention because two of the smaller windows had been stored at Richmond Hall.

He walked on, crossing a small green, the bulge of St. William's College at the edge of his eye-line. At the foot of the Great East Window, Danny stopped, stared upwards. The structure soared above him, an elegant, black arch to the heavens. The dark glass glittered and shone in the cold light of a new moon and, standing beneath, he felt small and full of possibility all at the same time.

He dared to wonder what it might be like to leave his home behind and come to live somewhere like this. He could not imagine himself working at the glaziers' workshop, with the grave clergyman barring the door like that, but perhaps he could secure a place in the Minster stone yard and learn to carve gargoyles and suchlike. Of course, they'd start you on easier jobs but right from the beginning you'd be creating history, something important, which people might admire. Stone dust was better than wood, he felt sure of it. The sky was wide and clear above him and he allowed himself, just for a moment, to think how it would be to have Lennie here by his side. As his love, he meant, and no-one giving it a thought or finding time to wonder about it because in a city people don't. She would be happy here, because no-one could feel trapped in a place like this, where there were bookshops filled with new poetry to discover, and the air was sweet with the rich smell of chocolate from the nearby factory. He would take her to the theatre and to the cinema, to the big tea rooms with the plate-glass windows and silver teapots and shelves full of fancy cakes. It was easier to make things beautiful in a city, where there was no dirt or wood dust ruining everything. People lived this way because they wanted their lives to feel better. Even the river, darkening beneath him as he crossed the bridge on the way back to the station, seemed more civilised than a country river, keeping the noise down the way it did and staying put between its banks.

Danny didn't dare open the poetry book on the train home. The man across the carriage was reading The Times, turning the pages in an impatient way and looking put out by the space that Danny's long legs took up, so he had to wait all evening, until his mam put down the sewing she took in and said goodnight, reminding him that he had work tomorrow. When the floorboards creaked above him, he fetched the book from his jacket pocket and, with urgent fingers, began turning the pages. The fire pulsed and blackened as he found what he had been looking for and then his lips moved silently as he read the poem Lennie had chosen in class that day:

She lives with little joy or fear.
Over the water, running near,
The sheep bell tinkles in her ear.
Before her hangs a mirror clear,
    Reflecting tower'd Camelot.
And as the mazy web she whirls,
She sees the surly village churls,
And the red cloaks of market girls
    Pass onward from Shalott.

Sometimes a troop of damsels glad,
An abbot on an ambling pad,
Sometimes a curly shepherd lad,
Or long-hair'd page in crimson clad,
    Goes by to tower'd Camelot:
And sometimes thro' the mirror blue
The knights come riding two and two:
She hath no loyal knight and true,
    The Lady of Shalott.

Hearing a movement on the stairs, he slammed the book shut and returned it to the pocket on the inside of his jacket, before climbing the stairs to bed, all the hope of the day gone out of him. Lennie had chosen this poem out of all others because she had wanted someone to rescue her, he felt sure of that. She was like an angel to him but what was he to her? A village churl, said the unkind voice in his head. Or worse still, nothing whatsoever.

Helena!'

For a moment she did not move. The silver dress lay in a heap on the bedroom floor beside her. Her mother's dress. There was a rip in the hem where it had snagged on a bramble. A piece of the past had been ripped apart and it was her own fault. The future in tatters too, but now Alexander was here, calling to her, his voice soft beneath her window.

'Come downstairs.' She could smell foreign cigarette smoke drifting up to her on the night air, dry and pungent. 'Please, Helena. I need to talk to you.'

Lennie rose from the bed and took up the cotton dress she'd been wearing earlier that day, which hung over the back of the chair like another discarded version of herself. Her feet were sore and cut in places from running down the driveway, yet it did not occur to her to refuse Alexander.

He was waiting by the door of the cottage, his cheeks hollow as if in pain.

'Oh my darling, I'm so sorry.' He grasped her hands. 'Forgive me. It's not your fault. I was just shocked to see you.'

'It was my mother's dress.' Her voice so small it seemed to disappear even as she spoke. 'I thought you'd like it.'

'I did. I do. You are so beautiful, you can't imagine. I'm an idiot.'

She could feel him vibrating with emotion. She went to speak, to reassure him, as if it were him in need of comfort, but

Alexander continued. 'For drinking too much. For being bloody to you. I didn't want those people looking at you, I can't explain. Such an awful evening with mother carrying on as though nothing had changed and Uncle James looking so fucking proprietorial.' He put his hand to her cheek, gave a pained smile. 'Do you know, I like this dress better.'

Lennie shook her head in puzzlement. It was a workaday dress she was wearing.

'The other one was beautiful,' Alexander said. 'But it looked wrong on someone like you. Vulgar almost. It's the contrast, you see.'

'Oh.' He must be right and yet for a moment she had felt powerful in that dress, striding across the damp grass towards the house, ready to claim the man she loved from the girl with the hungry mouth and horse's teeth.

'You're such a good girl, Helena. You didn't deserve any of that.'

'You said I was a whore.'

'Sssh.' Alexander dismissed it with a wave of his hand. 'Promise me you'll stay like this always.'

His voice was gentle and full of ardour. She was still his; everything she'd thought broken was still intact. Yet the world remained tremulous, as if it might shift and alter at any moment.

He caught up her hands again. 'Come with me to the grave.'

She stiffened. 'Whose?'

'My father's of course. People die around here and no-one seems to notice. I can't go on my own.'

'It's late, Alexander.'

She felt guilty for denying him, did not want to anger him either. How quickly they reverted to form, even after tonight's behaviour.

Alexander's hands went to his temples, pressing as if trying to contain chaos. 'I can't bring myself to go there. My mother and Uncle James . . . ' He grimaced into the moonlight. 'They spend so much time together and the way he looks at her is . . . I should do something about it. Only months since my father died and now it's like he didn't exist.' He looked at her. 'I'm starting to believe she's glad about it.'

'Oh no, Alexander.' Lennie tried to think in some kind of practical way. 'There must be so much to talk about with the farm and the estate, for both of them, I mean, there are all the new taxes. Father's been talking about them.'

'Why should it bother *him*? Come with me, Helena. Let's go right now.'

The moon sat high over the beech tree, leaves the colour of old blood, and all around, the call of the woods and the river, black and cold in the distance.

'I was afraid to see him die and then it was too late and now I can't even stand alone at his graveside. What a coward I am.' Alexander's voice rose with bitterness. 'I thought it was better after Greece but I keep dreaming about him and it's all mixed up with mother and everything else that's happened . . . '

He kissed her suddenly, as if it were the only way to put a stop to such thoughts. After a moment she felt his hands moving down to her waist and pulling her closer. More than anything Lennie wanted to go with him right then, out into the night where death and love waited. But *whore*. That word, ugly and angry. Had he really meant it or was she his good girl again?

He pulled away abruptly, as if confirming her fears.

'What is it?' she asked.

Lennie followed his gaze along the garden path to the gate. It was a quarter of an hour since the bells had chimed eleven and Peter Fairweather was home.

J ealousy.

Even now, Venetia could recall its precise geography, though she had not thought about it for years, not properly. The name *Marina* had simply announced itself in her mind when she'd been discussing future plans for the Hall with James, up in the office on the day of her birthday.

All the fuss with Alexander and Lennie out on the lawn last night:

'Leave us alone, mother! You don't understand.'

If jealousy had been at the root of Alexander's behaviour, she understood more than he imagined but must speak to him, she supposed, if only to mollify Fairweather, who seemed to have got wind of something. His face had been rigid when he had come to collect her morning tea tray just now. He studiedly ignored the cigarette smoke unfurling from the ashtray beside her and opened the window when he thought she wasn't paying attention. She'd not smoked for years but she'd found an old packet of Angus's in the office that morning. Now was as good a time as any to start again.

She was not unduly worried on Lennie's behalf. Venetia disliked ungentlemanly behaviour and public spats as much as Fairweather, but the young people were, well, young, not in control of themselves yet. Lennie would have to learn to speak up for herself or Alexander would think it fine to bully her, like her father and brother did. All of that would sort itself out in time. Still, something about the little scene had left her uneasy.

In the quiet of her private sitting room, a room which once had belonged to Thomasina and which she'd made her own—she closed the window to keep the smoke safely in, as if it might help her settle upon what it had been. That extraordinary dress, of course—which she herself had passed onto Jenny Fairweather all those years ago, having grown too thin for it after Alexander's birth and thinking it would suit her better. That, and every man at the party turning to stare at Lennie's beauty. Little wonder a drunken Alexander had felt jealous and behaved so badly. Venetia reached for the cigarette packet again. She had forgotten how much she loved to smoke.

Marina had arrived almost unnoticed in 1948, the year after Sir Laurie's death. Sent down from London by the bank, Angus said. Some relation of the manager who'd graduated from a provincial university several years ago, done something worthy for the war effort and was now back at the bank and 'working her way up.' Angus quickly pronounced her 'damned good' at her job but only her ordinariness had struck at first— thin limbs, puppy-fat torso; indistinguishable black clothing. On that first visit, Venetia invited her to dine with the family— Alexander being home from school for the holidays—but it soon become clear that the girl preferred to take her meals in her room and Venetia forgot about her almost. In retrospect, the only emotion Venetia could recall was a vague pity for this earnest young woman who seemed to have some kind of unhappy, ongoing situation with a fiancé back in London. Venetia registered this just enough to wonder if there was some unspeakable war injury to think about.

Marina—a grandiose name, Venetia had thought, for such a nondescript little thing, but she seemed useful in her way. It was good for Angus to have someone with whom he could share his worries about the finances. Someone who, it turned out, could make him laugh again.

My handsome boy.' His mam said, pushing a packet containing his lunch into his hands. 'Just like your Dad, you look. Don't go getting in any trouble now.' Well there would be trouble if Mary Stockton didn't keep popping up everywhere he went, when she was supposed to be engaged to Jackie. Hattie Merriot from up at the Hall was just as bad, always pestering about what he was doing at the weekend, how she loved going to the pictures on her day off. He wasn't sure he liked being thought handsome all of a sudden, not if it meant girls who'd once been friends, like Bridie who was working in her Dad's hardware shop, went all stiff and red in the face when he stopped to talk. There was no use being handsome if Lennie wasn't around to notice. Now that school was finished she was only likely to come when the shops were open, while he was stuck at the sawmill, right at the other end of the village. Once he'd felt sure the village was too small for the two of them. Now the distance between here and there seemed vast and he didn't feel certain about anything anymore.

Autumn quickened the air and it made him brave. As casually as possible, he enquired of Hattie Merriot about Lennie, came to hear about the scarlet fever. She wasn't in any danger, only taking longer to recover than people expected. Danny searched his mind for some excuse to venture up to Gatekeeper's Cottage, came up with nothing. Peter Fairweather wouldn't welcome some village lad asking about his daughter, and Danny hadn't spoken to Thomas in years, not properly.

The only feeling he'd registered, seeing him step off a train as he arrived home from university, was that someone that lucky in life oughtn't to look so angry all the time. Besides, it was Alexander he'd liked best when all of them were small. Thomas was too unpredictable to be fun, you never knew whether he'd be storming off over something.

He had to wait until Christmas to see her again when the staff party gave him an excuse to go up to the Hall. Lennie stood behind a trestle table, helping Lady Richmond to serve mulled cider and mince pies to the estate workers. All evening he waited, trying to find the courage to approach her, but when he finally made his way across that great, glittering salon, she'd disappeared. He drank until he could barely stand—Sir Angus being on ale duty and in typical generous mood—and then staggered home along the river path, barely noticing the cold. New Year came and went. After a fine start to the year, February came in raw and wet, day after day of weeping skies pressed down on Danny like a damp sod. His hands grew damp even inside his winter gloves as he walked home from the sawmill, rainwater seeping through the lace holes of his boots. By early spring it was no longer enough to read his book of Tennyson in the lamplight of the cottage. He needed to see Lennie.

She saved him a journey. The sawmill was just a hundred yards or so from where the last of the cottages petered out, but the shadow of the woods made the whole idea of a village seem insubstantial, a temporary aberration on the landscape. That morning the foreman was standing over Danny, making sure that he was planing his plank of wood correctly. Lady Richmond had commissioned a dresser for her sitting room, so it was important to take special care. Danny was in two minds about the task: he liked the way his hands moved more assuredly these days, his palms thickened in places, but he could hear the wind outside, stirring up the trees and it seemed a shame then, this reducing of nature to smooth, uniform portions. As if you could ever know the woods like that. He paused for a moment; saw Lennie standing right in front of him, in a slice of sunshine that fell across the gate of the sawmill. Forgetting the foreman, the dresser, he half-raised a hand in greeting and then let it hang in the air in case she hadn't recognised him, in his work-clothes and his skin furred with wood dust. But she smiled right at him, a beautiful serious smile that made his heart leap in his chest. Lennie stayed only a moment. He watched her disappear into the trees and carried on planing just as the foreman had instructed. Seeing and hearing nothing.

Why had she come? The track that led to the sawmill ended at a narrow bank at the edge of the woods. There was nothing that might have drawn Lennie along that dead-end road. She must have sought him out, gone out of her way to do it!

He slept fitfully that night and awoke in a state of anxiety, wanting to be out of the cottage as soon as possible in case she should return. He waited but she did not reappear. As the evenings grew lighter, he took to walking the river path in the direction of the Hall. He would liked to have gone home first, wash the smell of wood and sweat off his skin; his mam already thought it odd, him needing to go walking after work instead of coming straight home for his tea.

The weather took a turn, growing unseasonably hot. On one particular day, when he'd walked twice up and down the river path, almost to the front of Gatekeeper's Cottage and back, Danny stopped at the pool that lay safely downstream from the Stride. He stripped off his clothes and plunged into the water. It was cool and deep. Danny felt the heat and dirt of the day roll off his skin as he turned onto his back and allowed himself to drift, the faint currents that lay beneath the green surface taking him where they would. Back on the river bank, he shook the dust from his clothes and there was a strange feeling then, as if someone was watching him. He checked all around; no-one was there; no sound of feet in the undergrowth. It made him suddenly conscious of himself—the muscles in his thighs and arms and the new breadth of his chest from carrying planks at the mill. He hurried into his clothes and went home.

Just once he was lucky, on a day in early summer. He almost missed her because she was crouched down by the edge of the water, near the Stride. It took him a second to realise what she was doing: cutting roses from the scrubby patch that grew there, laying them down one by one in a dark pile at her feet. He'd been desperate for such a chance encounter but now a part of him wanted to shrink back, return home along the track through the wood, so that she might never know. He hesitated and the Stride quietened for a moment. Lennie turned.

'You should be careful,' he said, as she came towards him, onto the footpath. 'That close to the water.' He'd meant to show concern but the way he put it was all wrong, more like telling her off.

'I wanted these though.' She'd lost weight since her illness. How strange her beauty was, like something from another world.

'They're not really black,' he said, staring down at the roses she carried. They were darkest purple with petals like crushed velvet. 'People don't look properly.'

'No.' She shook that thought away. 'Wild things shouldn't be kept inside.' She smiled. 'But the flowers in our garden have no scent.'

'You don't believe what everyone says about them? Kids, I mean,' he added, trying to distance himself from the kind of ignorant superstition that someone who worked in a sawmill might harbour.

Lennie laughed. 'How could something so beautiful do any harm?'

He stared at her thinking: you do me such harm that I cannot go on with it. Wanting to speak so badly that the blood beat painfully inside his skull. All his life, the truth had come easily to Danny, straight out of his mouth without thinking, and now it stuck in his throat like something unnatural. Lennie bent down, gathered the rest of the blooms to her breast; was gone before he had time to think of a single thing to say in response. He arrived home, his feelings still wild and torn up by his meeting with her, to find that time had run out of patience with him. His mam was in tears and beside her on the kitchen table was his call-up letter.

Fishnet stockings. That had been the beginning. No, before then. But that was the moment when Venetia had acknowledged that something was wrong. Like a vague itching that had, at last, demanded her attention.

Marina had lost weight. As she turned at the top of the staircase, on her way to Angus's office, Venetia saw her in profile. For once she was wearing a properly fitted suit. The puppy-fat around her midriff had slipped away at some point during the weeks she'd been coming and going from the Hall, revealing a rectangular outline; heavy breasts; sloping shoulders; a body designed for harsh eastern European winters rather than the neatness of rural England. She was by no means pretty—there was too much of the masculine about her—but Venetia, standing on the landing beneath her, was suddenly alert to something that had been missing before, a self-awareness, some element of display. One of the stockings had a rip in it. Marina must have snagged it on the train journey from London that morning. Forever afterwards Venetia would wish that she had drawn attention to it, called up the stairs and gained some kind of victory over the girl.

Look how you are failing to disguise yourself! I see what you are. I am watching you.

'I do think Marina should join us sometimes,' she said to Angus over dinner that evening. 'It's feels rather odd, her eating alone every night.'

'She's working,' said Angus. 'There's a lot to do.'

He spoke little during the rest of the meal, left as soon as they were finished, needing to return to his office.

Alone at the dinner table, Venetia wondered, not for the first time, why everything must take so long. She understood enough to know that things were bad—with Sir Laurie gone, there were death duties to think about, on top of crippling new taxes. The roof on the garden wing was in urgent need of replacing too, and all of these things needed thinking about for a long time, with many hours at the books and walks around the estate to be had. There were stories in the paper every other week of country homes that could no longer support themselves, that were being sold off as hotels or even demolished. Yet it seemed to her that it ought to be simpler by now: either it was possible to carry on as they were, or it was not.

There was part of her too that could not bring herself to worry about a future that might never happen. It was far worse for Angus, of course, she understood that. Unbeautiful as it was, Richmond Hall was his home; the history of his family mapped out in the portraits and photographs in the hallway. Venetia had learned proprietorship too, yet there were moments when she wondered if all the landscaping, the duck-egg blue paint and fresh plasterwork in the restored salon, were only pretty icing over the past. She was not one for dwelling on unpleasantness though; neither had she ever questioned that she belonged here, beside Angus.

The next day, coming in from the stables, she saw Marina sitting alone at breakfast. The younger woman was wearing her black suit, this time with plain stockings and low heels. The bright morning air had rid Venetia of yesterday's unease. Birds were singing in the trees; the world brimming over with optimism.

'You must take one of the horses out sometime,' she said, stopping in the doorway of the breakfast room. 'While the weather's so fine. Just talk to the stable lads.' The sunlight through the window was citrus-sharp, cutting across the room in crisp lines. Despite her bountiful mood, Venetia stopped short—just—of offering her own horse.

'I don't ride.' said Marina, looking up from her coffee. 'Never had the opportunity, I'm afraid.' She smiled but her mouth remained tight around the edges, as if the rest of her face was resisting. Venetia felt herself flushing, angry at her own mistake. Angus had already told her that Marina had grown up in some part of Kent which was not like the garden of England but a place of flint and nettles and rusting barbed wire, of chalk pits blown out by bombs during the war. 'Or the time,' added Marina. The disdain was barely noticeable, but it was enough to turn Venetia's mortification to something colder.

'No. I suppose not.' She went upstairs to change.

Amphibious eyes, the girl had. A pretty shade of green but nothing beneath the surface. Eyes made for watching, not for giving away. Still, Venetia doubted her own instincts.

'You must miss London?' she asked her later that day. 'Your fiancé?'

When this and further attempts were steadily and subtly rebuffed, she gave up on it, assuming some inaptitude for womanly intimacy on one or both of their parts. Venetia had grown up in a man's world, with mostly her brothers for company on the farm. The few friendships she'd had in her youth were with girls from the neighbourhood who were too bound up with the practical demands of farming life to find time for the finely-gauged destructiveness, the obliquity, of teenage girls, while acquaintances since her marriage had remained just that.

If this made her naive about Marina, it became obvious only in retrospect, when everything was revealed in simplified form, as if time had stylised the edges of things. For now, Venetia was too busy with other concerns to dwell on her suspicions: Alexander needed urgent help with his lines for the school play, having not bothered to learn them until the week before term started; her mind was greatly taken up with plans for the garden too, most which had been given over to vegetable plots during the war. Food was still in short supply, but Venetia felt no guilt in claiming back one or two beds for herself. The world might be chaotic and ugly sometimes, but you could not just give up on it.

CHAPTER 20
Lennie, August 1955

I can't stay long,' she told him.

'Lie down for a minute,' said Alexander. 'The grass is quite dry.'

A crow bounced over a nearby grave and Lennie hesitated. 'Won't they mind?'

Alexander laughed. 'They're dead, Helena. And father won't object to us keeping him company. I don't know why I didn't come before.'

Lennie dropped down to her knees beside him. The graveyard was a peaceful spot on a day like this: sun-warmed headstones, butterflies rising and falling in a pollen daze. A lovely breeze shook the meadowsweet.

'Did you get into trouble with your father?' Alexander said, stretching lazily. 'Disobeying orders.'

'He was upset.' She chose her words carefully. 'He hadn't really understood about . . . us.'

'I hope you reassured him that my intentions are honourable.' Alexander grinned. He pulled up a long piece of grass and bit down on it. 'Well, fairly so. Anyway, your father *likes* to fret. Normally about Tom, so this must make a pleasant change.'

Picturing her father's face, white and troubled, she could not laugh with Alexander.

Alexander's expression switched to sullenness. 'Tom's become horribly earnest this last year, you know. Palled up with a bunch of politicos. They spend all their time holed up in some dank little printing press off King's Parade. Always banging on about Oliver Cromwell or suchlike. He's no fun at all.'

'Tom always takes things seriously. It's just his nature.'

Yet her brother had laughed off the news of her behaviour at the party, said it was about time she showed some spirit. Lennie sensed that it was the disruptive element of her behaviour—the part that had least to do with her normal self—that had won his approval.

'I feel so much better today.' Alexander said. They lay side by side, looking up into a sky whose depth of blue foretold autumn. 'The whole of last term I wanted to be somewhere else. I didn't know where.'

'Even when I came?'

'Not then. Greece seemed like a good idea but as soon as I got to Athens that wasn't right either. I kept getting on ferries, needing to be in the next place, and on and on like that. After a while everything started to look the same—same dust, same villages, even the faces started to look familiar. I grew quite sick of it.'

'Home is better,' she said. It was the closest she had come to admonishing him for his absence.

'I thought so at first.' His fingers drumming on his ribcage. 'Then I couldn't see the point of that either. Or anything else, come to that. Masters' dying has cheered me up though.' Lennie started. Danny's grave lay on the other side of the yard, just beyond the old mulberry tree; she had been sure to avoid looking. 'I'm joking,' said Alexander. 'But it has woken me up in a funny sort of way. I'd almost forgotten how to feel.' She felt for his hand, lying in the soft grass. 'I am *trying* to be a better man.' As if she had suggested otherwise. 'I suppose I owe that to father now that he's gone. He won medals in all sorts of battles, you know. I always encouraged him *not* to talk about it, partly because I loathe nostalgia. A bit peculiar for a classicist, I must admit.' He mimed dismay.

Lennie remembered Sir Angus and his kindness towards her and Thomas. His laughter that was large, seemed to include the world, making everyone feel easy in their own skins. It was difficult to believe he lay close by, just feet beneath the soil, his generosity all stopped up.

'Grandpa was at the Somme,' Alexander said, 'so there's all that to live up to as well. '*Your* father loves the war stuff, of course. All those bloodstains on the floor of the garden wing— his favourite stop on the tour. I always thought it great fun having all the soldiers here when we were small; I suppose you don't really understand suffering at that age. Imagine dying for your beliefs and nurses having to mop you up. It's so much easier to be a hero in wartime, I reckon.'

'Your uncle won a medal too, didn't he? Father said he was supposed to stay to keep the farm running but found some way round it.'

'God knows.' Alexander propped himself up above her. 'Anyway, who cares about him?'

His kisses always came out of nowhere, just when she had stopped waiting for them. His hair was hot and blond against her skin; hand on the curve of her hip. She thought of all the bones that lay beneath them, lodged in the dark soil. He moved his hand down to her thigh; long fingers beneath the hem of her dress, reaching. *Night scent of the woods. Leaf mould and the rich, giving earth.* But it was daylight.

'Alexander . . .'

He rolled onto his back again. 'The village boys reckon you're a cold bitch.' He frowned. 'I suppose I should be pleased.'

Lennie was on her feet, breath ragged. 'I'm leaving if you're going to speak to me like that again.'

'No, no!' He snatched for her hand. 'You're not to go. I'm only teasing you.'

She felt tired. She had longed to see Alexander; now she wanted to be alone, some place that was quiet, unchanging.

She sat down, knees tucked in, angled slightly away from him. 'I can't quite picture you at the Hall yet,' he said. He pulled a strand of grass from her hair. 'I always think of you in this kind of setting.'

'A graveyard?' She had not yet forgiven him.

'Outdoors. My mother said it took at least a year to feel at home at the Hall after she and Papa were married.'

Despite herself, a little thrill went through Lennie. Why would he talk about the future in such a way unless he really did love her?

'Of course, she acts like she owns the place now,' Alexander said. 'I suppose she does until I kick her out.'

'Won't your mother stay when we . . . ?' Lennie said. It was difficult to talk of the two of them as something solid and real, capable of affecting others, of taking up space in the world. Everything was still so delicate, a flutter of life within a translucent shell. 'It *is* her home.' Lady Richmond, cool blonde and imperious, self-possessed even at her husband's funeral. Lennie felt small, insignificant, even thinking about it.

'Oh, I don't know,' said Alexander. She had annoyed him in some way. 'I don't want to think about her right now. Tell me about *your* mother?'

'Alexander . . . ' She did not want to talk of such things when the sun was high in the sky, the world full of possibilities.

'I've asked mother about her once or twice but she hates talking about the past.'

'You already know. She was half-Italian—that's why Thomas is so dark—her father had a barber's shop . . . ' Lennie pulled up a daisy and pushed her thumbnail through the soft hairs of the stalk.

'No, about her dying. You won't actually remember any of it, but your father must know,' said Alexander. 'I always thought it odd that she went out in that kind of weather, let alone to the river.'

'Perhaps she didn't like having to stay inside for days on end. With just two little children for company, I mean.' Lennie paused while she pulled up another daisy and threaded its stalk through the first. 'I sometimes wonder if she was on her way to the woods. Thomas says it was her favourite place, remembers going there in autumn, chasing the falling leaves with her. I've always thought that strange when she grew up in the middle of Leeds.'

'It's supposed to be a pleasant way to go when you stop fighting it.' he said. 'Hard to believe though. There has to be a moment when you realise that you're not going to make it out. She must have died almost straight away in that cold.'

Lennie pulled the second daisy into place too hard, breaking the connection.

'I do think the world places awful obligations on us to stay alive sometimes,' said Alexander.

'It was an accident.' She tossed aside the failed chain. 'I've told you.'

'Sometimes I can't work out what the point of any of it is. Keeping other people happy when we can't be really sure we matter all that much to them.'

He was so beautiful, all sunlit and boyish in his perplexity. She gazed at him, quite sure that the past did not matter anymore: her mother was at peace now and poor Danny Masters was tucked up safely in a neat new grave. 'Silly boy,' she said, jumping to her feet and holding out her hand to him. '*We* are the point.'

CHAPTER 21
Danny, 1949

A day in summer. They four of them were in the grave-yard—Danny, Lennie, Thomas and Alexander. He couldn't remember why, only that they were eating mulberries straight from the tree, which was ancient, limbs lolling across the gravestones, resting where they might; propped up in places by wedges of wood. The mulberries hung in pendulous clusters, darkening from green to red to black, or lay half-broken in the long grass beneath.

Alexander was holding out a handful of the fruit to Lennie. An offering. He and Thomas were back from school for sum-mer with some new language of their own: Latin, rugger, prep. It didn't bother Danny, but he felt for Lennie who looked up to her brother, wanted to share in everything he did. Lennie shaking her head, adamant that she would not take a single one of the long, fragile mulberries.

And only Danny had understood.

Like clotted blood, she once said, of all the dead people in this graveyard. As if it had mixed together beneath the surface and come bubbling up, and then coagulated. Years ago that had been, when they were small, but even now she refused to eat a single one of those intensely fragrant berries that the boys guzzled so greedily, that were already crumbling to a purple mess in Alexander's palm.

Time to go. Thomas pointed at the back of Lennie's skirt: 'You've sat in them, you idiot. You've got them all over you.'

'That's not . . .' said Alexander, and then he broke off, staring.

What was the matter with them, Danny wondered, Thomas so stiff and awkward all of a sudden, gazing in the opposite direction, Alexander with his hands on his hips, colour rising on his neck, as though someone had challenged him? Danny had grown up seeing his mother soaking cloths in cold water and salt each month; could not imagine what was troubling them.

'Here,' he said. He stood up, took off the light sweater he was wearing, and passed it to Lennie. She took it in silence, tied it around her waist. The two of them set off together, leaving Thomas and Alexander to compose themselves.

'It's not the first time,' said Lennie, as the two of them walked along the lane towards Gatekeeper's Cottage. On either side of the pathway, the Canterbury bells were bending in the lightest of breezes. 'Only I wasn't expecting it today.'

'Just nature isn't it,' he said, as they reached the garden gate.

She handed the sweater back to him, went inside. His sweater was unmarked, yet all the way home he could feel her blood-warmth upon him.

S he watched them sometimes, Marina and her husband walking out on the Great Lawn, lighting cigarettes while they took a break from the paperwork. They walked in silence for the most part, quite separately, yet occasionally Marina would speak, a throwaway comment by the look of it, and Angus might laugh. Seeing that quick lift of the chin brought home to Venetia how troubled he had been in recent times. Often now, she woke to an empty space beside her, found him and James huddled together in the office with the accounts spread out before them, though there rarely seemed to be any kind of activity taking place. Once she stood at the door and watched as the pair of them stared at the books in frozen misery, which only lifted once Marina arrived, almost but not quite pushing past Venetia to enter the room, smelling of train journeys; London; cigarette smoke. There were no fishnet stockings that day, but stiletto heels clicked efficiently into place as she took a seat between the two men. Both of them were visibly relieved to see her and, at the same time, surprised to spot Venetia standing at the door.

'What are you doing here?' Angus said, with genuine puzzlement.

A reasonable question. After all, she had been bred for nothing that could be of any use to them now. A woman like her was made for ornamentation and motherhood. Yet others with backgrounds not too dissimilar to hers had sought more in life, insisted on an education or leadership in some form or other. And now here was Marina, a girl out of context, whose education and self-confidence made men nod in agreement when she spoke. Whose ability to support herself meant she could go where she wanted, become whatever she chose. It was not something that Venetia coveted exactly—there was something rather bleak, *modern*, about such an unconnected life and Marina did not strike her as a joyful person—yet she couldn't help admiring her nerve.

'I'm sorry,' she said to Angus at breakfast one morning when he'd failed to come to bed at all, saying he'd fallen asleep at his desk. Why was she apologising? It had not been her intention to start that way, but the question that was to follow was straying into perilous territory, the realm of the neurotic, unhinged woman intent on harm. She had never had been that woman, even in the bad time.

'Is there something going on with Marina? Something we need to discuss?'

Those words. That sequence. Ridiculous lines from a third-rate film script which cheapened everything. Suddenly Venetia was angered that she had been brought to this ugliness. She should have stayed down at the stables where the horses were being fed, everything simple and the air wholesome with shifting, masticating animal contentment.

Angus held her gaze: 'No.'

She believed him in concrete terms but it didn't matter now. The coldness in his eyes was worse than the alternative answer. He looked at her as if some kind of alien had entered the room and he was unable, for the life of him, to comprehend its purpose, how its existence might in any way dovetail with his own. His refusal to offer her further reassurance made it clear that it was she who was at fault. Still, she continued: 'She seems to be here all the time quite suddenly. Is there something wrong?'

'You know there is.' His voice was incredulous. 'She's helping me.'

At times she caught Marina observing her with an air of detachment, as if Venetia was part of an experiment she was conducting. Venetia stayed very still, not wanting to give anything away. Life was frangible now; moving too quickly or thoughtlessly might destroy everything. Instead she watched, listened, all her energies concentrated in her senses, in the surface of her skin.

Marina had transformed herself once. Could she do it again, reinvent herself as the next Lady of Richmond Hall, for instance? It was a ludicrous idea that would not die once Venetia had allowed it to form in her mind. Her natural logic told her it was not remotely possible that this nondescript girl had the power to bring about an alchemical change of that nature—and yet she could not help remembering what her brother Freddie had taught her: *water, ice, steam*. Energy could not be created or destroyed but it could shift its shape right in front of your eyes. It was sly like that.

Basic Training was hell, but he minded it less than most. You could keep your head down for the most part and if you didn't let the yelling get past the surface of you, it wasn't that bad. They did it on purpose: the brutal haircuts, the uniforms that didn't begin to fit, the viciously-administered jabs, plates of slop that passed as food, endless square-bashing and corporals all red in the face from bellowing the impossible rules. It was to teach you who was boss and quickly. Well, that was fine by him. Six weeks had to be filled some way or another, that was the game, so let someone else work out how to pass the time, even if their notions of how to do it weren't everyone's idea of fun.

Lucky for him that he was already strong from lugging wood around the yard all these months. Endurance didn't scare him either: long days helping out with the harvest or the Easter lambing had seen to that, with old Farmer Dowdy as bad as any NCO when it came to shouting and swearing at you for your pains. It was lads like Granger who had it harder. A skinny lad from the East End of London who'd been a bellboy 'up West' since he was fifteen and was all swagger until he was forced to run round the parade ground in the pouring rain with a rifle over his head. Dropped to his knees in a puddle. Curled up in a sobbing ball where he fell. Or Ludlow, a gentle, knock-kneed fellow who'd been a bank clerk in Coventry, and who found himself at the back of the pack on the early morning runs, his face white with the effort of unaccustomed exercise. Danny ran the way he lived during those six weeks, firmly in the middle of things, not too fast, not too slow, head down and don't draw attention. Don't go excelling too much in the gym either, that was setting yourself up for trouble. Just make sure you do everything that's asked of you and no shirking. If you did that and weren't too cocky, you could keep out of the worst trouble. It only took staff a few days to decide who really needed licking into shape, and after that you could leave it to mental cases like McLean, a Glaswegian with a dangerous look in his eye. McLean understood discipline as a concept; just not as one that applied to him. He spent half his time arguing about the degree of shine to his boots or point-blank refusing to clean the invisible speck of dirt in the barrel of his rifle, and off to jankers he'd go again.

At least it was summer, warm enough to go without lighting the billet's pot-bellied stove, which must always be blacked and pristine at inspection. The only use for the scuttle of coal during Danny's training period was as another form of punishment—McLean being ordered to paint each piece white after backchatting the corporal. Danny thought the lack of privacy would bother him, but he got used to that. The whole billet were jealous of Porter, a grammar school boy from Essex who'd been given the only separate room in their quarters, on account of his education and the leadership qualities that apparently came with it. But once he grew accustomed to the snoring, the odd homesick snivel in the early days, the shifting and turning bodies and night noises all around him, Danny wouldn't have swapped places with him.

He found himself well-liked in the billet, and even the officers made comments about his steady temperament, his straight way of talking. An only child, used to only his mother for company, Danny looked forward to the late-night card games, the practical jokes, good-humoured banter with people he would never have come across in the normal way of things. There was something soothing about the molten pulse of cigarette ends in the dark, the hushed voices, about one of the lads coming home all beery-smelling and wanting to tell anyone who was still awake about their girl back home, or some less respectable adventure. Stopped you dwelling too much on other things.

Some of it was downright funny too, like the day they were instructed how to fire a Bren gun and Ludlow lost all control of his, everyone diving for cover while he flapped around like a fish on a hook, peppering the field with ammo.

'What are you, Ludlow?' the corporal screeched, nose to nose with him.

'An absolute fucking disgrace, sir.'

There would be Trade Training after Basic. Everyone tested to see what they were good at and then off you'd go to some other part of the country. Some of the lads had strong views about this but Danny didn't care much what trade he was allocated. After that you might be sent abroad. Porter said you didn't want Germany; pretty dull with nothing much happening on the Rhine right now. The Commies were causing problems all over, or you might end up in Kenya with the Mau Mau to think about—that wasn't going to be resolved in any sort of hurry. Danny had been schooled well enough in geography to place Kenya on a map and he was pretty sure he could pinpoint Malaya—main exports tin and rubber—too. It was hard to believe these countries actually existed though, that someone like him could end up in some hot, strange land. He'd never even been to London.

The ugliness was what he hated and that wasn't something you could share with your new mates because they'd think you soft in the head. Danny hadn't realised how attached he was to the roll of the fields at home, the green haze of the woods all around, until he came to this flat place where the wind cut across the drill square with barely a tree to stop it until it reached the Dales. It was still Yorkshire but there was nothing of home about this place, with its barbed wire and its guard dog, the greyness of everything—grey billets, grey food, grey city faces.

He'd not dared to bring his book of Tennyson poems with him, for fear it being found in his kit bag or beneath his mattress, but he thought of Lennie every day. There'd been no chance to say goodbye to her—to explain why he should want to say goodbye in the first place. Everything had happened so quickly after his call-up letter. In the end, with an hour to spare before his train to Leeds where he was to meet the other recruits and be transported onwards, he'd found the courage to set off along the river path towards Gatekeeper's Cottage. He'd only just started out when he met Peter Fairweather coming the other way. Somehow he found the courage to ask if he might call on Lennie, mumbling something about returning a book she'd lent him. She'd taken the morning bus to Helmsley on some errands, her father said, eyeing Danny. He did offer to pass on the book in question. Danny went through some awful pantomime, pretending to search about his person for it; muttered something about having left the book at home and having to rush for his train.

There would be a weekend pass soon. Two whole days off at some point during the six weeks. The knowledge that he could soon be posted anywhere in the world, with no choice in the matter, meant Danny was determined not to waste any more time. He felt changed by these few short weeks at barracks. They said that service made you grow up. Well, Danny wasn't sure about that when you'd been forced to make up your bed pack three times over until the sheets and blankets were at perfect angles, or been consigned to the mess on spud-bashing duty all morning, but all of them were physically stronger now—you couldn't help it—and they'd become hardened to the bullying and deprivation. Danny pictured himself returning home with something about him, something akin to manliness or gravity which Lennie would notice. He thought about it so often that it began to take concrete form in his mind.

'You got a girl somewhere, Masters?' asked McLean from his bunk one night, rolling onto his back and lighting up a cigarette. Danny could smell whisky on him, and something faintly vegetal too. McLean had been chopping cabbages all day—punishment for leaving a trail of muddy footprints across the buffed lino expanse between billet door and bunk. The rule was that you could only walk on that polished floor with strips of blanket beneath your feet.

'Yes,' he answered, after a moment.

It was the first time in his life that Danny Masters told an outright lie.

Chapter 24,
Venetia, 1949

It was over so soon—the bite of land taken from the woods, red brick houses starting to fill the space, Marina back in London. The marriage to the on-off fiancé took place; there was news of a child on the way. Venetia wondered about that child and then berated herself for doing so. She did not truly believe the baby had anything to do with Angus, yet that kind of thinking had become a habit. Yet she and Angus went on in the usual way, neither of them bringing up the tensions of the previous year. Angus was happier; Venetia began to feel she'd been mistaken in her suspicions.

'That was Caro Levisham,' said Angus, after taking a phone call one morning. 'I've invited her to lunch tomorrow.' Seeing her blank look, he added. 'Caro. Ben's sister.'

'I didn't know he had a sister.'

'Surely I've mentioned her before? She was one of the Newnham set when we were at college.'

'I don't think so.'

'Well, she's passing through on her way to a wedding in St. Andrew's. I've not seen her in years.'

Caro Levisham was a barrister, divorced, sharp of tongue and very beautiful. She treated Angus like a mischievous but charming brother, made sure to include Venetia in their recollections of college mishaps. 'But *you* know what he's like.'

She was full of admiration for the restoration work in the salon.

'How wonderful,' she said, taking Venetia by the arm after

lunch. 'You've put such love into it. Makes my little flat look an absolute hovel. I've not had the energy to do anything about it since I moved in. It was just after the divorce, you see.'

'How did you find her?' asked Angus later, as Caro's car sped off at a frightening pace down the driveway, gravel flying in its wake.

'Great fun,' said Venetia, and meant it.

'I knew you'd love her. Everyone does.'

Venetia could not sleep. It was nothing to do with Caro and everything to do with her. Why had Angus never spoken of this friendship before? A girl that beautiful and funny was surely worth a mention? Had they been lovers when they were young? Why get in touch now, after all these years? The divorce. In her fingertips, Venetia knew the answer to each of these questions. There was nothing in Caro or Angus's behaviour to suggest anything more than a sibling-like fondness for one another. She would have known otherwise. She would have *known*. What was the matter with her, lying here staring into the darkness? In the early hours of the morning, long before the promise of dawn, something anchored deep tore free, headed straight for the surface.

The rage that came felt catastrophic in its violence, as if it might destroy her. She lay awake until sunrise, eaten up by thoughts of revenge. She would seek out Marina, crash into that carefully constructed life, just as Marina had crashed through hers. No-one could stop her once she started. What might a nebulous fiancé think of fishnet stockings and shared cigarettes; of eyes that watched, gave nothing away; of a silent dinner at Richmond Hall on her last night, which Marina had agreed to under duress, then made no attempt to hide the fact that she felt constrained by Venetia's presence? Of a child that might, if Venetia chose, be called into question?

I am not stupid, she would tell Marina.

You did not win.

Or she would inflict physical damage. That would surprise everyone the most, but Venetia knew she was capable of it. She was a farm girl, after all, strong and resilient, brought up to help with the lambing. All those hours spent reining in wayward horses too. She had been considered an honorary boy by her brothers, fighting alongside them against the village lads. Oh, she could still throw a punch if the occasion demanded it, she was sure she could, and the idea that she, Lady Richmond, might do such a thing made the laughter rise hysterically inside her, so that she had to cover her mouth for fear of waking Angus. She would call the girl a whore, or, racking her brains for the old insults, a cunt.

Cunt

Her mouth silently formed the word over and over again as Angus slept on, oblivious. The incantation restored the balance of power somehow, carrying her through the dark hours before dawn. She had hated the girl; she could finally admit it to herself. She had hated Angus too for his coldness, for choosing not to spare his own wife. She pictured a scene where she would tell both of them how she wished them all the bad things in the world, so that when misfortunes inevitably came their way, they would remember her words and wonder if they were, indeed, cursed.

T he butter was off. She dreaded having to return it to the shop, Mrs. Cuthbert always behaved as if Lennie had airs and graces that needed putting right, especially when there were other customers present. Lennie would find herself saying too many pleases and thank yous, escaping as soon as possible. She could hear father's footsteps on the stairs. She slid the entire pat of butter into the bin, pushing it down into the damp warmth of last night's scrapings, which already had the smell of rot upon them. It was a terrible waste but she'd rather spend some of her small savings on more, make up some story of a great batch of baking if Mrs. Cuthbert asked, than cast doubt on the shopkeeper's storage skills.

'What will you do today?' The brass buttons on her father's jacket shone like chips of sunlight. Even in the height of summer Peter Fairweather dressed formally, whether on duty or at leisure.

'Nothing special,' she said.

In the short space of time that her father had reconciled himself to his daughter's new attachment, just as rapidly he'd transformed it into a new source of anxiety. For the last few days he had wanted to know what arrangements she and Alexander had for the day, for next week, or for his return to university. Had they spoken to Lady Richmond about their *situation*? Others might have thought that this was social ambition at work, but Lennie knew better. Her father liked continuity, tradition. If people must move out of their allocated roles, he could not rest until they had settled into new ones. He would not be happy, Lennie suspected, until some kind of formal announcement had been made.

Her father dealt in certainties but Alexander could not be pinned down in that way. He had made no attempt to engage her father in discussions about the future, and Lennie was fairly certain that there had been no conversation with Lady Richmond. Surely he would have told her if that were the case?

Some days he was desperate to spend more hours with her than she could spare, yet gave her no notice so that she could plan for these sudden impulses. Then days at a time might pass without him calling by at all, when she could almost convince herself that she'd imagined a relationship between them. Only yesterday, she'd come across him on the river path as she returned from the village. She was carrying heavy bags home, having lost her nerve at the grocers; failing to ask Mrs. Cuthbert for her shopping to be delivered.

'I'll take those for you,' he said.

He kissed her; she could think of nothing else but his beautiful mouth, his hands deep in her hair. Afterwards, he seemed to forget about his offer, walking her back to Gatekeeper's Cottage with his arms swinging light and free by his sides.

They lingered at the gate, talking of a new film they both wanted to see, but then he seemed to grow impatient, said he had no time to spare, that he had a paper to research and write. He said he'd been putting it off all summer, what a bore it was, having to give up so many days to it now.

Lennie washed and dried the breakfast things, tied up her hair, then stepped out into the garden. The vegetable patch needed weeding. It was early yet but the sun was already a hard circle in the sky, flat as a tin tray. The heat of high summer had held steady for weeks. Now the earth was cracked and brown, like the surface of a fruitcake, the weeds holding their position with a show of tenacity before flying up in a sudden shower of dust. Lennie worked with her hands to begin with, the sun falling in a hot bar across her shoulders, onto the pale skin at the back of her neck. The heat did not trouble her. Though slender, Lennie was strong, the blood thumping in her body a hot, red pulse of life.

Her work took her towards the far edge of the garden, where the compost heap shifted and fermented in the heat like a small, dampish volcano. The smell of it, filling her nostrils, was familiar, but there was something else today, more potent than the usual base note. The smell of death, sweet and rich with decay, which even as a child she had recognised, passing a hedgerow or a ditch with hastily covered mouth and nose. Just inside the privet hedge boundary, hunched in upon itself, lay the corpse of a young rabbit, its body deflated and grey, like a sock without a foot to give it form and function. Lennie moved closer and flies erupted from the corpse. She could see the rabbit's silvery ears drooping to the earth, almost translucent in death, while the skin between its shoulders had begun to collapse in on itself, forming a dark, liquid furrow.

She must not be squeamish. She would move the creature before its rotting flesh liquefied, seeping into the row of lettuces growing in the nearby bed. She didn't quite like the idea of picking up the corpse with her bare hands, looked around for some kind of tool, thinking she might push what remained of the little rabbit through a gap in the hedge and onto open ground. If Alexander came to see her later, she could ask him to bury it for her, though even as the thought entered her mind she couldn't picture him doing such a thing. Never mind; the creature would rot quickly enough in the open.

Lennie fetched the hoe, inserting its sharp edge between the rabbit and the earth to lift the little corpse from its spot. It stuck to the soil. She exerted more pressure, pushing the hoe deeper into the soil, levering it up more forcefully. The rabbit clung on for another moment, as though its little paws had burrowed down into the earth, then gave up quite suddenly, flipping onto its back with an acrobatic flourish.

Whatever had attacked the creature must have had it by the neck, ripping out its throat, which was now a crusted mess of maggots and iron-dark blood. A fox probably. She must make sure the henhouse was secure, though they'd been no squawking in the night. The rabbit's muzzle was angled towards her. As she tried to roll the animal towards a gap in the hedge, its head suddenly shifted. She saw an empty eye socket, like a gaping extra mouth, the rabbit's eye dangling down its cheek in a viscous red drip.

The hoe landed with a thud on the dry earth. Lennie ran towards the cottage, trying to reach the path, the door. Anywhere. But it was too late: she fell to her knees in the dirt, vomited gobs of barely digested toast into her father's strawberry patch.

CHAPTER 26
Danny, July 1955

Hattie Merriot coming along the river path on her way home from the Hall; no way to avoid her.

'What are you doing out here, Danny Masters? Come to walk me home?'

'If you like,' he said. It wasn't far and there was no point being rude. Danny turned back in the direction of the village while Hattie took his arm and chattered on about everything and nothing in her usual way as they walked.

'Don't you look different with your hair all shorn! You almost scared me. My brother reckoned Basic was the worst bit. You'll be glad to get that over and done with. You look so grown up, all of a sudden.'

'I've two more weeks to go yet,' said Danny.' Just home for the weekend.'

He'd saved money by hitching, was lucky to be picked up by a couple of US servicemen who were heading back to base in Cambridgeshire after a trip to Scotland. They were from Kansas and South Carolina, might easily have been brothers though, tanned and healthful, with their mouths full of strong, white teeth and easy laughter. They took pity on the young English soldier in his ill-fitting uniform and a hungry look about him, plying him with cigarettes and chocolate and going out of their way to drop him at York, from where he said he could catch a train the rest of the way home. He'd dropped his bag at the cottage, given the chocolate to his mam, and then slipped out while she prepared a celebratory tea.

'You'll be finished in time for the ball then,' Hattie said, when they reached the High Street.

He nodded. The optimistically-titled Summer Ball was an annual event held in the village hall, organised by Miss Price, the schoolmistress, for the benefit of the young people of the parish. 'I don't know if I'll go.'

'Oh.' Hattie looked up at him and then away. He felt bad. At one time she might have been just the kind of girl he'd go for, with her freckled face and that lively way about her. He'd known her all his life, she was easy to be around, Hattie. Always a great one for laughing.

'You must see a bit of Lennie up at the Hall,' he said.

'Lennie Fairweather?' She'd heard him perfectly well, Danny knew. Was just startled by his question. Well, it was too late to take back his words. 'Not really. Anyway, I don't suppose she'll be coming.' Hattie was on the verge of saying something spiteful, he could feel it, and she wasn't like that, not really. If he wasn't careful, she'd be thinking he'd got above himself since he'd been away, fancying himself too good for the village.

'I just wondered, that's all,' he said lamely. Even the simplest things were difficult when they involved his feelings for Lennie.

'She'll be too busy waiting for her boyfriend to come home, I should think.' Hattie looked at him. 'He's overseas, they say.'

'Her boyfriend?' He could feel his face getting warm, knowing she had guessed something. Maybe this wasn't the first time she'd spotted him walking along the river path towards the cottage.

'Alexander Richmond,' a note of triumph in Hattie's voice. 'Everyone says he's crazy about her, even though she's only old Fairweather's daughter.'

'Who says that?' His voice was wild, he could hear it. His hand reached for the book of poems in his pocket, seeking comfort in its solidity. 'You shouldn't listen to gossip, Hattie!'

'It's not gossip! Why would anyone make up something like that?' She turned to face him as they reached the gate to her home. 'Besides it's been going on for ages. My sister saw him with her in the woods one day.'

He seized her arm. 'What was she doing, spying on people?'

'She wasn't spying! He was kissing her. Back when Sir Angus was not long buried and them all in mourning. And the girls in the kitchen reckoned she went down south to visit him too.' Hattie stared at him wide-eyed, imploring him to believe her. 'Anyway, he calls her Helena.'

Her final piece of evidence.

'I'm sorry, Hattie.' He let go of her arm and patted it awkwardly by way of apology. 'Go on inside now.'

'You'll come to the dance still? It's going to be a Hollywood theme. I might be wrong about everything I said.'

Poor Hattie. He had been hard on her and here she was, already wanting to forgive him.

'If I can,' he promised.

N ational Service was a waste of time, Thomas was saying, waving a butter knife in the air. He couldn't see the point of it now that Korea was over, but if one had to do it, the RAF was definitely the way to go.

'You're forgetting Malaya,' his father said. 'And of course Kenya shows no signs of being resolved.'

'That's the beauty of a young institution. With the army, you're either officer material or cannon fodder,' said Thomas. 'The RAF's about brains and competence. No-one gives a hoot where you came from. Jamie Markham says they're less silly about discipline too.'

This idea so outraged Peter Fairweather that he quite forgot to avoid conflict with his son. Discipline won wars and saved lives so could not be regarded as silly. He did not see why Thomas would be attracted to any institution that did not value it. Besides that, there was a family tradition of army service.

'Hardly a tradition,' said Tom. '*You* managed to duck out, so we're only talking about your father and his brother.'

Lennie's limbs felt heavy. She had slept late. Was she sickening for something? Other than last year's scarlet fever, she was rarely ill, had to think back to a childhood bout of chicken pox which had driven her half-mad with itching and left a little crater at her temple as a memento. Tom had teased her for days about the spots—great unsightly warts, hardening into crusts over her skin—and then fallen sick himself. She had recovered from the worst by then and had busied herself fetching cooling drinks for him and daubing calamine lotion onto his limbs and face, rendering him a chalky pink warrior.

'Want to come to York?' Thomas's voice cut across her thoughts, as she filled the kettle. 'I've some books to collect,' he said. 'I could do with a hand carrying them.'

'Oh. But I've things to do.'

'What kind of things?' Thomas gave a flick of his wrist: there was nothing in her day that could not be dismissed.

Lennie carried on spooning tea into the pot, thought how small her world must seem to her brother: this cottage with its little square of a garden, a doll's house. Suddenly she saw herself as if from above, busying herself like an ant in its nest, constantly in motion but to no purpose that an observer could discern.

'I would, Tom, but I really do have lots to do and Alexander has asked me to come with him to York tomorrow.'

'Suit yourself then.' Tom pushed back his chair and took up his jacket.

Their father left soon afterwards. She craved company yet she was glad to have the cottage to herself on days when he and Tom were at odds. Between the two of them, there was barely room for anyone else, she just was an insubstantial thing, to be pressed into corners. There was an strange feeling in Lennie's stomach. She wanted to eat and not eat at the same time. Scraping the bright eggy mess from Tom's plate did nothing to improve things. She poured tea for herself; sat down at the table to drink it. The hot tea hit her stomach before there was anything she could do about it; there was something wrong with the milk. An oily curdled taste coated the inside of her mouth. Lennie dropped her cup onto the saucer, covered her mouth and hurried to the lavatory to spit. What was Mrs. Cuthbert thinking? The big refrigerator hummed so confidently behind the shop counter, displaying its rows of dairy

produce with buxom pride, but it mustn't be working properly. She wondered if she could she ask her father to complain.
Mrs. Cuthbert must be poisoning half the village with her
stock!

And yet her father and Tom had taken milk with their tea
this morning and neither of them had complained of any foul
taste. In the kitchen, she sniffed the bottle. The milk seemed to
be perfectly fine. The contents had not thickened or turned
yellow at the edges. Perhaps it was nothing to do with the milk.
Maybe she really was becoming unwell. That wouldn't do
though. Alexander was taking her out properly tomorrow, not
just dropping by on a whim—she couldn't be ill. Lennie took
down a tumbler from the cupboard, poured a tiny splash of the
milk into the base of it, lifted the glass to her lips.

She hurtled towards the sink, bent almost double over it,
her body shuddering of its own accord. Once it had started the
shuddering would not stop. Her stomach wrenched itself
inside out, over and over. She was choking. Tears ran down her
face. She could not see. Until, eventually, she could stand
upright again, legs hot and shaky beneath her. She wiped away
the tears and the stringy mucus that was like some horrible
drool a dog might have produced, carefully washed out the
sink. She knew.

D on't you want to see your baby?' The midwife said when it all was over. The question, the laughter that accompanied it, surprised Venetia; in all the pain and commotion of the last few hours she had forgotten that this would be the outcome. The midwife finished what she was doing, while Venetia looked down at herself. Her stomach was no longer hard and proud but crumpled, like a tent that has been struck. Soldiers must feel like this, she thought, when the guns stop firing, and it is time to see what damage had been inflicted during the heat of the battle, what has been bruised or bloodied, what destroyed. She noticed that she was shaking.

'You've a little boy,' said the midwife, handing her a bundle of blankets. 'Congratulations.'

Venetia held out her arms to receive him, gathering him to her heart as mothers do. She gazed down at her newborn child, Alexander, they had decided to call him. She looked at his birth-pinched face, nose flattened, eyelids like a small lizard. She felt nothing.

The pregnancy had been straightforward. She had suffered no morning sickness, had only started to wonder when she missed a second month. Dr. Harrison confirmed what she suspected and life carried on as usual. She was busy with the renovations to the salon, still went out riding most days, much to Angus's concern, stopping only when she was too heavy to pull herself up into the saddle without assistance. She carried the

child well, people said, so neat and tidy, and while this survey-
ing and assessing of her body as though she were some kind of
municipal object made her uncomfortable, she had to agree
with the verdict. The baby had curled itself tightly beneath her
ribcage, while the rest of her body remained lithe and unaf-
fected. She was proud of her unabated energy, as if there was
some rectitude in not slumping into fat torpor.

'He doesn't like me,' she found herself saying, when the
baby was a week old. She hardly recognised the petulance in
her own voice. Angus smiled and shook his head at her, as if
she'd made a poor joke. She might have added: *I don't much
like him either*, but it would have been an exaggeration, or a
skewing of the truth. From that first moment she had remained
almost indifferent to her son. She looked down at him with a
blankness that was tinged only with the resentment of the very
tired.

'You need some rest,' was all that Angus said.

Well, exhaustion was partly to blame—she attributed the
odd sense of floating above everything to that—but she knew
she was right. Why else would the child keep crying out in
hunger and then refuse to feed from her? Already, it had
become a battle between the two of them, Venetia putting the
baby to her breast when he cried, holding her breath as he
took her nipple into his mouth. Seconds later, he would throw
himself off with surprising force, face crumpling into a howl,
features contorting like a small, enraged demon. The strength
of him was surprising. Like one of those strangely muscular
cherubs, or the Christ Child himself in a renaissance painting,
with the stature of an infant and breadth of a grown man. It
scared her, his capacity for rage, she who had not thought herself easily cowed. He was just a child she had to remind herself, a tiny scrap of flesh.

'Where's my lovely boy?' Angus would say, coming in from

his work on the estate, scooping Alexander up in his arms. A little part of her would be puzzled, wondering to whom he referred.

Night times were the worst, the bleakness of the early hours, until daylight pushed everything back into its right shape. Time and again she would repeat the process of coaxing Alexander to latch on to her breast, both she and the infant growing slippery from effort and agitation. Eventually he would suckle a little and then fall into a dissatisfied sleep, leaving Venetia staring into the darkness, the clock ticking smugly in the hallway below. She was beyond tired by that stage—her body still ached from the birth, and from the tension of trying to hold him in the correct position while he fed. Her breasts turned to hot, hard rocks, aching from the milk that Alexander craved but did not want. Still, she was unable to sleep, a knot of anxiety in the pit of her stomach, turning and tightening as she waited for the baby to wake from his fitful doze, for the crying to begin all over again. Angus would find the two of them slumped in the chair like wounded soldiers, daylight sliding through the nursery window bringing the pretence of new beginnings.

The midwife came to visit, wanted to know why Venetia didn't give the baby a bottle. Lots of women preferred it these days and that way someone could come in to help, especially with the night feeds. Sir Angus would likely be happier with that. You had to think about the father as well. Venetia said she'd think about it, just to stop the woman hectoring, but resolved to keep trying nonetheless. She'd grown up on a farm, knew about the bad ewe who couldn't give her newborn what it needed. Eventually, the small creature would be taken away and introduced into to another family, or else she or her mother would bottle-feed it. You'd think twice about breeding from that animal again. It didn't have the right instincts.

What she would have given to feel clean and contained and healthy again. She was leaking like some great-uddered milk cow. If she could just get herself organised and clean, stay that way for an hour or two, there might be a chance of taking control, instead of lying around in a hot, exhausted heap all the time, sweat running from her brow and temples, adding to the mess. It was unseemly. No wonder Angus kept urging her to rest, to leave the child with one of the maids for an hour or two. He must wonder what had become of his old wife, the one who had been self-possessed for one so young, with her smart clothes and the arch manner that had always amused him. He did his best to help, taking the pram around the Great Lawn, or to Sir Laurie's rooms. The crying didn't seem to bother him. Once she overhead him talking to Alexander about his plans for the estate. She might have teased him about it if she'd been capable.

'Failing to thrive,' the midwife said, one morning about two weeks after Alexander's birth. If things didn't improve, she said, eyeing Venetia meaningfully, then we'd need to have a good think about what's happening here. The midwife checked the scales again, Alexander's mottled little body swamped by his nappy, his limbs spidery, shook her head.

You read about it in the newspaper sometimes: mothers who neglected to clothe their offspring properly or bathe them, the children being taken away 'for their own sake.' Once she'd seen a story of a woman whose baby, like Alexander, would not stop crying. The woman had taken a cushion and held it over the baby's face until the crying stopped for good. At the trial she said that she loved the child dearly, was distraught by what she had done. The noise had been awful though. It was the only way to make it stop. Looking down into Alexander's cot, Venetia understood what had driven the woman to that point, though she had no urge to hurt her own child. He had lived inside her body for nine months in perfect peace, the two of them in equilibrium. Now everything was off-kilter and she did not know what to do about it. Crying was a ridiculous response, tears splashing on to the white blanket in the cot. At this rate she would wake him but the tears kept on coming. She covered her mouth with her hands, held her breath, but the noise wouldn't stop.

L ying on his bed, Tennyson's poems abandoned on the floor, Danny knew himself to be a fool because the thought had never crossed his mind. Alexander bloody Richmond. Lord of almost everything now that old Sir Angus was dead and gone.

A small, wiry boy he'd been, building dams across the river shallows in bright sunlight; who should have been cowed by the village lads but wasn't. Something to do with a sharp tongue, and, of course, no-one forgetting who his old man was. Danny hadn't cared about that, had liked him for his laughter, his grand ideas: they should dig a great network of tunnels between their homes, put on a play that the whole village would watch, recreate the Battle of Britain by gathering together as many model Spitfires and Hurricanes as possible. Alexander would come up with the next big idea while Danny's job was to realise it in line with the resources at hand. Alexander would clap him on the shoulder and call him his 'right hand man.'

Picture him now, Danny urged himself, sitting up on his bed and holding his head in his hands, as if trying to squeeze out the truth. Looks like his mother, that's what people said about him. His father was dark and thicker-set, with his perfect manners no matter who you were, everyone saying it was a sad day when he died. Alexander would inherit everything as soon as he was old enough, even the sawmill, so that Danny would spend the rest of his life in thrall to him. Set for life, his mam said only this morning, boasting to her sister about his apprenticeship at the mill. Not knowing how he longed to escape. A dream that now seemed impossible and pointless if Lennie wasn't to be part of it.

The Christmas party up at the Hall last year. That was the last time he'd seen Alexander. He was standing at one end of the salon by the great fireplace, talking to Thomas, who looked as sullen ever. There was something fox-like about Alexander now that he was older, Danny noticed, a sharper set to his face. Handsome though, with Hattie and the rest of the kitchen girls all looking his way. Danny had seen him out riding last winter too. On a day when the fields were iced with frost, the grass blades snapping beneath your boots, the sky blue and endless.

His broad clear brow in sunlight glow'd;
On burnish'd hooves his war-horse trode;

Danny felt sure that there would be a whole library full of poetry somewhere in the Hall for those who wanted it. Alexander would never need to take a train into York, talk too loudly in a second-hand bookshop just to get hold of a cheap battered copy that was losing its cover. His mouth would be full of poetry already and it would come easily to him instead of being all stopped up inside. The heir to Richmond Hall didn't need to dream ridiculous dreams about working in a stone yard and someone like Lennie settling for that. Danny saw how blinkered he had been by his passion. He'd been so sure that only he could comprehend her quiet splendour, that it had never occurred to him to search the horizon for rivals.

Danny escaped as soon as possible the next day, slamming the cottage door behind him in his hurry to be away. He caught the first train to York, intending to hitch the rest of the way to barracks. As no-one seemed to be driving any distance today, he worked his way there in stages, walking for a bit when he found himself on country roads. Though it was still early, it was going to be a proper summer's day. The birds were half-crazed with it, shrieking at one another from the hedgerows, while the spiders had been busy, stretching dewy webs across his pathway that glittered and trembled in the morning air. The beauty didn't get past the surface of him though. All morning he walked and hitched, the day settling into itself, hot and lazy. By the time he reached the gates of the barracks, evening was coming and the birds had quietened.

As he readied himself for bed that night, something came to mind which gave him a sliver of hope. He just needed to be sure. Square-bashing the next day was preceded by a punitive session in the gym and both acted like some kind of medicine, lifting Danny's despair still further. It was easier to think straight now that he was no longer locked up inside his own head.

'Porter!' he called across the parade ground as the recruits made their way into tea. Porter, who was walking ahead of him, waited for Danny to catch up.

'What's up, fellow? Good weekend home?' he said, offering Danny a cigarette.

'Yes thanks. I just wanted to ask . . . Your sister's at Cambridge, isn't she? The university.'

'Why, are you in need of a date?' Porter grinned at him. 'I'm not sure Cecily's quite what you're after.'

Danny reddened. 'No, not that. You said something about her being home for the summer.'

'Yes, and bored out of her mind after a month of being dragged to bridge drives and WI teas by my mother. She'll be desperate to go up again come autumn.'

So Porter's sister was home from college, had been for weeks. Yet Hattie had said Alexander Richmond had gone abroad. Why wouldn't he come home to see Lennie if they were supposed to be courting? It didn't make sense, yet he found it hard to believe that Hattie would tell an outright lie. The village was full of gossip, always had been; Hattie couldn't stop people telling her things that might not be true, especially that sister of hers who wasn't, everyone suspected, quite right in the head. It wasn't much to go on but it was enough to make a difference. Danny, tired from the day's exertions, slept soundly that night, despite McLean snoring like a donkey in the next bunk.

T here were voices on the stairs. Fresh sunlight was slanting through the window. The midwife was not due until
late morning.

Venetia could make out disjointed bits of conversation. The
nursery door was slightly ajar.

'Sleeping . . . ' Angus was saying. 'Don't know what . . . '

'Very much afraid . . . your wife . . . '

'Now then, what's been happening here?' the midwife
said, entering. Without waiting for an answer, she scooped
up Alexander from his crib, pulling the blanket from him.
Alexander was limp in sleep, his scrappy arms half sus-
pended in the air in protest, legs dangling beneath him. His
skin was blotchy and purple. He looked the opposite of
health.

Failing to thrive. Her child.

The midwife shook her head. 'This can't go on any longer.'

Venetia's dressing gown was open, her nightdress still
unbuttoned from the last aborted feed. She had not brushed
her hair or washed her face. She was too tired to argue.

The midwife misinterpreted her silence. 'Do you want this
baby to end up in hospital? Because that's what will happen if
you carry on with this nonsense.'

Venetia stared at her, and then at Angus who was hovering
in the doorway. Waiting for him to take issue with this manner
of address. There were still times when she had to remind herself that she was Lady Richmond, not just young Venetia from

the farm, but there was not a housemaid at the Hall who would dare to speak to her with such disrespect.

If only she'd had time to clean her teeth.

The midwife tested the warmed milk on the inside her wrist and then handed the bottle to Venetia.

'Brush his lips with it,' she said. Alexander was sleeping soundly for once, heavy in Venetia's arms. His mouth twitched as soon as the teat touched his lips. His eyes flickered for a second; he opened his mouth. Venetia nudged the bottle in. Alexander's eyes opened. He began to suck, slowly at first, wary of this new introduction to the whole business of feeding, but then more quickly, his temples fluttering. When he began taking great greedy gulps, she heard Angus laugh, relief in his voice. The midwife said:

'There! The poor mite was starving.'

'Good boy,' said Angus, stroking the baby's head. He did not look at Venetia.

'He'll be putting weight on in no time,' the woman went on, 'now that he's getting what he needs. I've left you more bottles downstairs and some formula. You'll have to get into a routine with the sterilising, of course, but you're lucky enough to have folk who can help you with that sort of thing.'

She wasn't to be trusted even with that task.

Part of her had imagined carrying on with life as usual—she would take the baby with her on trips to the stables, the kitchen, the garden, the obligatory visits to villagers in need. She would still enjoy quiet dinners with Angus, talking through the events of their day, the child a delightful appendage to their happy existence. She had been wrong. She understood that now. Motherhood was a form of combat and the better prepared she was, the more likely she was to triumph over this enemy child who'd turned out to have far more power than she'd thought possible.

'He needs a nanny,' said Angus, finding the two of them asleep in the nursing chair one day. 'Then you could get some rest.'

'We don't need one,' she said. 'I've told you.'

Fatigue made her tone so sour. She had vowed to watch herself for it, that wasn't the kind of person Angus had married, but every time he mentioned a nanny it felt like confirmation of a lack of competency on her part. It was a matter of pride and also of difference. All she needed to do was to take care of this one small child and of herself. How difficult could it be when the women in the village tended to half a dozen infants, scrubbed doorsteps, hung out swathes of nappies to dry with hands raw from work? Her own mother had never needed help either.

But in Angus's world, everyone had a nanny. To him it was quite straightforward; he would happily have engaged someone capable even before she had given birth. It was this, more than the estate, its buildings and all its acres that brought home to Venetia what was different about the two of them. Her husband's early years had been patterned by the nursery and the ordered rhythm of its day: a morning walk, riding lessons, teatimes and early to bed. Venetia and her brothers had scrabbled towards adulthood in a mess of limbs and sunlit impressions, their parents and elders existing somewhere shadowy and peripheral, like an afterthought. Angus's way wasn't something to disapprove of exactly, but she couldn't recognise it for herself, for her own child. When all was said and done, it shouldn't be hard to look after something so small.

'Put him in his pram out on the lawn,' the midwife said, when colic made Alexander draw up his legs and scream. 'Or in the hallway if the weather's bad.' She'd laughed, shaken her head at Venetia. 'You're making a rod for your own back, picking him up every time like that.'

How unfortunate, Venetia thought. A midwife who didn't like mothers *or* their babies. But perhaps it was just her, Venetia, and other families weren't so disappointing.

She walked through the village with the pram early one morning. Neither she nor Alexander had slept properly the night before but, determined to start the day on a brighter note, she'd made the effort to take him out for a walk immediately after breakfast.

Myrtle Brayshaw, postman's wife, mother of five, waved as they passed her cottage, left off picking gooseberries to join them. She gazed down in the pram at Alexander's fine blond hair, his eyes as blue as an autumn sky. 'Ah, love him,' she said, brushing her hands over her apron.

It was intended as compliment, an appreciation of her child's beauty, but it felt like a command, as if this capable woman could see past her neatly buttoned raincoat, to the empty heart within.

I was going to take you for tea at "Betty's" after the film,'
said Alexander.

'I'm sorry.' Lennie held onto the door frame. 'Something I
ate maybe.'

She could feel it again, like a bubbling in the pit of her
stomach. Already, she knew the pattern, how that stirred-up
feeling would build to something unstoppable. Tomorrow she
would get up early, try to eat something before Tom and her
father came downstairs. That way they'd be out of earshot if
she had to be sick. Dry toast was the thing; she'd heard that
once though she couldn't remember where or imagine why
she'd held onto it. *Something plain.*

'Some fresh air'll help.' Alexander looked at her. 'It's not
your bloody father being difficult again is it? Oh do come on,
Lennie, I really need to get away from here for a bit.'

'I'm sorry, Alexander.' The churning feeling was more
urgent. Any moment now her stomach would lurch, and she
wouldn't be able to control what came next. 'I've got to go.'

Lennie slammed the door in Alexander's face and ran.

Last night she had persuaded herself into believing that she
was mistaken, that her imagination was running away with her,
that the sickness was down to something she'd eaten and the
lateness wasn't worth thinking about yet, it being such a short
time since *it* happened, just a coincidence. She slept well but
in the morning the sickness had been there, waiting. She had
wedged shut the bedroom door with a chair; slipped off her

nightdress. The evidence was in the mirror, subtle yet unavoidable: a new roundness to her breasts, which felt hard and sore when she touched them. Her nipples looked different too, more pronounced. There was no change to her stomach—she turned sideways to check—she knew that it was too soon for that, and all the time she was examining herself, the nausea building.

The mere act of fetching a chair to reach the top shelf in the parlour made Lennie want to lie down and sleep. She had never felt so exhausted and ill in her life, not even when she'd had scarlet fever. This is what it must feel like to be old, she thought: drained by the smallest task, your body slowing down gradually until all the working parts stop. Or else to have a parasite living within you, leaching your strength away.

The cover of the book had once been blue but, with the exception of the creases in the spine which had retained their colour, it had now faded to grey. The pages were yellow, made of thick paper with a rough texture. As she turned them, some fell to the floor, floating down like desiccated wings. The book smelt of age and dust. It had belonged to her mother. Her father had, as far as she knew, never consulted it; his first response to any form of illness was to telephone Dr. Harrison. Still, she was familiar with it, had always thought it strange that her mother, who grew up in the middle of a city, would turn to herbal remedies. A gift, perhaps, given by someone because she was moving to the countryside? All Lennie could be sure of was that her mother had dug and planted out the cottage's little herb garden herself, must have wanted it even while honking taxis and pavements spilling over with people were still in her mind.

She read the inscription in the front of the book:

To Jennifer, from Margaret

It was undated. She must have seen it before; passed over it without interest. She had never heard her father speak of a Margaret. Girlish handwriting; an unknown person with a whole life of their own. Maybe dead now. Lennie felt she was putting her hand into a sack, rummaging blindly through the past. Once, when was small, she had watched a team of men digging just beyond the far edge of the estate. Looking for a Viking burial site, her father said, eyeing the men's beards and the dirt lodged under their fingernails with distrust. University men they might be, but Peter Fairweather saw no use in digging up the past when there was plenty to be getting on with in the here and now, and no harm in looking presentable while you were at it. Lennie had been fascinated by their project. Every afternoon she ran home from school across the fields to the spot where the men had been at work, where the tarpaulin covers baked and shone in the sun. She longed to see a glittering Viking sword, or a surprise cache of Roman jewellery hauled from the dark soil. In the end, the men found nothing, backfilled the exploratory trenches they'd dug in various spots. How hard it was, persuading Tom and Alexander and Danny to help carry on digging. They humoured her for an afternoon and then grew bored.

'What are the chances?' said Tom, abandoning the spade he'd borrowed from the gardener. Lennie remained certain that by joining the dots between the trenches, a thorough search of the area would unearth the bones of some giant Viking, his collapsed face covered by a great, golden death mask.

This little book with its inscription was a tiny borehole into the past. You might find nothing at all, or maybe if you dug down through layers you'd uncover the real thing, or else miss it by an inch or a mile. Lennie began turning the pages, disturbing pinhead insects that had lodged there. She knew what she was seeking in the alphabetical list of herbs and their uses—*angelica, calendula, chamomile, evening primrose, fennel, lovage*—yet could not have explained how she knew. She found it halfway down a page towards the back of the book: *Rosemary. Considered sacred by the ancient Greeks, Romans, Egyptians and Hebrews, Rosmarinus officials has been used in folk medicine for thousands of years to improve memory, soothe the digestive process, and relieve muscle aches and pains.*

To reduce pain: mix 2 drops of rosemary oil, 2 drops of peppermint oil and 1 tsp of olive oil. Rub on sore muscles and painful joints.

To heal neuralgia: take 2 drops of rosemary oil, 2 drops of helichrysum oil and 1 tsp of olive oil and rub on area.

She turned the page and found the lines that had been lodged in her mind from a time, perhaps, before she fully understood the meaning:

Rosemary is a herbal emmenagogue useful in stimulating the womb to bring about menstruation. Caution: traditionally, it was also used as an abortifacient and should be avoided during pregnancy.

The book had sat in its place on the top shelf for as long as she could remember. If her mother had consulted it in her presence, Lennie would have been too young to realise, just a baby herself.

A baby. Tilly Hartnett, who'd tried to drown herself in the river, had been pulled from the shallows just in time, crying and kicking like a great sodden baby herself. Or that girl from Branleigh who ran away down to London and died there. Some filthy backstreet place in Islington, they said. Might as well have finished butchering her then and there, rather than letting her suffer in agony for days afterwards. Her family had her buried somewhere in London where people weren't so bothered about such things. No plot in Branleigh churchyard for her. These stories were woven into the narrative of the village. No matter how sheltered a life you lived, there were tales of knitting needles, flights of stairs, coat hangers and all kinds of other horrors. You knew about those whether you wanted to or not.

Rosemary. The comforting, grandmotherly sound of it. How familiar to her, the sharp scent of its spiked leaves as she brushed past them in the garden, the innocent blue of its flowers.

To bring on menstruation: dry leaves thoroughly and cover with olive oil. Leave in a dark place for a month before use.

A small bottle of olive oil sat in the medical box beneath the sink, its neck gummed up and tacky from lack of use. Dr. Harrison prescribed it years ago, one summer when Tom had spent too many hours swimming and blocked up his ears.

A whole month. Plus the time it would take to dry the leaves.

It was impossible, even without the awful sickness. In trouble, they called it. All her life, Lennie had been the opposite of trouble. She would rather follow Tilly Hartnett into the river than face her father and Tom every day for all the weeks to come, having to smile and pretend that nothing was wrong. Lennie never prayed but, oh God! She sunk to her knees in the parlour, the book falling from her hands.

Another sentence jumped out at her.

Can also be infused in hot water to make rosemary tea.

That would have to do.

fterwards, she would barely recall the detail of the first twelve months of Alexander's life. As if the entire year had sunk beneath the surface, everything viewed through some watery murk where the sunlight couldn't reach. She must have functioned at some basic level, but with no energy left over. When Angus suggested a trip to London without the baby, or a drive to the coast, the thought of organising herself seemed overwhelming. It would have been pitiful to admit to that, so she made excuses—an appointment she couldn't change, Alexander sickening for something. She couldn't remember the last time she'd been to York, or even down to the stables to show Alexander the horses. In the rose garden, she watched him crawl on the grass but her senses wouldn't work in the way they once did—the perfumed blooms, the tumble of the rambling roses over the archways, might as well be rank weeds for all they meant to her. She ate because it was expected of her, tasting nothing. Sometimes she would pause mid-chew, wonder what substance was in her mouth.

'You're getting thin,' Angus said, watching her as she dressed one morning. She made an effort, not wanting to draw attention to herself, but each day there was less of her, her skirts swinging from her waist like loose bells.

Love him. She would give her life to protect Alexander. Sometimes, on the edge of sleep, a knot of anxiety tight in her stomach, scenes of disaster slid into her mind: a car taking a corner too fast and swerving towards the pram; Alexander slipping from her arms, falling from a bridge into a river full of rocks and boiling water. In every image she was there in an instant, throwing herself between car and pram, clambering over the parapet. Was that love, or merely anxiety turned up to an unbearable volume? Life was nothing but terrors and this was frightening to one who had always been bold. What had happened to the girl who would crouch down low over her pony's neck and attempt a jump before anyone else, who would follow her brothers into battle with the village boys? It was shameful to be so scared so Venetia did what she had always done when something was daunting, carried on as if she hadn't noticed. When Alexander was six months old, Angus asked her a question he had never asked before:

'Are you all right, darling?'

'Perfectly, thank you,' she said, having already decided on it.

Angus seemed to find their son endlessly amusing, liked to be charmed with stories about him.

'I tried to get him to crawl to me today,' she said one evening at dinner, hoping Angus wouldn't notice that she had barely touched her food. The pork chop on her plate looked monstrous, too solid to be edible, the frill of thick white fat at its edge sweating onto her plate. 'He seems to prefer rolling, gets about perfectly . . . '

She came to a halt, forgetting why she had begun. Angus took up where she had left off but noises and gestures meant nothing when she was too tired to decipher the signs.

'I think I need an early night,' she said, excusing herself from the table early.

She slept deeply and it was peaceful and empty. She would have liked to stay there for a long time, beneath the lid of unconsciousness. There was no point complaining about anything: this was her existence now, each day a series of tasks to be got through, and it was not a hard life or a traumatic one. She lived in comfort and security, with a husband who loved her and a child who was now thriving. The fault was in her, some flaw in her design which made her immune to happiness.

She took Alexander to see young Dr. Harrison. A vaccination was due and, like any responsible mother, she was punctilious about such arrangements. The injection was administered, Alexander sitting squarely on her lap. By the time she had fastened his clothes he had forgotten what he was crying about.

Dr. Harrison wasn't finished. 'And how are *you*, Lady Richmond?'

'Perfectly well, thank you.' The question surprised her, but Dr. Harrison was new and enthusiastic, as his father must once have been.

'Managing?'

She nodded, ready to leave.

'Because lots of women don't and there are things that can help.'

'What sort of things?' She didn't know why she'd asked. Alexander wriggled and she held him tightly, like a bulwark between her and the desk.

'Well, medication can be of use. There's some work being done on that for post-natal problems that don't lift of their own accord. ECT's remarkably effective too.'

'ECT? You mean electricity?'

'It sounds worse than it is, but the results . . . '

Her knees were shaking, even with the weight of the baby on her lap, as if some invisible doctor had already administered the treatment. She pushed her chin down into her chest, steadying herself. A thought occurred to her. 'Did my husband give you some idea that . . . ?'

'It's just one form of therapy. I'm not suggesting . . . '

The pram was just outside in the waiting room. She stood. 'Alexander's nap is already overdue. He gets fretful.'

Dr. Harrison sat back in his chair, looking younger and more defeated than she'd expected. She forced a smile to her face, wanting to comfort both him and herself. 'I'm perfectly alright, you know. I certainly will be.'

Venetia marched home along the river path with the pram before her like some chariot of war, staring resolutely ahead. That kind of illness was for weak people who weren't fit for purpose. Or it was inherited like some poisoned legacy. She would not think of it again. Besides, she knew herself better than Dr. Harrison, better than her own husband, if indeed, he had intervened.

The anger seemed to help, like a call to arms. In the weeks that followed the underwater feeling left her as gradually as it had begun, a lifting of the skies above, as imperceptible as when they'd first pressed down, pushing her beneath the surface of herself. She did not believe in some chemical shift that a scientist could pinpoint. All she knew was that walking through the woods one morning, her step felt lighter, her feet no longer weighed down by invisible concrete. The feeling of lightness was like a memory of someone else's life, at once familiar and strange. Could the electricity have produced this same effect? Perhaps. She picked up the newspaper one day, became absorbed in an article about Germany's leader, Adolf Hitler, his new laws for the Jews.

'You're reading.' Angus smiled at her as if this prosaic act was some kind of phenomenon.

'Why ever not?' she said. Something like pleasure flickered in her all the same.

Venetia stood on the lawn. The sun was no longer a brassy bar, a rod for her own back, weighing down upon her shoulders.

Alexander was playing nearby. He heaved himself to a standing position before setting off across the grass, his small face furious in concentration. She found herself smiling at his unsustainable pace. He stumbled, stared at his feet with a comical air, as if they'd played a trick upon him, undeterred set off again. Something in his determination caught at her. She dropped to a crouch.

'Alexander!' she called, holding out her hands. 'This way.'

He stopped, looked over his shoulder at her in surprise. As if a stone or a bush had spoken to him. Then he changed direction, heading towards her in another great spurt of energy. His eyes were blue as the sky, bright with the joy of movement as he wavered, fat little hands steadying himself on unreliable air. 'Come to me,' she said, a twinge of anticipation or perhaps it was excitement growing in her stomach. And then, out of nowhere, love for her child crashed over her like a wave that had been quivering above her all this time. 'Come to mother, Alexander!'

A butterfly flitted in front of the child, its wings primrose yellow, almost transparent in their delicacy. Alexander, distracted, reached for it. She called again, opened her arms to him. He stared at her for a moment, thoughtful, and then waddled after the butterfly, chasing something more certain.

S he rose early, tamped down the growing nausea with dry toast and tea. Tom was going to Leeds to meet a friend so she could be sure of being alone. First, though, he wanted eggs and bacon. Lennie tried not to inhale as she stood over the stove but the hot, porcine smell of rendering fat found its way into her nostrils, her throat, and the sight of raw eggs, plopping into the pan with a foetal weight, sent her hurrying to the lavatory. She vomited as quietly as she could. It felt as if her ribs were wrenching apart. Her stomach ached from the silent heaving. She washed her face and hands and returned to finish her task. Thankfully, her father wanted only his usual porridge made with water. Lennie stirred the beige slurry, grateful for something so bland and inoffensive, though the slop of it dropping from spoon to bowl nearly undid her again.

Tom spoke little over breakfast, his mind already elsewhere. It had always been that way with him: his thoughts travelling ahead of him, disengaging with the present. Lennie had felt it ever since they were small. When Tom was preparing to go off to school each term, he never seemed to think twice about leaving. In his mind he had already departed. It made everything he left behind feel drab and less significant, somehow devalued by his indifference. There was a bit of Tom that existed separately from this cottage, this family; she wondered how it must feel to have the freedom to change your world for another whenever the fancy took you. If the world was to change overnight, turn in some new way that shifted the balance of everything, would she have the courage to exercise her new-found liberty, to lay down her sewing basket, the pots and pans for dinner, walk out of the door of the cottage without a backward glance? She wondered if that sort of thing might not require practise, and she had never even got started.

Lennie filled the kettle, put it on the stove. Then she went out into the garden. It was a sprightly morning, still fresh at this hour. She stepped between neat humps of thyme, curled in upon themselves like small mammals, sage plants bursting from the dewy earth in artless bouquets. When she reached the prostrate rosemary bush, its scarecrow arms marking the centre of the herb garden, she took out scissors and began snipping, taking sprigs from the established, woodier parts of the plant, rather than the soft new growth whose properties might be less concentrated. Returning to the kitchen, Lennie stripped the sprigs of their needle-sharp leaves. She fetched her rolling pin, the bread board. Using the end of the pin she began to pound the little heap of leaves. Soon, the chopping board was green and oily from the smashed leaves, and the air was filled with a pungent, medicinal scent. The process felt ancient and satisfying and womanly; on any other day Lennie might have smiled or sung to herself as she went about the simple task.

The kettle started to whistle, Lennie scraped the pulverised leaves into a jug and poured the boiled water over them. She wasn't clear about quantities—the book hadn't specified. Neither did she have any idea how long the process of infusing might take. Five minutes or five hours? She waited until the liquid was cool enough to drink before straining it carefully into a teacup, took a tentative sip.

The rosemary tea was watery, yellow in colour but less unpleasant than she'd expected. She had been anticipating something foul and undrinkable, like pond water. She took the unexpected outcome as a sign. It was not so different to lemon tea. Lennie picked up the cup again, drank it down slowly but steadily, fearful of making herself sick, fearful that she might have to start all over. She was surprised to find that her stomach did not threaten to reject the liquid and she finished it without any trouble. She washed and dried the cup, replaced it in the cupboard, suddenly buoyed by how easy it all was.

Her mother's book of remedies had given no indication of what to expect or how long things might take. Lennie decided to go about her morning chores as best she could, her body already having learned to move more cautiously than usual, as if it wanted to protect the very thing she was trying to expel. With slow, deliberate strokes, she mopped the kitchen floor, the repetitive, mindless motion and her lightened mood setting her thoughts free.

How different things might have been if she and Alexander were already married, joyful even. Hard to imagine when she felt like this all day long, her limbs granite-heavy, the sickness simmering away inside her like a witch's cauldron, always on the point of boiling over. She'd finished ironing the last of the sheets, when she felt it. Like a fist gripping her insides and then after it a familiar ache, like the one she had each month, but this time concentrated into the small of her back, as if someone had kicked her. She put away the ironing board, folded the sheets into the cupboard, went upstairs.

Her room was cool, peaceful, the curtains easing in and out of the window in the breeze. It was definitely happening now. The contractions were coming from somewhere deep inside her and the ache was spreading. Lennie felt almost giddy with the relief of it. Bad things happened sometimes but then they were over and you were allowed to go on living. The world would be a blank and wonderful place again, where any story might yet be written. Tomorrow, she would go up to the Hall to find Alexander. She wouldn't wait for him to come to her.

With the release came a wave of tiredness. Lennie closed her eyes, drifted. Alexander on the river bank, his mouth moving silently. She knelt down, trying to hear what he was saying above the roar of the water. It was not Alexander, just a small boy. Danny Masters gazed up at her from the lip of the river. He was calling for help. Lennie stroked his hand, comforting him, and then, one by one, she prised his fingers from the crumbling soil.

It was just the three of them and they were lost in the woods. Not in a bad way because if you kept on going you'd eventually see something you recognised and work it out, but at this particular moment nothing looked familiar, which could only mean they still weren't anywhere near home. They walked on until they came to a clearing. A group of lads was building a den in the middle of it. Not much of one—the branches they'd used to form a wigwam shape looked flimsy, like they might buckle any minute, and they'd shored the thing up with greying planks, deeply ridged, stuck with rusty nails, that threatened to send the structure toppling. A fire smoked to one side of the den, a small boy crouched over it, poking.

'Where do you lot think you're going?' Danny recognised the lad who stepped forward. Danny's mam, who knew everyone on account of her midwifing, had pointed out the family in Helmsley one day not that long ago, when he'd gone to help her with the shopping. Kids allowed to run wild she'd said, and they'd looked it to him, a pack of wiry, walnut-brown creatures in mish-mash clothing, something wild and hard in their eyes. From Branleigh, they were, which meant that he and Alexander and Lennie shouldn't be standing in this clearing, on someone else's territory.

'Go where we like, can't we?' he said.

There was no point admitting fault now. The best you could hope for was a stand-off. Adults acted like that was the wrong way of going about things. There was no point explaining to them that all those ideas they tried to teach you in school and at home—doing unto others, that kind of stuff—went out the window as soon as you were in the woods. None of that worked here, which the grown-ups must know, having been young themselves once. Forget about kindness and fairness; work things out for yourself.

'You can leave yer girlfriend if you like.' The lad, the one who was the ringleader, sniggered and lifted his chin towards Lennie. 'Want to come inside my den for a bit?'

His mates all laughing, drew together behind him. Danny was calculating. The lad was shorter than him, just a bit, but weirdly muscular in his arms and across his chest, like he spent his time swinging through the trees or punching walls. Lennie looked straight ahead as if the boy hadn't spoken. Her chin tilted up, just a fraction. The lad looked around at the little crew behind him. 'Fancies herself a bit, don't she? Just as well, cause nobody else does.'

His friends howling with laughter, way more than it was worth. Danny's fists clenched now, ready.

'Don't speak to her like that,' said Alexander, stepping forwards. Danny could feel him there, a slight golden presence beside him. The Branleigh lot clocked the accent right away. Danny could hear it as if through their ears, sharp and honed as a well-cared-for tool. Like he was hearing it himself for the first time. Had it got stronger since he had been away at school or was it just that they were here, in this clearing, where differences mattered more? 'Anyway,' Alexander's voice grew sharper, posher, 'we'll go where we bloody well like.'

Was that a tremble in Alexander's voice? Danny noticed it, picked up on fear behind the brave words, which were greeted with more howls of laughter from the group. There was a tension in the air now. The Branleigh lads hadn't worked out who Alexander was, Danny could see that. Would it make a difference? He couldn't be sure and Alexander wouldn't thank him for letting them know, not one bit.

'Mouthy aren't you?' said their ringleader. His tone was jovial but his eyes were dark and fixed all of a sudden, like a mad person's. A line had been crossed and everyone knew it. 'Well, I've got a bigger mouth and bigger fists than you, see?' It was true, Danny thought, checking. The boy's fists were enormous.

'What are you going to do?' said Alexander. 'Hit me, or suck me off?'

The fight, when it came, was quick and brutal. The Branleigh kid lunged towards Alexander but Danny got there first. He was angrier than he'd thought, a mad kind of blur in his mind for a minute or two. Then it was over. The other kids had retreated to a kind of log seat in the trees where the brambles grew long and whippy, and he and Alexander and Lennie were turning back towards home, instinct taking over now they needed it, being sure to go slowly to demonstrate that it was choice not necessity that sent them in that direction.

Danny's face stung from the blows he'd taken.

You didn't need to do that.

Alexander never said it, but Danny could feel the unspoken words hanging between them as they walked. It wasn't like he'd made a choice, he told himself. Sometimes things just happened. What were you supposed to do about it? Lennie walked between the two of them, as if it was best to keep them apart. He could tell that she was upset, as if it had bruised her skin in some invisible way. It made him angry again, with the wild Branleigh kid, with Alexander, with Lennie even. Something had shifted between the three of them that he didn't want to think about. He wished he'd been with one of the lads from the village, some other girl too, Bridie say or even Hattie, who would have silenced the Branleigh kid with some mean answer. They'd have been laughing about it by now, same as they always did when trouble came along and they survived it.

But after a while the woods were theirs again and Danny felt his shoulders relaxing. They skirted the great oak that had been charred by lighting years before and turned onto a familiar track towards the river.

'Are you all right?' said Lennie softly.

'Fine,' he said, because he was now.

When they reached the river path, she seemed to hesitate. For one moment it felt to Danny that she wanted to go with him, towards the village. She looked at him, went to say something, but then just smiled and shook her head, as if catching herself at it. She turned the other way instead, following Alexander towards Richmond Hall.

T here was blood. Thin and watery, but there it was. The contractions in her womb had stopped. A relief that there was something. She hadn't known what to expect, had not allowed herself to think about what might emerge from her body. There was just this. No little limbs, no hands like peony fronds clawing up through spring soil, no unblinking eye staring up at her, no unformed, pulsing blob, none of the monsters of her imagination. Silly to have been so scared. It could only have been a matter of weeks, could barely have been a real thing. With the future back in its rightful place again, Lennie flew through the rest of the day's chores on light feet. She went out into the garden to gather some of her father's awful marigolds for the dinner table. For some reason she felt extraordinarily grateful to him, as though he'd had a part in rescuing her.

They had a pleasant time over supper, just the two of them, Tom having left a message to say he would be late. Lennie made a special effort to reassure her father, knowing that he worried about the company Tom kept. The secretiveness, which their father took as a personal affront. She knew from experience that it was best to let her father voice his concerns. With patience, she knew that his attention would eventually turn to happier subjects. She had found his fretting wearisome lately, all her thoughts taken up by Alexander, her own trouble, but tonight Lennie felt herself overflowing with sympathy, capable of dispensing goodness to the whole world.

When she washed the dishes she saw that the lights were still shining up at the Hall. It looked like a great ship against a dark sea. She wondered if Alexander was still cross about the missed trip to York. She would have to make it up to him somehow. She climbed the stairs to bed, lay for a time, staring up at the ceiling.

When had loving Alexander become so difficult, a jangling up of her once-peaceful cells, the world off-kilter all around her? People talked about love as though it was a blissful state; to Lennie it seemed something taut and perilous:

Why are you dressed like a whore?

But no. She placed her hand on her stomach. Flat, warm, empty. The universe would be on her side from now on. Alexander loved her; she loved him. The world had moved in precise ways to make it so.

The girls had gone to a lot of effort, hanging up bunting and streamers and stars cut from silver paper all around the village hall. Someone had found a bit of red carpet, stained only down one edge, to lay out in the entrance, and the high windows of the hall were covered with coloured paper to keep out the early evening sunshine. By the time Danny arrived the band was already playing, on a stage decorated with swags of gold material. They'd been hired in from York, Bridie Martin said, all flushed from balancing on a chair to cover the last of the lights with red crepe paper.

The village boys arrived in twos and threes, hair brushed back and ties knotted too tightly, daring anyone to comment, the girls growing self-conscious and shrill in their stiff new dresses. A good few of the lads wanted to know about training, how long he was home for and suchlike. Danny was happy to answer but already he felt older, set apart from these boys yet to be called up. Just a few days ago he'd said goodbye to the rest of his billet and already he was nostalgic for the friends he'd made in those short intense weeks. He felt adrift, as though he didn't belong anywhere.

A glass of beer in his hand, he moved closer to the stage. The band was playing numbers sedate enough to satisfy the odd parent who put their head around the door. When he looked closer he thought that if you took away their smart suits, the lads looked a bit rough around the edges. He could imagine them later, when the violent orange punch had taken effect, taking their chances when the local girls grew tired of the familiar old faces. Mary Stockton and Jackie Bracegirdle were dancing just in front of the stage, already clinging too closely to one another. Bridie and her friend Dorothy danced together, giggling at themselves as they swung each other round.

'Not dancing then?' said Hattie, arriving at his side. She handed him a beer, took a ladylike sip from her own glass of punch. She was wearing a yellow dress with big skirts that showed off her small waist, with thin straps at the shoulders. Quartered bits of orange floated in her punch, with some murky-looking leaves of some kind.

'Not yet,' he said, taking the beer from her. Hattie's mouth went flat with disappointment. He felt bad. 'Maybe later.'

'The band are great, aren't they?' said Hattie, cheering up. 'Better than last year's anyway. Oh, look who's here.'

'Who?' But he knew from the way her expression had fallen again.

He hadn't, for one moment, expected Lennie to come. The party was an annual event, eagerly waited for by the young people of Starome, yet Lennie had never once attended. He had only come along himself to avoid being alone—it was amazing how quickly army life got you accustomed to the company of others and then you couldn't do without it. Yet there she was, standing in the doorway, wearing a dress with blue flowers on it, looking down at the run of red carpet beneath her feet as if puzzled to find it there.

Danny looked away, forced himself to listen to Hattie, though he heard nothing, saw nothing. When, at last, he trusted himself to glance over his shoulder again, Lennie had moved away from the door, was speaking to Miss Price, their old schoolmistress who had organised the party, and who had dropped by to make sure all was well. He should walk across the room, speak to them both. What would he say? Could he

ask Lennie to dance? No, not that, here in front of everyone
they knew. He watched as they were joined by Sandra Taylor
and Jeanie Patterson. Sandra had left off her glasses for the
occasion so that her face looked all bare and twitchy, like an
excitable mouse. Jackie Bracegirdle came across with another
beer, flinging his great arm around Danny's shoulder, wanting
to know where he was being posted to next.

'Norfolk,' Danny said. 'Day after tomorrow.'

For no very good reason, Danny had put his name down to
train as a mechanic. He had no thoughts about Norfolk either,
except to think that it sounded a decent enough posting.
McLean's older brother had been at the same barracks, said it
was pretty lax. Some glitch in administration meant they'd not
been expecting him, so the elder McLean had spent his first
two weeks sunbathing on a nearby beach and flirting with the
local girls. The idea of anyone related to McLean flirting was a
terrifying concept, but the story had the ring of truth about it.
Danny had already said goodbye to his mam. She was staying
in Malton for a few days because Danny's cousin Valerie was
already overdue. When she'd gone, he found his rucksack by
his bed with everything laundered for him and a tin of toffee
in one of the side-pockets. Weeks of training must have taught
him something, because he moved it, for the sake of tidiness,
into the wardrobe.

Lennie was standing on her own, drinking punch. She had
a wary look about her, like an animal when it senses danger at
hand but can't pinpoint its source. Some of the other girls were
talking about her, Bridie and her lot huddled together by the
stage. He'd spent too many years in their company not to know
what they were about. How lovely Lennie was with her hair
falling over her shoulders, the pale oval of her face like the
Virgin Mary in the illustrated bible they'd read when they were
children, back in school. He stared at her, he couldn't help
himself, her body slender and upright as a young birch. All the

girls he'd once thought pretty seemed commonplace and clumsy next to her. Why had she come tonight? She had no friends here, not really. Even Joan Nicholson had moved right away. His mam said she had some mad idea of going to university. When Joan's dad said no, get a proper job, she went off to join the WRAF, just to show him. Besides, if everything Hattie said was true, Lennie should surely have been at home right now, waiting for him to come back.

The band seemed to wake up once darkness fell outside. The music was modern now and rawer, getting into your bones. Danny talked to people without knowing what he said, signalled yes to more beer. Miss Price left, waving goodbye to people, and the beer and punch must have been doing their work because more people were dancing. Jackie and Mary were locked into one another at the edge of the dance floor. They'd be disappearing soon, off somewhere secret before Mary had to be home.

The lights went up. It was time for the band to take a break, for the food that had been set out earlier on trestle tables to be uncovered. Lennie was going now, he could see her outline in the doorway. Hattie was making her way across the hall towards him, a determined look in her eyes. He needed to move.

'Lennie!' He was outside the hall, the darkness gathering him in.

She waited for him to catch up.

'I'll walk you home,' he said.

As easily as that, they were walking together. He'd pictured it in his head many times but now that it was actually happening it felt less real that it had in his imagination. Behind them, he heard little balloons of noise as people came and went from the party.

'The band weren't so bad,' said Danny, trying for any kind of conversation. The book of poetry was in the inside pocket of his jacket, one corner of it digging into his heart. He carried it like a talisman but wished he hadn't brought it with him tonight; he didn't need it now that Lennie was here, right next to him. They passed his home, came to the stile that led to the river path. Lennie was agile, needed no help to climb the stile, but she took his hand when he offered it.

'You were watching me,' Lennie said, holding onto him for a moment longer. 'I've noticed before.' There was no way of telling if she was angry or happy about it.

'I'm not the only one,' he said, then wished he'd kept his mouth shut.

They were approaching the roar of the Stride.

'You like me, don't you, Danny.'

At first he thought she was teasing him.

'I do,' he found himself saying. He stared at her, knowing that all his desperation was there to see. It was too late to stop now. 'Don't you know?'

'People act a certain way sometimes . . . It's hard to know what to believe.'

She had drunk too much of the punch, her words were sticky with it. Him too. His head felt heavy, as if the beer had thickened his senses.

'I would never . . . Why did you come tonight, Lennie?'

He had to know.

'I saw Miss Price and she said it would be good for me.' She shrugged. 'I don't know why. Even my father said I should go. Usually he likes me to be at home.'

'Don't you get lonely? With school over and you up there all on your own?'

She shook her head. 'No. I mean, I never used to. I hadn't spoken to anyone all day though. I knew I wouldn't enjoy the party but I suppose I grew tired of waiting around.'

'Like the Lady of Shalott,' he said.

'What?' Lennie laughed. 'Oh yes, I suppose so.'

Dusk clung to the bracken, damp-fronded and green on either side of the pathway. Lennie came towards him and the night closed in upon him. They kissed and she tasted of oranges and cheap rum. He felt her hands on his chest, pushing him away.

'Danny?' she asked, as if, in the darkness, she was uncertain of him.

He could feel the blood crashing in his eardrums, in his chest. He could barely speak and yet it didn't matter: Lennie had taken his hand in hers and was leading him off the pathway into the trees, stopping only when they reached a clearing.

'Here,' she said, as if the clearing was a gift that had been waiting for them. Her eyes were shining in the black light. 'I watched you once,' she said 'When you were swimming in that pool downstream.'

'I knew.' Looking back it felt like a certainty. Though it was dark, he flushed at the memory of his nakedness.

'You were lovely.' Lennie reached out the fingers of one hand, placed them on his chest, and Danny's stomach lurched in agony. Hardly aware of what she was doing, she seemed, her hair glowing in the gloom of the clearing. Ghost hair. A ghost girl, all pale like the moon. 'I wanted to keep on looking.'

Lennie put her arms round his waist, pulling him towards her. They kissed and he was lost after that: awkwardness of clothes; unpractised mouths; yielding undergrowth and the smell of some acrid wild herb rising up. She was wilder than he could ever have imagined, not the saintly creature of his dreams, but a girl who sunk her teeth into the flesh of his shoulder, drawing blood, who lifted her throat to the blade of the moon.

Danny dressed in a hurry. He helped Lennie search for her clothes. They were soon back on the footpath, man-made and civilised, the woods to one side of them and the great churn of the Stride on the other. The air was damp and in motion. A sweet, dark smell came to them on the breeze. Danny stepped off the pathway towards the river bank, dropping to a crouch by the patch of dark roses, her favourites. He wrenched a trio of blooms from a thorny branch, held them out to Lennie. Now she would have to say something to make this new, awful silence come to an end. In his heart he knew it to be a cheap gesture. Roses had nothing to do with what had just happened, out there in the woods.

'I love you, Lennie,' he said.

Worse even than flowers. The words came out before he could stop them. He let go of the roses. The thorns had hooked into his flesh like sharp little teeth. Danny cupped his palm, watched the blood pool, dark and shining, like an offering. Lennie took a step backwards, turned in what looked like panic. 'I'll walk you home,' he said, trying to take her arm in his, as if they were courting, as if what had happened had not happened. She shied away from him, pushed him with such force that he staggered, fell to his knees. He could see the river bank falling away beside him.

T he room where Angus had died, this bedroom had belonged to both of them until it had seemed obscene to continue to lie beside him at night, as though she was easing herself into her husband's coffin. Here, on one side of the oak bed—made up since by one of the girls, with cream sheets and the jacquard bedspread—was the armchair where she had kept vigil. No-one would ever sleep in this room again. How ordered and civilised it now looked, this place where a life unravelled. Whoever had cleaned it had forgotten to plump the chair cushion, the only detail out of place. The chair had creaked whenever she had moved in it. Perhaps the noise had been one of the last things that Angus had properly registered, an everyday irritation on the edge of nothingness.

She crossed to the window, her eyes following the line of the sycamores along the driveway. How often had she left the house during those days, taking the path that led towards the stables? She must feed the chickens, see to the horses, she would tell James or the nurse, though the chickens were thriving and the horses managed perfectly well without her, fed, watered and exercised by the stable lads. What she had really wanted was to breathe normal air again, to remind herself that life, in all its joyous mundanity, still continued.

Venetia turned abruptly from the window. She no longer wanted to be in this room where the minutes still passed at a slower rate. There was too much time to think here. The bedroom door had been closed for months. She did not know why, today, she had chosen to enter the room again. In her hurry to leave, she caught her foot on the corner of a chest of drawers, one of a pair which flanked the bed. The chest echoed against her shoe, but wasn't quite empty. Something rolled around inside the top drawer, back and forth, before coming to a halt. She did not need to look. She could picture what was inside the drawer precisely: it was an infant's cup of innocent blue, with a spouted lid and a transfer of a teddy bear on the side, the bear's red and yellow jumper half worn away. The cup had belonged to Alexander when he was a child. Later, she had retrieved it from the back of a cupboard in the kitchens, brought it here in case it was needed. Someone—not her—must take it away again.

CHAPTER 38

Lennie, September 1955

I n the cool, blue light of a new morning she was determined that she would no longer think about the past. Lennie dressed quickly and went down to the kitchen. The tap screeched as she filled the kettle, she must get someone in to look at it. She began making her father's porridge, tipping oats into the saucepan, salt, water, and then lighting the stove. The gas popped into flame, chemical-blue and orange, vaguely sulphurous. She turned it to its lowest setting, moved around the kitchen in her usual way, putting out plates and cups, fetching spoons and knives, the butter dish, returning to the stove from time to time to stir the porridge or add a little more water.

Something made her stop what she was doing. She would not have been able to explain it. Lennie went to the breakfast table with a knife, she made a small, clean cut through a corner of the new pat of butter, then dabbed the blade onto her finger. She lifted the chip of butter, already melting to yellow oil from her body heat, onto the tip of her tongue.

The knife fell to the table.

Lennie ran to the lavatory, it was almost too late, the sickness catching her just as she'd elbowed open the door and then coming in great, voluptuous waves. She made it by throwing herself forwards, sinking to her knees and there she stayed until the spasms of sickness were done, tears were streaming down her face, mixing with the mucus from her nose. Crumpled on the cold lavatory tiles, Lennie closed her eyes, listened to her own breath heaving in and out of her chest. From the kitchen came the unmistakable smell of burnt porridge.

A ngus was crestfallen, as if dying was a character flaw, a failure of good manners.

'Nothing they can do, apparently. At most, they can buy me a bit of time with treatment.'

They talked mostly of practical matters. How long? Nobody could be sure. Months not years. The estate finances were still messy. If only he had another year or two, he said. But there was much that could be done in the time he had left. James must help at first, until Alexander finished his studies and his National Service. They would have to tell James right away, give him fair warning. Venetia agreed that there was no way round that. What to do about Alexander?

'Wait till after Christmas,' Angus said, and Venetia did not argue.

By December Angus had come through his first two sessions of treatment without side effects and with no clear worsening of his health. At the Christmas party, he was in festive mood. Venetia watched him joking with Nathan Lacey, the head gardener, as he served him beer. Later, after his speech, he made his usual round of the salon to wish every member of staff and their wives or husbands a happy Christmas. Perhaps the initial prognosis had been too pessimistic, thought Venetia, as the salon emptied and she and Lennie began collecting plates and stray mince pies, stacking the plates in neat piles on the trestle table. Lennie was wearing a forest-green dress and she had clipped a sprig of holly in her hair. Alexander stood by the fireplace and watched intently as she moved about the room, as if he had only just noticed her.

Venetia told Angus when they were getting ready for bed. 'We should wait a little longer,' she said. It seemed cruel to destroy one form of Alexander's future when another version might be taking shape. And what if the doctors were wrong about Angus?

The early weeks of 1955 were crisp, bright distillations of themselves, more poignant, more lovely, than they deserved to be, given the presence of death on the horizon. February was rain-sodden, windy, unusually mild, but in early March everything changed. There was a morning when the sky was flat and heavy, with an ominous brassy quality which foretold snow. As Venetia returned from the stables, the earth was unyielding beneath her boots. Silence all around, as if the world were waiting for some momentous event. Across the hedge she saw a tractor making its way up and down the far side of the field, James ploughing in the winter manure. The farmer's daughter in her took satisfaction in the sight of good work almost completed so early in the day. Soon the earth would be unworkable, a hard mass of frozen roots. But there was something desolate in the scene too, the small vehicle doggedly scraping away at the surface of the landscape. James appeared a lonely figure there, a reminder of the life he had chosen for himself, living alone all these years. She thought of his farmhouse, all heavy male lines except for a ridiculous china shepherdess simpering on the mantelpiece. The shepherdess had been left behind by the young woman James had met and swiftly married on his return from the war.

'This is Cynthia,' he'd said, bumping into Angus and Venetia outside the Post Office one afternoon. Venetia had the feeling he would have avoided them if it had been possible. James gestured to the girl who stood beside him.

'Nice to meet you,' said Cynthia in a soft whisper of a voice which smoothed the edges of her London accent. She was dressed in a Land Girl's uniform, belted tightly around her waist. She had a pretty, heart-shaped face, was built like a child.

'Cynthia's working up at Stockton's,' said James. He took her hand, pulled her closer. 'Not for much longer now.'

Venetia and Angus asked appropriate questions though there was little they didn't know already. Starome was too small a village for the movements of a newcomer to go unnoticed, especially one as pretty as Cynthia.

She had thoroughly disliked working as a Land Girl, she told Venetia on her first visit after the wedding, which took place just weeks after the post office meeting.

'Hated every moment of it,' she said, shaking her Veronica Lake curls so violently that her teacup rattled. A poster on the Underground had given her the idea: 'Come and Help with the Victory Harvest,' it had said. Beneath the writing was a picture of a young woman with a heroic look about her and rippling wheat-coloured hair. She held an abundant armful of cartoon-bright hay and the sky topping the rural scene behind her was a perfect Californian blue. The poster had borne little resemblance to the mud and stinking silage Cynthia found at Alfred Stockton's farm that winter. Farmer Stockton had set her to rat-catching on her very first day— 'Oh those rats!', she said to Venetia, shuddering and wrinkling her doll's nose. Even more terrifying than rats were the pigs she must feed each morning, with their devil's trotters and great pink bulk. The creatures gazed at her through pale lashes as she approached and Cynthia felt sure they knew exactly what she'd been about in her previous life, slicing bacon behind the counter of Swain The Butcher—Quality Meat, Affordable Prices—in Whitechapel.

Venetia came to feel sorry for Cynthia, who would never be

at home in the countryside and clearly thought the whole place could be improved by paving it over. Cynthia truly believed that her handsome new husband needed nothing more than bringing out of himself. She adorned their farmhouse with frills and frippery, tried to jolly him along with parties, but the war seemed to have hardened something in James and it had been no surprise to anyone when, just a year after the marriage, Cynthia returned to London, leaving only the china shepherdess as a reminder of her existence.

As Venetia turned the dog-leg in the lane the wind caught her; it began to snow, as she'd known it would. Snow flew over the bare brown hedges in stinging handfuls, forcing her to wrap her shawl across the lower half of her face and bow her head as she hurried back to the Hall.

At lunch Angus had only just begun to eat when he stood up abruptly and hurried from the table. By evening his skin had turned an odd shade of yellow. Against his wishes, she insisted on telephoning Dr. Harrison.

'It won't be long now,' the doctor said, coming out of the bedroom.

'This is the first time he's been sick,' Venetia said. 'He walked all over the estate yesterday. And we were in York just the day before.'

'I believe the cancer has spread to the liver and into the bowel. All the evidence points that way. He says he's not in pain but that seems unlikely. I've given him something to help if he should need it and I'll call again tomorrow, but you must ring me immediately if he's uncomfortable. Do you want a nurse to come?'

'Here? What for?'

'Lady Richmond, I should be frank with you.'

'Please.'

'We'll do everything we can to alleviate the pain, but he's

going to get weaker quickly and he'll need help to move around and dress. He seems quite adamant about staying at home, although he may well change his mind about that at things progress. In the meantime, a nurse would make life easier for you.'

'No.' She didn't want a stranger in the house. 'Fairweather will be here each day. He can help me.'

'What about Alexander?'

'He's on a study tour in Italy. We were going to wait until . . . '

'You should bring him home.'

CHAPTER 40
Lennie, September 1955

'What can I do for you, Helena?'

Only Dr. Harrison and Alexander used her full name.

'I've not been well.'

She concentrated on the stethoscope that sat on the desk between them, remembering the reassuring feel of that cool disc against her chest when she was small, what a marvel it had seemed that the doctor could know everything that was happening inside of you.

'It's a couple of weeks now.'

How desperate she had been, waiting for her name to be called, so that she could get out of the waiting room, which was really a parlour at the front of Dr. Harrison's house. In that cramped little space, the Ingram twins sniffled and crawled over their mother, the old people groaned as they took their seats, passed the time by listing their various sufferings to anyone who would listen. Lennie had sat in terror that someone would ask her what she was doing there.

'What's been the trouble, my dear? You're certainly looking rather pale this morning.'

The paternal kindness in Dr. Harrison's voice made her eyes swim. She had been sick on the way there, worse than ever, hunched over in the undergrowth on the edge of the woods, so exhausted all of a sudden, so overwhelmed by what was happening to her that she wanted nothing more than to crawl into the trees out of sight and curl up beneath them. Her limbs were so heavy that she felt she could rest there forever.

'I'm . . . late.' Lennie looked down at her lap, at hands that grasped one another as if seeking comfort. 'I can't remember quite when . . . but it's definitely late now. I thought I'd started but then it stopped too soon. I've been sick too and not just in the mornings.'

'Oh, Helena.' Dr. Harrison's eyes were fixed on her now, his voice grave. Then: 'I will need to examine you. To be sure.'

She moved to the couch behind the screen, lay down on the blue paper that covered it, lifted her dress. The screen was patterned with blue and orange flowers, simple in shape, monstrous in size; some blooms wouldn't fit an entire section of the screen, like some tropical experiment that had got out of hand. How ashamed she felt, lying there exposed in broad daylight, with half the village in the waiting room outside. Foolish too. *Caught with her knickers down.* That was the expression people used.

Lennie closed her eyes while Dr. Harrison pushed down on her stomach with the flat of his hands. Her stomach was sensitive and a hard little rock all at the same time. They didn't speak until he was finished and she was back in the chair, clothes rearranged.

'Well now, Helena, you're definitely pregnant, I'm afraid. Have you spoken to your father yet?'

'No! And please don't say anything to him. To anyone.'

How disappointed he looked. He'd known her since she was small. Everyone said she was a good girl but the truth lay elsewhere, in a clearing in the woods.

'You must tell him as soon as possible.'

Dr. Harrison's voice was solemn and careful. For a moment, she was so scared that she could not speak. She did not know what she'd expected, coming here on this bright summer's morning, but part of her had perhaps hoped that there might still be a way, some narrative she'd not yet imagined, which might yet lead her to safety.

'There's nothing . . . ' She stared hard at the blind-covered window which swayed in the summer breeze. A fly was trapped behind it. She could hear its buzzing becoming more frenzied as it batted at the glass behind. 'Can anything be done?'

Dr. Harrison peered over his glasses. Everything was long about him: torso and arms rising up from behind the desk, fingers, face and that nose like a curved beak. His legs were hidden from sight but she knew they'd be twisted around one another in his customary fashion.

He sighed. 'You're lucky in some ways. Lots of girls have to go away until it's over. Mistakes happen but if the wedding comes soon nobody will be any the wiser.' He looked at her. 'If it would help, I'll come with you to speak to your father.'

'Oh no, I can't, not yet.'

'He'll be upset at first, but your father has faced worse. People will always find something to talk about, then it passes. I presume the child's father is already aware?'

The fly was desperate now, batting repeatedly at the blind. It was far too hot in this small room, sweat was dampening her armpits, running down the base of her spine.

'Thank you, Dr. Harrison.' She was on her feet, wanting to be out of the surgery, away from those eyes, that voice.

'Please, Helena,' he held his hand up in something approximating a halt gesture. She had obeyed authority for too many years of her short life to ignore it now.

Dr. Harrison removed his glasses, placed them on the desk in front of him, hands still grasping the stems. Lennie gazed at him. Everyone in the village knew what that meant. It was the gesture he reserved for imparting the worst of news: an unexpected death, a lost heartbeat or some disease that was multiplying in every cell.

'My dear, you are very young still. The most important thing is that you have help around you at a time like this. I can't stress that enough. Delaying the matter will only make things more difficult for yourself and for your family. Do you understand?' She nodded silently. Outside, one of the Ingram twins was crying in a half-hearted yet persistent way. Dr. Harrison picked up his glasses, examined the lenses as if he held suspicions about their clarity.

'Thank you, Dr. Harrison,' she repeated.

'It's early days yet, Helena.' The glasses hovered just beyond the end of his nose for a moment, before he lodged them decisively back in place. 'But there will come a point when you can't hide it anymore.'

T he morning after Dr. Harrison's visit, Angus rose from the breakfast table in a hurry. He left the lavatory door ajar but she waited for him to come out all the same. She heard the running of water.

'Not good,' he said, wiping his mouth.

In the hallway she placed a telephone call to Italy, but the hotel clerk in Rome said that the group from the university had gone south, to Sorrento, he thought, though he could not be sure. He would do his best. If all else failed, the *signore* had rooms booked for their return in a week's time.

'He is needed now. His father . . . '

Yes, he understood the urgency, *Signora*, would do all he could, but to Venetia the promise sounded as empty as the echoing line.

The following day Angus dressed as usual but did not want even his morning tea, only to sit in the chair to read. At lunchtime he insisted on joining Venetia at the table again. She had ordered soup and bread to be served, something simple, but Angus ate only a few mouthfuls before his spoon clattered in the bowl and he stumbled from the room.

A nurse came that evening. She seemed terribly young for her responsibilities, Venetia thought, but she was quietly efficient, seemed to understand more than her years might warrant.

'Let's see if we can get him more comfortable. Sir Angus

said you have a son. So at least you'll have some help soon. Someone to look after you too.'

Angus made no attempt to dress the next morning, though he washed and shaved and put on the fresh pyjamas she brought for him. His skin was that sickly shade of yellow again, like the sky before a storm. She offered to fetch the newspaper.

'Might need something close at hand first, Venetia, for the sickness.' She went down to the kitchens, found an orange plastic bowl in the dresser. She had bought the bowl for Alexander when he was small and liked to bake things, the cook's china bowls being too heavy for his little hands. There were scratches in the base of the bowl, around the sides, where he had tried to scrape out the mixture with a knife instead of a spoon.

'I think I could eat some toast,' Angus announced at lunchtime, looking more cheerful. More like himself, she thought, and then wondered what she meant by that. 'And some tea.'

He was several mouthfuls in before he grasped for the bowl, which she had placed beside him. When the spasms eased, she saw that he was trying to shield it from view. 'Fetch Fairweather,' he said. But she had already taken it from his shaking hands. 'Sorry,' he said. The contents, viscous in the base of the cheap plastic bowl, were black.

I n the darkness of the auditorium, she gripped Alexander's hand, willed the film to finish. The air was thick with tobacco smoke and, beneath it, the faint odour of frying from the fish and chip shop next door. She'd refused ice cream, concentrated now on her breathing. Why did they call it morning sickness? The threat was there all day long, a bilious volcano.

Alexander had wanted to drive but she'd persuaded him to take the train.

'My father will worry less.'

On the way home from York, they had the carriage almost to themselves, just an elderly couple finishing up their sandwiches who then fell into a doze in the corner. The carriage window was half open, a breeze softening the air. Alexander hadn't thought much of the film, *To Catch a Thief*, but he was in one of his playful moods, stealing kisses, keeping his arm around her throughout the journey.

It was late by the time they arrived at Starome station. The High Street was empty and quiet, just a spill of light and faint voices coming from the Black Swan. Her father would be on his second Friday night pint by now, with his back to the door as usual. All the same, Lennie kept her eyes down as they passed. Seeing a light on in the downstairs window of the Masters' cottage, she glanced across at Alexander.

'Mrs. Masters is thinking of moving away. Father says she might go to her sister's.' She didn't know why she had mentioned it. Only that it had bothered her to think of winter coming, the graveyard bleak and bare, Danny's grave unvisited. She hoped Mrs. Masters might still make the journey to tend it. 'Do you still think about what happened to Danny?'

'Not recently.'

The river was glass-green and still tonight. Even the Stride seemed to have quietened to a distant whisper. Silence hung in the air as though everything had paused, as if the world was waiting for something to happen. Overhead, the stars were steady and sure, Lennie's dress glowed like a flower in the twilight. Could it really be so difficult when Alexander loved her and she loved him? In the beauty of the summer's evening, the great obstacle in her way faded to nothing. Lennie turned to Alexander, holding up her face to be kissed. He put his arms around her and she held him tightly.

'Let's not go home yet,' she said, taking a step off the path into the deep shadow of the trees. She held out her hand to him.

'You'll get into bother with your father again,' said Alexander.

Her father's feelings had never bothered Alexander before. Why did he care now? It should have been a sign.

'Do you love me?' she said.

'You know I do.'

'Then it's for us to decide.'

Alexander frowned, looked over his shoulder as if searching for answers on the river bank.

'You're in a strange mood tonight.' He pushed his hands down into his pockets as if steadying himself for an argument.

Lennie planted her feet between the ancient roots of an oak tree. She would not move. He laughed then, the sound harsh in the deep green silence.

'Not such a good girl, after all,' he said. 'You'll have people talking at this rate.'

'But what can it matter if we're to be married? Whatever happens . . . '

'Who said anything about marriage?'

Her power left her in that moment. As if Alexander had physically knocked it out of her. Lennie could not breathe, was crying without knowing that she had even begun. Alexander tried to take hold of her arm. She recoiled, stumbling over the tree roots.

'Oh, come on now, Helena!' There was irritation in his voice, as if she had forced him to be cruel.

'Leave me alone. Please.' She had sunk to a crouch in the soft green undergrowth, arms wrapped around herself, her breath coming in great jags.

'Do get up. I just wish you'd make up your mind, that's all. Half the time you push me away—'

'When?'

'Just the other week, when we were in the graveyard. And now you're behaving like this. I don't understand.'

Like a whore.

'You said you loved me.'

Alexander threw up his hands. 'I don't know if I trust you. I don't know if I can trust anyone.'

'All these years, I don't understand how . . . '

'This is ridiculous.' Alexander turned away from her, then swung round again. 'You're ruining a perfectly nice evening. I don't understand why.'

She shrank at his anger, but she was not going to back down now. Crouched like an animal in the undergrowth, her belly soft and vulnerable, it felt like her entire future was at stake.

Lennie rose to her feet. 'You said we would marry.' With great effort she made her voice stay low. 'I haven't made that up. Or have I gone mad?' She steadied herself against the immense trunk of the oak tree. It proved, beyond doubt, that the past existed, she hadn't just imagined the whole thing. 'You talked about it . . . We both did.'

Alexander shook his head. 'I'm not sure I believe in marriage anymore, that's all. It doesn't seem to mean that much to people.'

'But you said . . . What are we doing then?' she whispered. Why should he care about other people? Did he know that in a few harsh sentences he had destroyed their future?

He feigned boredom but she could see that he was trembling. What had happened? Did he suspect something? Was there some other problem, something that had nothing to do with her after all? With a word, or a gesture, he might still put everything right again.

Alexander stayed where he was and would not meet her eye. Lennie felt something dislodge in her mind, like a book dropping from a shelf.

H e's getting weaker so quickly,' she said, motioning to James to close the bedroom door behind him as he joined her on the landing. Angus appeared to be sleeping at last, but it was difficult to tell. 'You can see how much weight he's lost since you last came. Alexander has set off from Rome now apparently, but I have no idea how long he might take to get here.'

James looked at her steadily, though his expression remained customarily guarded. 'I'm not sure he'll last till then. You say he's not keeping anything down?'

'People can survive for weeks without food. He's drinking water constantly and he craves ice. I get them to crush it for him downstairs. Fairweather is desperate to do more but Angus doesn't want the servants to see him in this . . . like this.'

'No good for anyone, him hanging on like this.'

The baldness of the statement appalled and liberated her all at once. She thought of Ptolemy, her old favourite among the horses, who'd broken his leg jumping a fence one day last autumn. She had buried her face in his rough mane for a minute before the gunshot solidified the life in his eyes.

'Have one of the girls make a bed up for me here,' said James. 'At least you can get some rest that way. Sam and the lads can manage well enough without me at the farm.'

'I don't need rest.'

'We'll do it together,' said James.

'A blockage,' said the nurse when she visited the following evening. She was not the young one but an older woman with a thin, mean look about her. She dropped her hand down to her stomach and clenched her fist to illustrate the point. 'Nowhere for anything to go.'

'I see,' said Venetia. The news came as no surprise, when she had made numerous journeys between bedroom and bathroom in the last few days, the priestess with the orange plastic bowl. She removed a heap of bedding from the corner of the bedroom and went downstairs.

When she returned, James met her at the top of the staircase, signalled to her that Angus was sleeping, should not be disturbed. With the promise of a few hours of peace, they went downstairs for dinner. They might have had food sent up to Venetia's sitting room, just along the landing from where Angus slept, but the small proprieties of the dining room—a set table, the good glassware and china, the shining cutlery— seemed to matter tonight. In the formality of the dining room, with its marble pillars, the vast stretch of the walnut table, Venetia found herself ravenously hungry. They both drank wine and then James, visibly relaxing as the meal went on, opened a second bottle. Venetia accepted another glass, savouring the ruby dryness upon her tongue. The alcohol was getting into her blood, numbing the surface of her skin. She realised how exhausted she was.

They talked of Alexander.

'You'll want him to carry on at university, I presume,' said James. 'Angus seems set on that.' Angus had made no mention of the matter to Venetia. Perhaps he sensed her need to keep a narrow focus—change the sheets; turn the mattress; ask the nurse for this. 'The finances are better than they were,' James continued. 'We'll manage.'

We. So, there were three of them now. Or did he mean two? She looked across the table at him. It occurred to her that she knew him barely any better now than at their first encounter among the greenery of the McAndrewses' conservatory. Did he miss female company, she wondered, living up at the farm on his own? He'd never mentioned anyone since Cynthia and that was years ago. Before Cynthia he'd dated a small number of women from his own social set, most relationships petering out after a short while. There had been no animosity in these endings, as far as Venetia could tell—James was never, by all accounts, anything but gentlemanly—only frustration on the part of the other. Lydia Faversham, the one girlfriend who lasted almost a year, once remarked that James was 'awfully self-contained' and left it at that.

'Do you ever hear from Cynthia?' she said. She hadn't planned on asking, but found herself curious, aggravated almost, by the mystery of his life. 'I suppose I never quite understood what went wrong. Though you and she seemed very . . . ' Venetia gestured with her hands *apart*.

'What's to tell?' said James. 'She came, she went. You know as much as me.' He poured the last of the second bottle into their glasses, glanced towards the drinks cabinet as if already considering a third. 'Anyway, it wasn't her fault.' he said. 'I'd just got back from Africa if you remember, so perhaps I seemed an exciting prospect, even with my injury.'

'Did you love her?'

'I thought so, at the time. You met her, Venetia. You couldn't help but be charmed by Cynthia if she decided . . . ' It was astonishing, Venetia thought, how many perfectly sensible men were happy to overlook vacuity if it came in a pretty enough package.

'It all happened so quickly. The marriage, I mean.'

'Yes well, I couldn't risk hanging around. Angus was home on leave.' Seeing the look on Venetia's face James said, 'I am joking, you know.' He laughed, proving it.

'I'm glad to hear it,' she said, attempting archness but

unable to keep the ice from her voice. She wanted to get up from the table, to leave him there. She knew it would be a ridiculously dramatic thing to do.

'Angus has always got everything he wanted.' James pushed back his chair abruptly, and went to the fireplace. A small fire danced and snapped, keeping the spring chill out of the air. 'I don't know how he manages it.'

She thought for a moment. 'You do understand that he's dying, don't you?'

'I'm not an idiot, Venetia.'

'The Hall hasn't always been a blessing,' she said, unsure if James was becoming angry or maudlin. 'You know that as well as anyone.'

'Oh, I never wanted the Hall. Not just the responsibility, all the decisions to be made, but the whole Lord of the Manor game wouldn't have suited me, having to be everything to all people every time you step outside your front door.'

Was it the heat of the fire or the wine causing the flush to rise on his sallow skin?

'I ought to go and check on Angus,' she said.

'Do you know, he was the most popular boy in the school when we were young?' said James. He took another bottle of wine from the drinks cabinet, opened it without bothering to look at the label. 'I'm sure that doesn't surprise you. Not the best at any one thing in particular, or even academic, but just one of those people . . . I remember that when I got there, I discovered I had this kind of *cachet*, right from the word go, just because I was his younger brother. But then what happens is that people become disappointed. You start to see it in their eyes. You're not what they expected you to be.' His fingers were tapping out some odd rhythm on the mantelpiece, as if trying to place a pattern over the past. 'So, it didn't really matter that Angus had been married to you for however many years by the time I met Cynthia. The point was that once she'd come face to face with Angus, she wouldn't think about me in the same way again. Nobody ever does.'

'That's ludicrous, James. As you say, Angus and I were married by then; we had Alexander. I'm sure Cynthia barely noticed Angus. '

'I'm not saying that it's intentional—this casting of spells he does with people. Taking what he wants. Only that I was wary because he already had form.'

He was staring at her so hard that it felt like an assault. Venetia looked down at the tablecloth and for a moment concentrated on the raised pattern of the embroidery.

'He doesn't know that about himself, I don't think.' She felt a need to explain herself too. 'We don't choose who we love.'

'Oh, I understand that, Venetia.' He turned away from her and stared down into the fire, the flames pulsing and stretching. 'But you can see why I might hate him.'

S he ran all the way home and Alexander did not follow her. She vomited as soon as she got through the door, scrabbling on her knees to clean up after herself when it was over. Then she went upstairs and laid down on her bed, with the sour taste of vomit still in her mouth. She cried silently, tears running into her hair, soaking through to the pillow below.

The moon rose outside her window, cold and certain. She stopped crying. In the wake of tears came clarity, a new resolve. A shape was forming inside her body, like a photograph swimming into focus in a dark room, and no amount of rosemary tea or hot baths was going to change that. This was the price to pay for a night when instinct had taken over. It had come from inside of her, animal and urgent, and also from the trees, from the roar of the river. Loneliness too. Danny wanting her so badly. She was not a good girl, had turned out to be quite the opposite. She must face the consequences.

Her father would be devastated and there was no avoiding it. She was supposed to be the easy child, the one he need never worry about. She would tell him everything, not lie to save herself, or push the blame on Danny. She would have to go away soon. Her father would arrange it in some way that would shield her from the worst of the village gossip. He would do this even though she had let him down so terribly, because he loved her. She couldn't bring herself to think about Tom. She was just thankful that he was in London—at some sort of rally against the new government, though their father said Eden was doing a splendid job.

You're my girl, Alexander had said. Words meant nothing. Only actions mattered and look where they had got her. She must go as far away from Alexander as possible, even though it felt like it would kill her to leave him, but staying here was worse, if she was no longer his girl, his nymph of the woods, just the daughter of a servant who meant nothing to him, a girl he couldn't even bring himself to touch.

Tired to the bone. She pulled the covers over her without bothering to undress. Tomorrow was Saturday, in the evening her father would be home. This was the one thing left in the world of which she could be certain. She would go to Helmsley to buy something nice for his dinner and then she would tell him.

F airweather came to her at a quarter past seven.
'I've instructed the kitchens to delay dinner, ma'am.'
His voice was full of some meaning she did not yet
understand. Venetia sipped on her gin and tonic, which was
already taking the edge off the day, and waited.

'Master Alexander is still in his room,' said Fairweather.

'Would you mind running up to him? He must have forgotten our arrangement. Then you really must go home.
Lennie will be wondering where you are.'

'He's not answering his door, ma'am, I'm afraid. And he's
taken it upon himself to lock it.'

'You're quite sure he's in there?'

'Hattie Merriot says he sent her away after she'd lit a fire for
him yesterday and hasn't come out since. She knows he's in the
room because she's heard him moving around.'

'I'm surprised no-one mentioned this to me until now?'

'That's exactly what I told Hattie. And nobody needs a fire
in this weather. I've already spoken to Mrs. Abbot on the subject and you can rest assured that it won't happen again.'

How delighted he was, standing beside her fireplace, to
have uncovered such a transgression amongst his colleagues.
How had Angus put up with him for all those years? He had
been different once, she remembered, picturing the young
man with thick blond hair she'd met when she first came to
Richmond Hall. Fairweather had always been conscientious,
but this had seemed to spring from an eagerness to please

rather than an obsession with rules, correctness. Venetia stopped herself from reaching for the gin bottle again, unable to bear the pantomime of dismay that would follow if she managed to serve herself before Fairweather could step in.

'Do go home now, Peter.'

'But what about the dinner arrangements, ma'am?'

'It really doesn't matter. It was only a quiet supper. There was no need for you to stay in the . . . '

'Good evening, mother!' Alexander reached for the back of an armchair to steady himself as he entered the room, squinting against the light.

Reluctantly, Fairweather withdrew, one eye on Alexander as he closed the door behind him.

'Poking his nose into everything.' Alexander found his way to the drinks cabinet and poured himself a generous whisky. 'Why don't you get rid of him?'

'Your father relied on him.' Venetia said. 'I would have thought you might find a way to be civil, given that he's Lennie's father.'

Alexander dropped down into an armchair, slumping into its depths with the whisky glass resting on his chest.

'I'll have them send up supper,' she said. 'You've been drinking. You ought to eat something.'

'I'm not staying.'

'You've been hidden away in your room since yesterday. What about going to see the Markham boys tomorrow? You've barely seen them all summer.'

Alexander shook his head. His face was reddened as if he had spent too much time in the sun, or else in front of the fire. The alcohol caused his handsome features to slide towards silliness. 'What, so they can report back to you?'

'I don't see why you'd think I'd want to spy on you,' she said.

'Anyway, there's nothing to know. I just didn't want to talk to anyone. I don't see the problem. Helena's better off without me too. I've told her. At least, I will.'

He slumped still deeper into the chair. Venetia felt irritation rising in her. How childish he was, locking himself away and indulging in self-pity. She thought of her brothers, bounding off to war at the first opportunity, of Angus and James too, who had done the same, if more soberly, but with the same unflinching intent.

'What can you mean, Alexander?'

'Oh, we get on well enough, I suppose.' Alexander sat up abruptly, taking holding of himself. 'I did think of taking her to a play next week in town. Do you think she'd like that?'

'Perhaps.' She spoke evenly, sensing that she was being led down a set path. 'As long her father's happy for her to go.'

'Yes, yes, naturally.' He waved the idea away. 'It's *Tis Pity She's a Whore*. Do you think she'd get the message?'

'What on earth is the matter, Alexander?'

'Well, I don't love her. At least I don't think I do. I don't like women at all.' He looked at her and then gave a bark of laughter. 'Oh it's not *that*, mother. My inclinations are entirely straightforward, if that's what you want to call it. Helena's probably the best of the lot of you—she's an angel really—but you're all whores in the end.'

Venetia set down her glass. 'Just because your father isn't here to—' She hesitated, enraged to find that there were tears in her eyes. 'I won't tolerate that kind of talk.' She turned to the Grinling Gibbons carving above the fireplace for a moment, as if in need of something unchanging. She gathered herself, looked back to see that Alexander was trembling. To her great discomfort, he too began to cry, proper crying, shoulders heaving and his mouth in a grimace, unconstrained as a child. As a drunk. '—Terrible person,' she thought he said but his voice was thick with tears, it was hard to understand. She moved across the sitting room with the intention of comforting him, to place a hand upon his shoulder perhaps. He reached out a hand to her as she approached, then, with a sudden and surprising force, he dragged her down beside him and rested his head against her body. She knew she ought to respond, but something in her could not bear to do it. She found herself repelled by this unexpected physicality of her son. She freed herself, collected her glass, and went to the drinks table.

'What kind of mother *are* you?' said Alexander.

'Alexander, that really is enough now. You've been drinking and I'm too tired for puzzles. Go and sleep it off. We'll talk again tomorrow.'

'Perhaps we should have invited Uncle James to join us tonight. A little family gathering.'

She had known this moment would come. She might as well face it now. 'I'm sorry, Alexander . . . ' She faltered, loath to speak of something so intimate to anyone, let alone to her son. She pushed her chin down into her chest. 'James has always cared me. Before your father even.'

'So he has some kind of prior claim, you mean?' Alexander was on his feet now, staggering towards her. He moved quickly, despite his drunken state. Venetia took an involuntary step backwards. She should have waited until he was sober. It was too late now.

'What I mean,' she said, 'is that I have watched too many people die: my parents, my brothers, your father. There is nothing we can do once they are gone except to go on living.'

Alexander at the drinks table, refilling his glass with a slop of rusty-coloured whisky. He lurched towards her, nearly losing the contents of the glass in the process.

'You must find yourself disgusting though, mother. When you look in the mirror, I mean, or go to his graveside. I have bad dreams about him all the time, about all manner of things, but, Christ, they must be nothing compared to yours!' His face was right up close to hers. She was aware that it must look like

a kind of distorted reflection of her own: the angles of cheekbone, the straight brow. She could feel the heat of his breath
on her skin, the sharp smell of whisky and the contempt. 'It
seems like you must have hated him in some way. Or maybe it's
just that you're all whores in the end. You,' Alexander
mummed an awful, simpering tone: 'little Lennie Fairweather.
You might have waited till he was fucking cold in his grave. '

The door opened with a crash. Peter Fairweather had hold
of Alexander's arm.

'What the hell are you doing, you stupid fool? Let go of
me.' Alexander turned white in the face. The contents of his
glass were now a dark stain across his chest. The shock of
Fairweather's entrance appeared to have sobered him up. 'You
were listening at the door, I suppose,' he said clearly.

'Peter, leave us alone, please.' Venetia tried to come
between the two men. 'I'm perfectly fine.'

Alexander laughed. 'It's his daughter he's worried about,
not you.' His voice wavered and for all his bravado Venetia
could see that he was close to tears again. 'Helena's the only
truly good thing in my life but you want to keep her all for
yourself. A lovely thing like that.' He spun away, tried to extri-
cate himself from Fairweather's grip. 'I won't have people
interfering and spoiling everything that's precious to me.'
Venetia placed a hand on his arm, partly a gesture of comfort,
partly one of restraint. Alexander wasn't finished. 'You should
be careful, Fairweather,' he said, shrugging both of them off.
'Keeping her all to yourself like that. People will start to get the
wrong idea.'

'Alexander,' she said.

'You mustn't stop me.' He swung round to face her, pain
not anger in his eyes now. 'Jealousy makes people do terrible
things, mother. They can't help it.'

Fairweather looked as though he was about to lunge at
Alexander, but instead a fit of wheezing stopped him.

Venetia went to fetch him some water from the drinks table, hoping that at the same time she could also usher him out of the door. Alexander stood with his arms folded in an apparent show of patience. The wheezing became almost theatrical and then Fairweather doubled over. Dropping to his knees, a constricted noise was the only sound he seemed capable of making.

'Help him!' Venetia cried, as Fairweather fell forward.

T he over-lit corridor gave everything an air of heightened reality, like a film set. Trolleys rattled by transporting patients from ward to ward, from ward to theatre and back again, the strip-lights blanking out their differences so that everyone appeared grey-faced and hollow-cheeked, tired amalgams of flesh that might or might not be revived. The last time she had been in this hospital had been for what turned out to be Angus's final consultation. Venetia had a sudden image of Fairweather lying on the stretcher as they lifted him into the ambulance, skin like old paper. A man whose worries had worn him down.

Jenny Fairweather had once told her the story of their courtship. It began, she'd said, in the barber's shop where her father cut and trimmed and shaved, Italian opera playing so loudly that a shy young man might never worry about making conversation. Jenny had been in charge of sweeping up hair and working the till.

'I knew he was coming for me,' she had said, thumping her breastbone; the diffident customer with thick blond hair and the English manners her father had taught her to admire. 'Nobody needs their hair cutting as often as that!'

Whenever Venetia thought of the young bride that Fairweather had brought home to Richmond Hall all those years ago, the word 'sexy' sprang into her mind. Jenny's mouth had been wide and laughing, her nose too upturned by conventional standards, but she had a lush, compact little body, a mass of spiralling dark hair that seemed to emit sexual energy.

Her mother had run off with a salesman years before, she told Venetia, leaving Roberto to bring up their only daughter by himself. Venetia could never decide whether it was that lack of motherly criticism and containment or the Italian blood in her veins that allowed Jenny to inhabit her sexuality quite so freely.

In the beginning, Jenny and Peter had had their own set of rooms at the Hall. Jenny spent her time wandering at will between servants' quarters, the kitchen, and the main house, chattering to anyone she met without any notion of transgression. There was none of the hushed reverence about her of those who came to Richmond Hall on one of the infrequent tour groups, the cringing middle classes, crippled by their own status. In the early days of pregnancy, Jenny would barge into Venetia's rooms to complain about feeling sick, never mind any timid tapping at doors first.

'What on earth is *that* thing?' she said, the first time she saw the sitting room. She gazed up at the Grinling Gibbons carving above the fireplace, recoiling in horror. Venetia, who wasn't sure she exactly liked the carving herself, though tracing the intricate workings of the craftsman's chisel could be soothing, didn't know whether to be offended or amused. Their natures were too different to allow true friendship to develop, but Venetia admired Jenny's spiritedness: happily hitching a ride home from the village on a tractor, pointedly ignoring some visiting lord or lady who'd offended her in some way. Sir Laurie openly adored this new addition to the household, finding her refusal to engage with anyone to whom she took a dislike, her unguarded behaviour, hilarious.

The cottage had been Venetia's idea, though it was Angus who had put the thought in her mind. Times were changing, he said, one morning after Fairweather had left the room. He did not see how one could justify any longer having a valet to wait upon one's every movement. Gatekeeper's Cottage had already been renovated after standing empty for some years. Venetia had taken it upon herself to oversee the work on the interior, so that by the time the project was finished the cottage was a snug little abode, decorated in an understated style and with every modern convenience, just right for a small family in need of a little privacy.

Once he had been made to understand that the move to the cottage and the change in his duties from valet to private secretary was in a no way a demotion, Peter Fairweather was grateful for the belated wedding gift. In truth, a man so sensitive to correct behaviour might have felt relief that his lovely yet outspoken young wife was to live at a slight remove from his place of work. Proud of her efforts, Venetia was anxious to show Peter and Jenny around their new home. Both she and Jenny were heavily pregnant by then; the two of them climbed the narrow stairs of the cottage to inspect the bedrooms, taking care to hold onto the new handrail. It was only when they stepped out into the freshly-dug garden, though, that Jenny seemed to wake up.

'I can put anything I want here?' she wanted to know, turning with an effort to Venetia. In her flowing white maternity dress she looked like a little ship in full sail.

Venetia was surprised by the question, not knowing that Jenny had horticultural leanings, but pleased to see some spark of enthusiasm. She'd played down her part in the project yet couldn't help feeling put out by Jenny's lack of interest. 'It's yours to do with as you wish.'

Jenny nodded, her habitual flashing smile still absent. 'Then I shall plant my herb garden here.'

The lights in the wards across the atrium had been turned

down. Venetia's tea grew cold beside her, an oily film forming on its surface. She looked for a nurse, wanting to ask if she might place a telephone call. Neither Lennie nor Thomas had been at home when their father was taken ill. Someone from the Hall ought to run down to the cottage to check again. Venetia sat alone and silent, her handbag on her lap. She searched the bag, wondering if there were cigarettes, but found only her purse and a postcard that Alexander had sent her from Athens earlier that summer in one of the side pockets. 'Cape Sounion,' it said in white, curling script, across a photograph of a ruined temple, with just a row of pillars remaining. There were no trees to soften the skyline, just dry earth and a mean-looking sun. She couldn't remember how it had found its way into her handbag.

She'd never quite understood Alexander's fascination with the past, particularly one that had nothing to do with him. What could Greek columns and Roman basilicas baked to biscuit by the Mediterranean sun mean to a small English schoolboy brought up in the grey light of the north? There was his name of course, but she had chosen it without a thought for the warring hero, because it was a name she'd always liked. Angus hadn't objected: there was some great uncle in the Richmond family with the same name.

As a little boy, Alexander had taken a liking to a book of myths that she bought him for Christmas. After that came children's versions of *The Iliad* and *The Odyssey*, though he hadn't been interested in Achilles or the other great warriors, only Odysseus, with his wiliness, his cunning brain that could outwit a Cyclops. At school he excelled at Latin, and later Greek, with its alien letters, slabs shored up against one another like temples, Venetia thought. Yet she was not convinced that Alexander was much attached to anything, let alone his childhood; had been surprised when a relationship appeared to be growing between him and Lennie. Venetia had always been fond of the girl, everyone was, but it occurred to her only now that what she really liked about the relationship was that it made her son seem more human.

'Go,' she had told him earlier this evening, running back upstairs after she'd telephoned for an ambulance to come. Alexander had turned from the window as if surprised to see her again. 'Just for tonight,' she had said. The situation had been bad enough without having to explain the argument between Fairweather and Alexander to anyone.

'Righto,' Alexander had said, and then stepped around Fairweather without looking down at him. Minutes later, Venetia had heard the car engine start on the driveway.

Alone now. The nurses and the ambulance men and their clanking jumble of stretcher and instruments all gone. They had delivered her father home and then driven away. Lady Richmond had gone too, after driving Lennie back from the hospital. She had offered to stay but Lennie panicked and said no, no thank you. Alexander's mother was always kind to her, but she had taken fright at the thought of passing a night in the cottage with someone so regal.

It had been different last night at the hospital. Sam Bracegirdle had driven her there at great speed and then she had sat beside Lady Richmond into the early hours of the morning and all of today, with doctors talking at them and nurses coming and going, doors swishing in their wake; a space that belonged to nobody but the sick. She couldn't imagine what they would talk about in the silence of the cottage's little parlour, crammed as it was with dark furniture and stiff with the formality of a room rarely used, the couch stuffed so tightly it seemed to reject your presence. Of Alexander, perhaps, who had disappeared again, or Thomas, who was somewhere in Scotland but hadn't been tracked down. How ridiculous to worry about topics of conversation when the fabric of her life had been wrenched apart and the threads left hanging.

A light summer rain fell outside, a chill little wind curling in through the bedroom window. Lennie pulled her knees in to her chest. She felt insubstantial, as if the wind might blow her away altogether. In the bedroom she had inhabited since she was a child, she sought something indisputably real, something solid. The cuckoo clock. Up there on the wall. Look at it. Thomas had brought it back from a trip to Salzburg when he was still at school.

'Didn't know what else to get you,' he had said, thrusting at her a package of soft tissue paper, fastened with a satin red ribbon.

Inside was a gaily-painted clock, like a gingerbread house from a fairy tale. Her father hung it on the bedroom wall for her. It had stayed there all these years, the passing of childhood reliably measured by its cheerful ticking, which at first kept her awake, but which soon became familiar, a soothing rhythm in the background.

Lennie had never seen proper mountains. She closed her eyes now, tried to imagine a snowy landscape, all brightly-lit chalet windows and skating figures on frozen rivers where nothing bad could ever happen. She couldn't make it real.

The music box on her dressing table. A birthday present from her father, her eighth or ninth birthday it might have been. She kept it out only to please him, though at one time she had been entranced by it. If you lifted the lid of the amber-coloured box, the figure of a little ballerina would pirouette on a podium, accompanied by tinkling music. The box was lined with pink velvet. If you rubbed the nap of the velvet it made your fingers itch. The dancer had hair the same shade as Lennie's, wore a stiff net tutu sewn with tiny glass beads that glittered as the ballerina turned. Lennie used to wonder what the ballerina did when no-one was watching. Perhaps she carried on smiling to herself in the darkness. Day after day, Lennie would ease back the catch of the music box with exaggerated care, then snap open the lid in the hope of catching the ballerina in some other pose, or gone altogether, an escapee from her pink tomb. She surprised the dancing figure all the time, a

relentless ballet mistress, making the ballerina dance on her little podium over and over again. One day it had suddenly
seemed like a bad thing to do, forcing the dancer to twirl on
and on like that, expression unchanging, simply for Lennie's
own amusement. She had rarely opened the lid of the music
box after that.

A music box; a clock; the acanthus ring that Alexander gave
her. Real, solid objects that definitely existed.

Lennie slept. When she woke, it was with a start. Outside,
the sky was clear, the first stars were visible. She had no sense
of how long she had lain there, only that she must go downstairs at once. They had put him in the parlour, the ambulance
men and the nurses, not in his own room across the landing.
She could not remember why at first, though she knew there
had been talk. She must go down immediately, light the lamp
so that he was not lying in darkness, draw the curtains against
the night. Without the fire lit, it might be cold down there too.

A crescent moon had risen above the beech tree. In the
churchyard, Sir Angus was falling away from himself beneath
the earth. Danny Masters, still fresh in his grave, would soon
follow suit. Danny. Features bloated and dumb, with no story
to tell. Had he become himself again, once the tide of water
went out of him? Gentle eyes upon her. His jacket hanging on
a tree, still holding his shape.

She would have to do things for her father for now. They
had done their best for him at the hospital but that was over.
She hardly took in the list of instructions the nurse had reeled
off yesterday because surely *for now* was a lie, to make her feel
better. Just once she touched him, her hand going to his fore-
head to smooth his hair into its rightful place. He stared at her
fixedly, no gratitude or recognition in his eyes. His skin felt
dense beneath her fingertips, like marble. His jacket and
trousers—purchased, like all of his possessions, for quality and

serviceability—were folded neatly and placed on the bureau. Perched on top were his highly-polished shoes. They looked too big, clown-like. The edge of his blanket had ridden up, she remembered, exposing a pale shin, bone-white like something they'd dug up in the woods as children. She pulled it down again, covering him from view.

Lennie's feet were bare, stiff with cold. For a second, in the darkness of the stairwell it felt like death was in her nostrils, took everything in her not to bolt back to the safety of her bedroom. The fire had indeed died in the parlour. Someone— who?—had lit the candles on the mantelpiece. They had burned to low stumps, dirty yellow wax pooling and hardening into new shapes at the base of each. Her father's eyes were closed, she was thankful for that. His head lay at an odd, constraining angle, making the breath rasp in the back of his throat. *The stairs.* That was why they put him down here on the couch. She remembered that now. *Because he wouldn't be able to.* She did not know where the blanket had came from, pale blue and shiny, like the puffy lining of a coffin. Like some girl's ball dress that had nothing to do with her father.

Lennie took the armchair by the window, on the far side of the parlour, pulled the fur stole more tightly around her shoulders. She must have fetched the stole earlier, half in sleep, could not recall going to her mother's wardrobe in search of it. The smell of the stole, trace of animal, musty like old carpet, pricked her nose. Yet it was soft and body-warm. Did it still remember its old, living shape? Lennie imagined it sliding from her shoulders, an orange streak slinking away into the night. *He'll need your help for now.* A body could start to decay even before death. After you were dead they did something to slow the process, so why not before? Blue liquid branching through her father's almost-corpse, glowing in the darkness. She had dreamed of his death once, but in the dream he had come back to life and no one remarked on this phenomenon as strange or unprecedented. She had woken empty and wracked with grief.

Bone-white moon outside. A summer ball, swish of dresses, baby blue, sugar pink. It was hard to imagine her father in such a setting, yet he used to take her mother dancing when they first met. He had told Lennie about it when she was small and had asked about the dresses in the wardrobe. Pale arms shivering against the night chill, young cheeks hectic with excitement. Lennie saw herself as a child again, perched upon her father's feet as he executed a slow waltz, moving faster and faster until she was giddy with laughter, hanging onto his waist. The image was a lie. It was Thomas who had taught her how to dance and not in that fashion. The idea must have come from a story, or perhaps she had inserted herself into a scene from a painting or a film.

Her father shifted in his sleep, moaned a little. Lennie stood in order to view him better without moving closer. His shoulders, never broad in life, appeared to have shrunk away from the bedclothes, like a cake from its tin when fully baked. It was hard to believe he was really so small, so lacking in significance. Only the breath rattling in and out of his throat made him real. And yet air was nothing, just an emptiness to be taken in and discarded. Nothing.

Where was Tom and where was Alexander and why must she be alone here with a father who was no longer a father, alone with something monstrous and unstoppable growing inside her?

A ngus?' She flicked on the light switch.
'Here.'
She had to look twice. He was on the far side of the bedroom, almost out of view, on his hands and knees on the floor.

'You should have called for me,' she said.

'Needed the loo.' He blinked up against the harsh overhead light, his words slurred by sleep or drugs or pain. His eyes had retreated into his skull.

'James is here too,' she said, hearing the creak of bedsprings in the nearby guest room.

Between the two of them they got Angus to his feet. Once he was standing, they could begin to move him. It was awkward to start with. Either side of him, they managed to manoeuvre him round the foot of the bed and through the doorway. They made their way along the landing in a kind of lopsided three-legged race.

'Getting there,' said Angus with a show of cheerfulness. 'Speed it up a bit though.'

Venetia had walked this landing so many times that she could negotiate her way along it with her eyes shut. Here was the slight dip in the carpet, here the creaking floorboard, the cool touch of the balustrade. It must be harder for James but at least the landing was moonlit. Angus was moving more purposefully now. Two steps more, past the window seat, then the lavatory door would be in reach. They would work out what to do next when they got there.

Angus came to an uncertain halt, something incoherent escaped from his lips. She turned towards him. He was staring down at himself. Venetia followed his eyes down to the wet leg of his pyjamas, the pool of wetness on the carpet.

'You were too slow, you fucking *idiots!*' All the light that had been absent from his eyes blazed in that moment. 'Didn't you hear me yelling for you?'

Sister Coombs came to speak to her the next morning.

'I've increased Sir Angus's pain relief again and the anti-sickness. It will make him quite sleepy, I'm afraid.'

'Good.' Seeing the young nurse's eyes widen, Venetia made an effort to speak less baldly. 'Do you know . . . ? Can you tell how long it will be? Only our son is arriving soon. I think I told you about that.'

The nurse shook her head. 'It could be days or it could be weeks, it's really hard to say at this stage, Lady Richmond. I wish I could be more helpful.'

Hattie knocked on the door. She was sorry for the interruption but wanted to know if she could let the kitchen know about supper arrangements. Venetia spent a minute discussing this and another housekeeping matter until she heard a noise from the bedroom behind her.

She found Angus gesturing weakly at a glass which lay on its side, ice melting darkly into the bedspread. Sending Hattie away, she helped him into a chair, changed the sheets and blankets. Then she went downstairs, and then down again to the cellars where racks of wine bottles shone dully beneath their shrouds of dust. She bypassed these, pushing aside bicycles of various sizes, Alexander's old pram, until she came to a row of wooden shelving. On the bottom shelf, a dark, unwieldy bundle was wedged against the cellar wall, like a loosely-wrapped body. This was the tent they'd bought when Alexander was small, at a time when Angus was still trying to interest him in outdoor pursuits. On the shelf above the bundle was a large rucksack. Venetia pulled it down and unknotted the rope at its neck, which was cold and slightly damp to touch. She felt around inside the rucksack and then drew out an enamel mug, one of a pair that had been packed away for years. It was white with a blue rim. The other one, she remembered, had a chip in it. She lifted it experimentally. Far lighter than crystal glassware, with a handle to grasp.

'That's good,' said Angus when she had washed the mug, filled it with cold water, and taken it up to the bedroom. He lifted it to his mouth successfully, though his hand was still shaking. 'Mouth gets so dry.' Then he scrabbled for the orange plastic bowl.

Alexander stood in the hallway listening again to everything Venetia had already told him over the phone, nodding his head like a schoolboy receiving instruction. He was lightly tanned from an early Mediterranean spring, looked out of place in the grey light of the hallway, as though someone had painted him from a different palette. He was unusually passive, with no questions to demand of her once she finished. She took him upstairs to see his father. Angus looked like he was sleeping, yet must have been conscious on some level because he started, then murmured to himself as his son entered the room.

'Oh, Papa,' was all that Alexander could say.

'Why is Uncle James staying here?' Alexander wanted to know, nodding to the guest room where James's coat was slung across the bed. They were waiting on the landing while the nurses were about their work in Angus's bedroom. Venetia could hear the two of them conversing, the creaking of the bed, the tear of paper, plastic. She was grateful for the relief they administered, the quiet words of advice, yet she had started to resent the way even the kindlier of the two appropriated death so readily. She wanted their work to be over as quickly as possible, so the house might return to itself: a private little world of suffering.

'I needed him,' she said. There was a depth of sorrow in Alexander's eyes and she knew that nothing she had told him over the crackling phone line had prepared him for the sight of his father, flat and grey as a shadow on the bed. 'Your father must have someone with him the whole time.'

Angus moaned in his sleep that evening, shifting and turning, plucking at the sheets as if the weight of them agitated him, all the while carrying on some feverish conversation.

'Do you think he knows I'm here?' said Alexander, standing over his father. 'What does he want?'

Angus's eyes flicked open, his gaze drifted past them as if they did not exist, lost in some space between sleeping and waking. Beneath his breath he whispered to an invisible audience. They caught only snippets of his agitation: lost train tickets, Suki and Tinker scratching at the door to come in, though his beloved dogs had long been dead, their bones resting beneath the dark soil of the rose garden. Until now Venetia had thought dying a linear process, something gradual, with steady stages, landmarks to be passed, not this trickster that shifted shape overnight, before you had time to get used to its last form.

'I don't know,' she said.

D own on her knees, up and down the small patch of earth, Lennie moved like a supplicant between the rosemary and the clumps of purple sage, the thyme and the creeping marjoram, the bronze fennel that glimmered in the sunshine. She dug, with her back turned to the cottage where her father lay, his eyes staring at the ceiling, breath so slow. Two nights since it had happened. Thomas knew now. Lady Richmond said he was hurrying home as fast as he could. Their father could hang on for years, they'd said at the hospital, or go in a moment.

She dug, trying to get to the root of things, grubbing around the dandelions that held onto to the earth so tenaciously, plucking at the more delicate weeds that sat like green froth upon the surface, came away with a gentler pull. She pushed her hands deeper into the earth, fingers moving like blind worms through the dark soil, blood and bone of everything that had once been alive. The earth could not lie: her hands would find out the truth.

Dark earth shifting, the taste of blood on her tongue. Damp air rising from the river.

I love you, Lennie

The river had roared, wanting to snatch the words from his mouth, to drown them. She had not understood. Danny Masters was a good, kind boy; she had kissed him because he was handsome and she could see in his eyes that he wanted her to. She had taken him by the hand and led him into the clearing in the woods. It had nothing to do with that love. It was the night air and the moon, the clean-sweat smell of him. Like the day she had watched him swimming in the woods, Danny's long body pale beneath the surface of the river pool, the smooth strokes of his arms cutting the water, how she could not move for the sight of him.

Love lived in her imagination and on the surface of her skin, her senses, the golden haze of Alexander almost blinding her. It was private but public too, with rules to be followed. With her hands deep in the earth, Lennie knew that there were parts of her love did not touch. It did not go bone-deep.

Danny holding onto her as if trying to keep afloat on the sea of the forest floor. Dark petals falling on the river bank; blood blooming in his palms like stigmata. How surprised he had looked, staring down at the blood, at her. She had pushed him away, run through the black trees till all the breath was gone from her lungs, slammed the cottage door shut behind her.

Hands in the earth. Small white hands, pushing Danny Masters to his death.

But no. She sat back on her heels, blinking at the sky. Was there something else, some other truth? It was hard to think straight with the little music box of a cottage at her back, waiting to contain her again. Danny lowering himself into the cold black rush of the Stride, his own fingers letting go of the wet rock? Whichever way. Everyone said she was a good girl but she made bad things happen. Brought trouble to others and to herself. Lennie bent forwards, pushed her hands down into the earth again, deep as they would go. It told her the only truth there was: the world makes its choices and it does not care.

CHAPTER 50
Venetia, Spring 1955

She did not mind the crocuses on the Great Lawn, they signalled the coming spring in a delicate, almost apologetic manner, and the snowdrops were white waxen tears, offensive to no one. It was the daffodils she loathed, so full of self-assurance, thrusting their sulphurous, penile buds out the ground.

At least it came quickly. The words of some well-meaning relative later, at Angus's funeral. Not fucking quickly enough, she had wanted to shout, and then to laugh hysterically all in the same moment.

Angus's body fought death long after the game was up. Even in sleep his ribs heaved, pulling useless spasms of air into failing lungs, his dried throat rasping. Always it was too hot for him in the room, despite the open windows and a good breeze lifting the curtains. It was as if his body was flushing out the last of life. Day and night they sponged his hands and face with cool water. When he managed to speak it was in whispers, half-sentences, but he lifted his face like a flower to the sun, submitting to her care, to the enamel cup lifted to his dry lips. It was all she could do for him, now food and language had become too complex for his regressing body to process. Water, touch. The instinct of the first blind, single-celled creatures on the littoral of existence, reaching out into the unknown. She wondered if that felt any different from reaching back, to the time before one began.

Lucidity came in odd flashes, just when she'd given up expecting it.

'Speed it up!' A sharp little joke that astonished her one morning when she took too long to pour fresh water into the enamel cup.

Later he swallowed, wincing at the effort. 'Alexander . . . home.'

'Yes.' Alexander would be happy to hear that Angus had registered his presence. Yet she had noticed that he would not be left alone with his father, went straight to his own room after dinner each evening, leaving her and James to care for him through the night. She could not find the energy to ask her son if he was scared of death or of the dying.

'Worse than I thought.'

'You should rest.'

Still his ravaged body was not ready to release him.

'He is a strong man,' said Dr. Harrison in a low voice. They stood in the doorway of the bedroom. 'Anyone else by now . . .'

'He's lost so much weight. You know he's not eaten for days. Surely it can't be long now?'

In her hands, a sodden pyjama top. The water she had given Angus had slipped straight from his mouth.

'What about a child's cup?' the nurse had said yesterday, watching as Venetia tried to help him drink. 'One of those with the lid and a spout. Somebody round here must have one.'

'I don't know.' Venetia had said. 'Perhaps.' She'd waited till the nurse had gone before going downstairs to hunt in the back of the kitchen dresser.

'Hard to tell,' said Dr. Harrison. 'It may be that his heart just gives out at some point.'

She hesitated.

'And there's nothing you can do? He gets so agitated.' Angus slept nearly all the time now, but to call it rest was an outrage, for it resembled nothing more than the troubled sleep

216 - KAREN POWELL

of the damned. For hours at a time he groaned to himself, crying out loud, or carrying on a fretful commentary beneath his
breath, little of which she and James managed to catch.

Dr. Harrison was slow to respond.

'All I can do is continue to increase the morphine and the
tranquillisers in increments, in order to make him more comfortable.' They watched one another, both of them knowing
there was only one comfort left for the man who lay in the bed.
'Eventually, of course, the combination of the two, and the
weakness of the body . . . but there are no guarantees.' He
looked at her steadily, then glanced towards the windowsill, his
eye caught by the blue plastic infant's cup which sat there,
unused.

'You should use that, you know. Less mess.'

In the chapel, Venetia prayed in a way she would have
despised as theatrical had she been able to view herself, down
on her knees, hands clasped in supplication.

Make it stop.

The baldest of requests. She could not specify death in her
prayers, and any kind of reversal would be nothing more than
a reprieve.

Till now she had thought of death differently: a noisy, visceral mess on a stretcher, like the soldiers in the garden wing,
poor brother Ned, during the fall of Crete, or else a shadow
descending somewhere close by, like a hand passing in front of
a lamp. This wringing out of a life, day after day, had a singular horror of its own. Exhausted, she fell asleep in the chair one
night when she was supposed to be watching him, awoke to
see transparent fingers clawing the air. She ran downstairs to
fetch more water, more ice, to assuage his incessant thirst.
Keeping him alive when his body had long since announced its
wish to die.

S nap. Her limbs were made of plastic, pink and shiny and snappable, like the dancer's in the music box. Little ballerina spinning round and round until the lid closed down with a slam. Across the parlour, her father was a rag doll crumpled on his bed, lopsided eyes staring. Upstairs, the cuckoo clock chimed. Nobody came.

Snap.

Just twigs breaking beneath her feet. It was colder here, among the tallest trees, the sky a distant green and gold above. She had never been afraid of the woods. Black roots clawed at the earth. Her ankles were beating a sure path through the undergrowth and her arms were pliable, strong, like young hazel branches. She pulled the fox stole more tightly around her, butting her cheek against its animal warmth. How lucky her mother had been to own such a beautiful thing.

You are like a dryad, Alexander had said. She had not known what he meant, saved up the word to check with Thomas later.

I'll walk you home.

Not Alexander but Danny Masters. A young girl like Lennie ought not to be at home on a Saturday night, said Miss Price, making Lennie feel sad for herself, then angry. In the village hall, the girls with covetous eyes, their smiles sticking to their teeth. She did not need walking home but she liked the feeling of him beside her, tall and certain. The roses are like spice, she told him on the riverbank. Afterwards, he straightened his clothes and helped her to her feet. The sky was violet above and the undergrowth snapped as they walked back to the river path in silence. She had wounded him. She knew that but she did not comfort him.

I love you, Lennie.

How his voice shook. Words that had nothing to do with the smell of him on her skin, the blackness swirling round the base of the trees. She tucked his words away in the collar of her dress where no-one could find them and then ran all the way home in the dark, slamming the cottage door shut behind her, pushing the lock into place with a snap.

It's happened now.

It had happened and it couldn't be undone.

S he must throw away the cup with the teddy bear transfer on it. It was a simple enough act, she should have done it before now—open the drawer, remove the cup, take it downstairs. She shouldn't delegate it to someone else. She was about to approach the chest of drawers when a movement caught her eye. From the bedroom window she saw that a taxi had pulled up at the bottom of the driveway, outside Gatekeeper's Cottage. She watched as Thomas got out. Even at a distance, she could sense urgency in his movements, the staccato thrust of money, the seizing of his luggage from the boot of the car. Visiting Lennie and her father again had been next on Venetia's list, but Tom would want some time alone with them now. She left the bedroom, closing the door behind her, went down the stairs and took the side doorway out into the garden.

Many of the plots were still given over to vegetables, with rationing only having been lifted the previous summer. Venetia wasn't much interested in the vegetable plots, leaving them and also the formal rose garden to be taken care of by Nathan Lacey and his crew, but she had reclaimed a number of beds for herself over the years, including a wide gravel-edged border which faced southwest and was sheltered by the high wall that separated the gardens from the rest of the grounds.

She walked the length of this border, checking each plant as she went. In the sharp light of the September afternoon the garden was hushed, like a stage set between scenes, or a mirage that might waver into nothing. The border would not reach maturity for another year or two but she had planted it generously and with her favourite things, a soft palette of white, pink, blues, against a background of cool greenery and silver grey foliage. Here were the last stems of snowy phlox, their delicious perfume drifting on the air, asters, as simple and charming as a child's sketch. There was lychnis elbowing its way in wherever it could, mounds of common sage, leaves rough and leathery as an old cat's tongue.

If it had been earlier in summer or even just a month ago, Venetia might have deadheaded as she moved along the border, or have been tempted to go and fetch her shears so that she might cut back here and there, in an attempt to bring shape and order to the planting. But so many of the plants were at their peak now: the leggy verbena branching out at shoulder-height, its small lilac flower heads trembling in the warm currents of air that the earth gave back at this time of day, the catmint, which was flowering for a second time, tumbling over the edges in clouds of hazy blue, even some of the dog roses were still blooming, producing fresh green leaves like little pleated skirts. All along the border plants twisted and intertwined, scrambling up neighbours, clambering over one other, all angling for the light, the last heat of summer. It would be wrong to contain them when winter was such a long time. You could never tell which plants would survive. In a garden youth and beauty counted for little. Strong roots were required to make it through a Yorkshire winter. Even the most gorgeous and abundant plant might be slayed by a harsh frost.

Venetia stooped to run her hand over the feathery foliage of the achillea that she had planted last summer. How well it sat against the spikes of mauve hyssop. Towards the back of the border, the pale, open faces of the Japanese anemones peeped through the purple branches of angelica where, earlier in the season, the honey bees had swarmed in pollen-fuelled ecstasy all day long. The anemones, she noted, would be ready for dividing soon.

She heard the sound of gravel being scattered on the other side of the wall. Whoever was coming up the driveway towards the house was moving quickly. She heard the front door being slammed followed by a commotion in the hallway. She heard Lennie's voice. Venetia retraced her steps along the border, hurrying in case Peter Fairweather's condition had worsened. Where on earth was Alexander when you needed him? Yes, it had been her idea that he should leave, but it had been three days now!

Lennie stood in the centre of the hallway, her extraordinary hair spilling over her shoulders. She was still in her nightdress, which gave weight to Venetia's concerns that there had been some new emergency with her father. Sunlight shone through the thin cotton of Lennie's nightdress, outlining her frame, the darkness between her legs. Something must have happened for her to have left the house without changing or even stopping for a dressing gown. Venetia was relieved to see Thomas at the doorway behind her. He was breathless, chest heaving.

Venetia sensed that something else wasn't right even before her eyes confirmed it. Thomas was looking back and forth between the kitchen girls, Hattie and Sarah, and the stable boy, Olly Sampson, for help, but none of them moved. Lennie had her hand behind her back and a kind of weighty garment draped over one shoulder which fell to the floor and which she dragged stiffly behind her. There was something familiar about it. Venetia drew nearer and saw with a shock that it was the Turkish rug from the floor of the cottage parlour. Her eye had traced the traditional pattern as a distraction during the hours in which she had sat with Peter Fairweather when they first brought him home from the hospital. Venetia approached warily.

'My mother said to give you this,' said Lennie. In her other hand was a rosemary bush which must have been wrenched from the ground just recently. Lennie shook it and soil spilled from its tattered roots. 'Though it doesn't work anymore.'

'Lennie, come home,' said Thomas, stepping forward, holding out his hand to her. 'If you'll just stay indoors . . . ' To Venetia: 'She wants to go to the woods.'

Lennie snatched her hand back, proffered the rosemary bush once again to Venetia.

'What's the matter, Lennie? Are you ill?' Venetia spoke carefully, trying to imbue her words with a calm she did not feel. 'Has something else happened with your father?' she said to Thomas.

'It stares so,' said Lennie.

'What does?' Venetia said. 'Did something frighten you, Lennie?'

Behind his sister, Thomas was white-faced.

'The rag doll in the parlour. Where the roses grow I left him. Not your boy with the pretty mouth but the other.' Lennie giggled. 'They took his jacket and hung him from a tree.' She shook the rosemary impatiently now at Venetia. Like dark snow more soil fell onto the pale stone of the hallway.

Venetia took the plant from her because it seemed she must. The pungent oil from its leaves filled the hallway. On Lennie's face was the same glassy expression that had unsettled Venetia on the night of the ball. Lennie in her mother's silver dress, gazing down at her hands as if they belonged to someone else.

'Alexander will be home soon, Lennie,' she said. 'And Thomas is here to look after you now.' She looked over the girl's shoulder and signalled calm to Lennie's brother, whose hands were frozen in a gesture of disbelief. 'You mustn't worry about anything.'

'Worry!' All of them jumped at the screech, which seemed to come from somewhere visceral. 'Why should I worry?'

Lennie spun around to her audience. 'It was me who took him and I didn't care about my dress being torn.'

'Did someone hurt you, Lennie?' Venetia said. 'Come upstairs and we can be quiet together, just the two of us. Thomas will fetch the doctor for you.' She motioned to him as discreetly as possible.

'Soaked to the skin, they said. That's why you fall to pieces when they heave-ho you up the river bank.' Lennie raised her eyes. 'Poor soul.'

A shaft of sunlight pierced the lantern window above Lennie's head and held her in its circle. She seemed confused for a second, letting slip the threadbare rug from her shoulders. The nightdress was torn from one shoulder, exposing one small, high breast. Venetia started towards her, wanting to shelter the girl from the gaze of others, but in that sudden blaze of light from above Lennie's slight frame seemed to grow in stature, the pathetic flimsiness of the cotton nightdress, the bare breast, no longer of any significance. Venetia forgot to be frightened for her, of her, only thought: how magnificent she looks, like a wounded goddess.

A cloud passed over the window. The light faded for a moment. Lennie frowned as she seemed to notice the point of her own breast for the first time. She plucked at the frayed edges of her nightdress with an air of distraction, as though trying to weave them back together again.

.'Come with me, Lennie,' said Venetia once again.

'They wanted to keep me in a box, but I went to the woods for my *sins*. They said I was safe with the lid pushed down but look at my poor hands!'

Lennie gazed down at her outstretched palms, then covered her eyes. Mud streaking her lovely cheeks, she began to sob.

CHAPTER 53
Venetia, 1955

W hy can't I see her?' Alexander came at her across the small sitting-room. 'What exactly is the matter with her, mother? I'll go down there right away.'

'I've told you all I know,' said Venetia. 'She's sedated. Dr. Harrison says she needs to rest. Besides, Thomas won't let anyone else in the cottage. Believe me, I've tried. I wish I could help him when there's Fairweather too, but . . .'

'She'll be better then? Once she's rested. I came back as soon as I got the message. Stupid night porter put it in the wrong pigeonhole.'

Venetia was not sure she believed him, or his story about meeting up with an old school friend in York by chance. It didn't matter now. 'I can't get any answers, Alexander. All Dr. Harrison will say is that she's had a terrible shock. We made a mistake, letting her be alone with her father like that.'

Her words didn't even graze the surface.

'It wasn't my fault though, was it? What happened with Fairweather. You said I should go away.'

'The blood clot could have been there a long time, apparently. It could have been making its way towards his brain for we don't know how long.' How odd, the thought that something so insubstantial could destroy all the subtle accretions of mind and memory formed over a lifetime in a matter of minutes. Little knot waiting in the darkness, biding its time.

'So they're sure it had nothing to do with me? You didn't tell the doctors about the argument?'

'Sit down, Alexander, for goodness sake!'

She could not breathe with him standing over her in that way, making her repeat herself all the time, wanting her to shoulder his own agitation. As a small boy he had been just like this, following her from room to room whenever he needed reassurance about some mishap or other. She could hear him now: *Everything will be fine, won't it, Mummy? I won't get into trouble, will I?* Over and over again. Words of comfort had meant nothing to him when he was in that state of mind, the badgering continuing until the very act of it exorcised whatever demon it was that was troubling him. Once, Venetia remembered, when she could stand it no longer, she locked herself in her own dressing room to get away from him, afraid of what she might do, afraid that she might strike him if he did not leave her be. She had sat with her back against the dressing room door, praying that Alexander would find Angus or one of the housemaids to torment instead. And still he had not been done with her, his little fists beating against the door.

'Tom'll have to let me in,' said Alexander. 'I'll make him.'

He ran his hands through his hair so that it stuck on end in a parody of shock. 'I want to *do* something. Not just sit around here like this. It's unbearable!' It would be fruitless to point out that he had not sat down once since he had entered the sitting room. She waited, as she knew she must. At last, a cooler voice: 'She'll be better once she's slept. That's what Harrison told you. I suppose Fairweather's going to need looking after from now on?'

Venetia nodded, relieved that his belligerence was blowing itself out. As it always did eventually. 'Of course. James and I have already started to think of ways . . . '

'What's it got to do with uncle? I don't see why he must have a say in everything now. It would have been better for Helena if Fairweather had died, really.'

'He's her *father.*'

Alexander had the grace to look startled, as though the fact had not been known to him before now. Venetia watched as he crossed to the window and stared out across the Great Lawn. Deep down, she couldn't help but admire this creature who had emerged like a chrysalis from her body, even while she despaired of his selfish ways. Alexander placed his outspread palm on the glass, as though seeking some connection with the closed-up little cottage in the distance. Then withdrew it, giving up on the idea.

Later, she made him walk with her, over the fields, away from the cottage where Lennie still slept and her father lay in his frozen state.

'Thomas will let us know if there's any change,' she said. 'He promised that at least. And it will do you good to walk.'

Yellow clouds smothered the sun. The midday heat was oppressive. They passed the entrance to the farm, started to climb the bridle path up to the ridge. Soon Venetia found her breath coming in small gasps. Sweat ran down the base of her spine. Alexander moved with small, quick steps up the hillside ahead of her, appearing not to feel the heat at all.

'Will you marry him?' He stopped and turned to her, taking advantage of the height he'd gained. 'Uncle James.'

She waited until she was alongside him before answering.

'I hadn't thought of it.' *It hardly matters* is what she wanted to say.

'I'm not enough for you?'

'I don't understand.'

'I mean if Helena . . . When we marry and have children and so on . . I would have thought that would be enough company for someone of your age.'

She forced down a laugh at this outrage before answering 'You've not been quite clear about your intentions until now.'

'I've hardly had time to think about it since father died. Don't you want us here?'

'I've never been sure that you cared for the place, Alexander. Not in the way your father did.' As she spoke, she knew that this had troubled her for a long time. She could not say how he felt about Richmond Hall. Her son seemed to exist in his head, skimming over the surface of his surroundings, captured on occasion by a particular trick of light or a beautiful ruin. It occurred to her only now that this might explain his desire to travel, to be in constant motion with only so much connecting expected of him. 'You've never shown much interest, you see. It gets more and more difficult to find staff, that sort of thing, but we must try to go on as we did before.'

'It can't be like before.' Alexander pushed ahead again, striding up the dusty hillside. Venetia let him go. He was not yet finished with her, she knew, but there seemed little point in exhausting herself in pursuit. He spun round just before he reached the apex of the ridge. '*Must* you marry?'

She could not help but smile though it was no time to joke. 'Some might think so. For propriety's sake.'

'It's that important to have a man in your bed, so soon after my . . . ' Alexander's voice cracked.

The smile left her lips in an instant. Never that, she wanted to say. She had loved the clean lines of her husband's body but had never been a sensual creature by nature. There was no way in the world that she would discuss such things with her son. It was outrageous that he should ask such intimate questions of his own mother. Was there something wrong with him? She had always felt her son's otherness—so unlike either of his parents with his scholar's mind, his obliqueness—and had thought this a good thing. Now she wondered if she had should have snapped at his heels, worried him towards the prosaic. Had she made some dreadful error of judgment?

When they had both reached the top, Venetia stopped to gather her breath. The village sat to their left, within the loop of the river. Before them lay half the county.

'Did you hear that the Hirons must sell Scawton Place?' She gestured to a grey smudge in the distance. 'It's to be a hotel. And the Favershams are struggling to find staff too. No one wants to stay at home these days. Not since the war.'

'It's difficult sometimes,' said Alexander. 'Home.' She waited for him to elaborate, sensing a softening of mood. 'They say we're a dying breed, you know. Us landowning types. That's what Tom and all his new friends bang on about anyway.'

'Nonsense.' Fear made her brusque. 'They said just that after the Wall Street crash and here we all are years later. No-one can just announce such things and expect everyone to give up.'

'I do wonder if we've had our time, mother, as if there's something rotten at the core of all *this* now.' His hand swept over the horizon. 'Last time I was in London everyone looked so grey and defeated. It felt as though we'd lost the war.'

'It takes time to recover.'

'Yes, but all civilisations think they're indestructible and then they're not, so maybe this little piece of history is up, our bit, I mean. I don't believe you've never thought of it too. Tell me, why is Helena's mother buried where she is?'

'I don't understand.'

'Right at the edge of the graveyard, away from the rest of the Fairweathers. Almost as if no one wanted her there. When I tried to talk to Dr. Harrison about Helena this morning, he said something about her being highly-strung like her mother, and then seemed to think better of it.'

'He didn't mean anything.'

'There was something wrong with her. Did she kill herself? Tom and Helena never seem to like talking about her.'

'You're not to speak about it to either of them!' Her voice was sharp on the breeze. Venetia thought for a moment before continuing. 'The fact of the matter is that Jennifer, Lennie's mother, wasn't well by then.' She spoke carefully and it was right, because words like *insane, running mad* belonged only in Gothic novels, not here, on this green hillside in late summer.

It was Mussolini's fault though no-one could have predicted that on 10th June 1940, the day that Italy declared war on Britain and France. Jenny and Peter Fairweather had been settled at Gatekeeper's Cottage for a number of years by that time, with Helena toddling around like a little fairy child in the wake of her dark-haired brother. Settled wasn't quite the right word, for Jenny never seemed quite at home in the cottage.

'It is so quiet down here,' Jenny said. While Thomas and Alexander played with toy soldiers on the kitchen floor, Helena, whose name had already been shortened to Lennie, snuffled in her carrycot. It was clear that Jenny did not consider the peace an asset.

'Everywhere is quiet,' Venetia said. 'With the men gone.' And then wished she hadn't said anything. Peter Fairweather had failed his fitness test for the army because of his asthma, would have to stay at home, dealing with the small amount of correspondence required in Angus's absence. But Jenny was too distracted by her own problems to perceive any slight.

'Up at the Hall there is always something going on. Sometimes a whole day goes by here . . . '

She found a little solace in her new herb garden. She was not much interested in cooking, but a school friend had given her a book of herbal remedies as a wedding present and she was often to be found with it open on the kitchen counter, making up batches of rosemary oil for bruised knees, or else brewing chamomile tea which she liked to press upon a reluctant Venetia, swearing that it was good for the nervous system.

Venetia would wonder later if there might have been a different outcome had Jenny lived long enough to see the hospital set up at Richmond Hall. She would have been far more suited than Venetia to tending to the young soldiers, would have kept up their spirits with her lively ways, her quick laughter. The work would have given purpose to her days, as well as the companionship and variety she craved and which two small children, however sweet, were incapable of providing.

Angus held out the newspaper to Venetia over breakfast one morning. 'Collar the lot,' said the headline. Beneath it was a picture of Churchill and an article about the Italian immigrants who were no longer welcome in Britain now that their country was in league with the Nazis. Later that day she mentioned it to Jenny, who said it was a shame but did not worry herself about it: her father Roberto and uncle Federico had lived in England all these years now.

'Papa loves this country,' she would say on more than one occasion that summer. Had he not given his only daughter an English name, had he not been overjoyed when a tall, quintessentially English man in the shape of Peter Fairweather came asking for her hand in marriage? Roberto Carloni even dressed like an Englishman, though all the tweed in the world could not disguise his southern European heritage. Venetia met him once or twice, a small, neat man whose open delight at seeing his daughter in so English a setting had charmed her

'Everyone loves Papa,' Jenny would say fondly after his visits. But loyalty to one's adopted country counted for little in the summer of 1940. An employee at the barber's shop telegrammed to say that Roberto had been interned. Jenny tore up to the Hall, made frantic calls all that day, but no one would tell her where her father had been taken.

Just a week later, Roberto's brother, Federico was also taken in. Arriving in England in 1913, Federico had started out selling ice cream from a handcart. Within the year, he opened a small ice cream parlour, then an eponymous milk bar just a few streets away from his brother's barber's shop in Leeds. Now the shutters were pulled down on both *Federico's* and the barber's shop, the other shopkeepers having little to say about the disappearance of their no-longer-loved neighbours. Venetia, thinking to help, made enquiries on Jenny's behalf about both the men, but the most she could ascertain was that some Italians were being held on the Isle of Man.

'Never heard of it!' Jenny said. 'I have to visit my Papa.'

'Wait a few weeks,' she said. 'Until things calm a little. Your father and uncle won't come to any harm.'

On July 2nd, 1940, the *Arandora Star*, sailing off the coast of western Ireland, was hit by a single torpedo fired by Gunther Prien, captain of U-boat U47. The ship, once a luxury cruise liner, was transporting 'enemy aliens' and German prisoners of war to Canada, including over a thousand Italian immigrants. All 15,000 tons of the *Arandora Star* went to the bottom of the ocean, taking with it those who failed to escape in time, some sucked down in its wake. There were rumours that the crew fired holes into the lifeboats to prevent their passengers from escaping to safety.

For weeks afterwards the sea returned the dead, an evil-smelling, bloated tide rolling in across the shores of Donegal. Exactly ten days after the sinking of the ship, Jenny, searching through the lists in the newspaper, learned that the body of her uncle, Federico Carloni, had been recovered, dragged out of the shallows by some local fishermen. In the months that followed, she grew desperate for information about her father, trying to discover if he'd been lost with the ship, or he had been sent, like the rest of the survivors, straight back to Liverpool and then on to Australia. Another possibility was that he was still interned on the Isle of Man or elsewhere.

She was never to know: Roberto Carloni disappeared like so many of his countrymen that year, never to reappear. In the barber's shop, the seats stayed empty, his comb and scissors still lying where he had set them down, mid-customer, when they came for him.

Jenny began to worry about Thomas.

'They'll want him next,' she said to Venetia, who came to offer condolences for her uncle. 'My little boy.'

'That's not possible, Jenny,' Venetia said. 'No one is interested in the children, let alone grandchildren.'

'Look how Italian he is!' said Jenny, grasping a handful of her son's dark curls. Thomas concentrated on colouring in an aeroplane. 'I've seen how they stare at him in the village, you know. They say there are informers everywhere.'

'I'm sure that's not true,' said Venetia.

Jenny made no reply, her expression blank.

Peter Fairweather asked to see Venetia. His wife, he said, was concerned about security at the cottage, was insisting they have new locks installed on the doors and windows. Had something happened? Venetia asked. No. Fairweather would arrange for the work to be carried out himself, he only wanted to reassure Venetia that no structural changes were to be made.

People would always think of the winter of 1939–40 as punishing in its severity, but it was the following one that Venetia would remember. Starome, along with the other villages that sat in the shadow of the moors, had a climate of its own and 1941 brought day after day of snow, followed by harsh winds that packed the snow into seemingly permanent drifts along the country lanes. On many days, the villagers had to dig their way out of their homes, emerged blinking into the weak sunlight. Livestock was kept inside so that the fields were empty of all movement, except the occasional hare bounding across the snow.

The confinement did not trouble Venetia greatly. She was

busy, with the help of Sir Laurie, with arrangements for converting the garden wing into a hospital, did not notice Peter Fairweather's strained look, nor that he was less exacting about his work than usual. Alexander was in bed with a severe cold and there was no thought in Venetia's mind to tramp down to Gatekeeper's Cottage in the snow and icy winds. She might even have avoided it, not wanting to have various foul-smelling remedies pressed upon her, with the insistence that they would cure a common cold

She saw Jenny only once in those weeks and that was from a distance, when Venetia was on her way home from the stables. The wind was whipping up a stinging flurry of snow and she was in a hurry to get back to the warmth of her sitting-room. She spotted Jenny at the doorway of the cottage with the pram. Thomas was jumping up and down in the garden, dark curls standing out against the white backdrop. Venetia waved to them a couple of times, but Jenny didn't notice. Venetia carried on up the driveway, her mind preoccupied with plans to reallocate beds from guestrooms to the garden wing. Her only thought for Jenny was that she would not get very far with the pram in this kind of weather.

S he took the children out to the woods,' Venetia said. 'She hadn't dressed them properly. Lennie was only in under-clothes in the pram. Thomas had bare feet, the poor child. Fairweather saw them and there was some sort of fight. No one really knows why Jenny ran back to the woods, what happened at the river. She might have slipped or fallen or . . . ' Venetia looked at Alexander steadily. 'All of us agreed it was an accident.'

'I don't understand why you wouldn't tell them the truth.' Alexander stared at her with all the fierceness of youth.

'Dr. Harrison said it would be better for Thomas and Lennie that way. For Fairweather too. Reverend Jones agreed to it too.'

'She will be all right, won't she?' Alexander said.

Venetia thought of Lennie in her torn nightgown and bare feet, that glassy expression. She did not know. It was Thomas that everyone had kept an eye on. Thomas who looked so much like his mother, who had, they thought, inherited her volatile nature. All these years Fairweather had fretted over his son, placated his every mood, while Lennie sat silently by.

'She needs to rest.' Venetia wanted to walk again. She set off along the ridge at a fast pace, despite the heat. 'I've seen too many people die over the years to dwell on the past, Alexander. My parents, my brothers. Your father. We owe it to them to get on with all the things left to do, not feel sorry for ourselves.'

'Helena will be all right, of course?' Alexander said, almost repeating himself. 'I've not always been kind to her, mother. I don't know why. I don't know what to do.' He shook his head, stared out across the horizon. 'I did a terrible thing.'

'You are not to blame, Alexander. I've told you what the doctors said about Fairweather, and none of us could have known that Lennie would become so distraught. These things run in families sometimes, though all of us had hoped . . . '

'I saw him picking those roses and I knew.'

'Fairweather?'

'Danny. I saw him picking them and I knew straight away they were for Lennie.'

Venetia stopped. 'I don't understand.'

'I killed him, mother.'

CHAPTER 56
Danny, July 1955

W ho's that?' Sharp across the darkness, a voice came
from the river path, where it looped just before the
Stride.

Only yesterday he'd stood here with Lennie. Danny didn't
know why he'd come back or how long he'd been standing on
the river bank, his skin cold, his muscles stiffened. He was broken up inside, pieces of misery and pieces of happiness coming
to the surface and then drifting away again. He was joyful and
wounded and he did not want to move. He felt as if some part
of his body had been shattered and that he must assess the
damage before shifting and making everything worse.

'Masters, isn't it? What the hell are you up to?'

He knew, even before the figure emerged from the gloom.

Alexander Richmond—golden-haired, taller than he remembered. All lean angles too. Plain, well-cut clothes. Danny felt
clumsy standing there, like a carthorse next to a thoroughbred.

'Why do you ask?' Danny said.

'Huh?'

For a moment Danny almost expected him to say that this
land they stood on belonged to Richmond Hall, to him, but
any lord-of-the-manor air disappeared as Alexander came
closer. When he spoke he sounded more like his father, Sir
Angus: 'Oh well, you can do what you want, I suppose. Gave
me a fright, that's all.'

'Nothing to be frightened of here.' Danny stood his ground
as if a dispute over it meant something.

'Well, I know that, of course.' Irritation crept into Alexander's voice. 'Not much of a welcome home from an old friend but never mind.' He took a little bow and gave a theatrical wave. Danny could smell whisky on him, understood now that he was quite drunk. 'I bid you good night, young Masters.'

If there was mockery in his words, it was faint. Something harmless at most. It was the wave though, the hand swirling too close to Danny's face that did it. His skin felt too sensitive, the lightest touch would harm him.

'Get off me.' He pushed at Alexander's chest. It was fine-boned, like a peacock's or some rare game bird's, not thickened as his was by labouring.

'What the hell's your problem, Masters? Lost your manners for some reason?'

'I've manners enough for them who deserve them.'

Alexander peered through the darkness. Focusing wasn't coming easily to him. Danny waited for a blow, a shove, something that would make everything simple.

'Get yourself to bed if I were you,' Alexander said. 'You'll feel it in the morning.'

The elder boy stepped back onto the path, turned away, putting distance between them.

'I'm not drunk,' Danny called after him. 'I came here to get roses for Lennie.'

Alexander stopped. Danny could feel the tension in him and relished it.

'How could you know about the roses?'

'It's no secret,' said Danny. They were face to face again. 'Lennie's the only one that likes them, always did.'

'Well, she's quite capable of picking them for herself, you know. No need for you to go to any trouble.'

'Someone has to look out for her.' Danny had started, it was too late to turn back again. 'All alone, she is, up at that cottage.

It's not right.' The taste of her seemed still to be on his tongue, his ears still ringing with the shock of what had happened between them.

'How on earth can it be any business of yours, what Helena does? It's nothing at all to do with you.' Alexander's voice was sharp again but Danny recognised the beginnings of fear in it.

'I love her.'

And there it was, laid down between the two of them. The truth sounded too simple. Like a child he was, a village idiot with not a drop of poetry or learning in his blood. Alexander would have found the right words, he was sure of that.

'You love her.' There was laughter somewhere in that voice. Danny felt the heat rise in his face. 'Helena?'

'No-one calls her that!' He had to stop him, stop Alexander from making her into someone else, not the girl who had lain down in the woods with him last night.

'Just to be clear. Is she aware of this passion of yours?'

Careful. He had to be careful.

'No. I don't know.'

'I see.' Even in the shadow of night, Danny could sense the other boy relaxing. Alexander sounded like his father again. 'Well look, I don't mean to be unkind, but Helena really won't have thought of you in that way. You always did say things straight, which is good, but I don't want you to embarrass yourself.'

'You don't know that.'

Alexander wagged a vague finger at him. 'Now Hattie Merriot's a different thing altogether. I heard her talking about you back at Easter.'

The friendliness finished him. In that moment Danny understood that he never had a chance: he was just an apprentice carpenter with wood dust ground into his soul. What had happened with Lennie was an accident which she would have regretted the moment it was over.

'You don't deserve her,' he said miserably.

'Not really for you to decide, is it?' said Alexander. 'Helena's a good girl and she'd be kind to you if she knew. That's why I don't want you bothering her.'

'I wouldn't. I never have.' It was a lie, but it felt like the truth. What happened couldn't be reduced in that way, turned into something ugly.

'Good.' Alexander nodded. His voice was still cool but even in the darkness Danny could sense something unsure in it, some weakness beneath the surface threatening to break through. 'I'm thinking of marrying her, so no point you wasting your time hankering after her. I'm only telling you because I always liked you, Masters.'

His love, all his precious and fine feelings reduced to hankering! And the arrogance of Alexander, talking about marrying Lennie so casually. As if he had any number of choices and might as well settle upon her as anyone else.

Danny took off his jacket, threw it on the ground.

'What are you doing now?' said Alexander.

'I told you, you don't deserve her.'

A bark of laughter. 'Surely you're not going to beat it out of me?' Alexander took a step backwards and held up his hands in mock-submission.

'No.' Danny took a step back himself, bent to pick up his jacket which, only a moment before, he'd dropped to the ground. Suddenly he was too tired, wanted only to go home and sleep beneath the cottage eaves. Not to think until morning.

A blow caught him in the ribs as he stood up. Light and fast it was, not enough to wind him, but the shock of it caught him off guard. Alexander was staring at him as if he himself couldn't believe what had just happened. At least Danny had an excuse now. He drew back his right fist but before the punch formed, Alexander connected with a second blow, this time to Danny's stomach. He wouldn't have felt the pain, even if the punch had been a practised one, but it was just enough to make him step back, instinct kicking in. One foot back and then the other, second foot finding nothing. It took only a second to understand that he was on the edge of the river bank, his arms flailing, trying to find his balance, trying to create some forward momentum so that he could grasp at something. Grass, stone, water, all rushed by in a blurry mess. And then the roar of water in his ears. The world turned black.

Danny surfaced seconds later, gasping at the cold. He could see Alexander high above him, crouched down on the river bank. His mouth was moving, an arm reaching over the edge, but Danny couldn't hear. The water pulled him down again. The second time he surfaced he was further downstream. He could no longer see Alexander. His head dropped back, he could see the black sky above, the stars that glittered cold. He went under, came up again, then struck out with all his strength, with everything in him that was young and alive and full of hope, pulling blindly towards the river bank with one arm, then the other. He could hear his legs thrashing wildly. His head turned from side to side, seeking out air, but the water wanted him and would not let him go. Danny made one last effort and then the river took him for its own.

A t least I think it was my fault.' Alexander said. 'At first I was pleased because I've never had a fight in my life. The only time it nearly happened was when we were kids and Danny himself stepped in, so I never knew if I was man enough. But then it all got mixed up in my head after we found his body. Did you see him yourself, mother? I can't remember. Seeing him like that made it all real again.' He frowned. 'But also less real, just a bag of flesh that had nothing to do with anything alive.'

'You're saying you fought with him on the river bank?' She must think logically.

'I'd been travelling back from Greece for two days, drunk rather a lot waiting for a train in York. I suddenly wanted to see Helena very badly, so I walked from the station rather than call for the car. That's when I saw him.'

'I don't understand. The roses could have been for any-one . . . '

'No. The villagers all think they're cursed or some such nonsense. That's what we used to say when we were kids. Only Helena liked them. Besides, the fool told me exactly what he was doing when I asked. Said that I didn't deserve a girl like her and that I was to blame for neglecting her!'

'Such a quiet boy always, I can't imagine . . . ' said Venetia. 'I'm presuming you haven't told anyone else about this. Anyone but me?'

Alexander shook his head as if trying to knock his thoughts into some kind of order.

'The problem is that I've thought about it and dreamt about it so much that I can't work out what actually happened.' He gazed at her, shook his head once again. 'He said something about Helena being better off with someone who would look after her properly, or words to that effect. I remember his hand on my shoulder and not being able to bear it, being so enraged. I knocked the roses out of his hand and I think I pushed him too, but I can't be sure now. He might have stepped back of his own accord. We were on the edge of the bank by that time, then he was gone, quite suddenly. It was almost as though he'd done it on purpose, mother, as a joke, was waiting just below the bank. Or that the water had risen up for a moment because it was racing beneath us the whole time we were struggling . . . None of it makes sense except that all at once he was in the river. I could have helped him but I didn't.'

'You didn't fetch anyone?' A stupid question. She already knew the answer.

'He didn't look like he wanted it. I can't explain. He'd left his jacket on the bank. I hung it on a tree, came home.'

'You would both have been killed,' Venetia said. 'No-one goes in the river that close to the Stride and comes out alive.'

'So you think it wasn't my fault, after all?' Alexander held her gaze urgently. 'You think he must have fallen or didn't care that much about living? Everyone knows that Helena loves me.'

Little fists beating against a door.

'I can hardly tell.' She hesitated. Alexander looked as if he might bolt at any moment, like a startled horse. She needed to think straight. Poor Danny was dead in his grave, with only his mother left to mourn him. Nothing could change that fact. What comfort would Mamie Masters take from the knowledge that her son died in misery, sick with love for a girl he could not have, the result of a pointless skirmish on the river bank? Wouldn't it be better to go on thinking it just a drunken stumble, the water closing over him before he even realised that he'd lost his footing? 'It was a terrible thing that happened, Alexander.'

'Yes.' He nodded slowly. 'I always liked Masters, you see, when we were small. The other boys from the village kept away because of who I am, or else were too keen to be friendly. Thomas was no different than now—always looking for something to be upset about. Danny was straightforward though, never afraid of me. That's why he couldn't help but tell the truth that night. You know, you might marry before Helena and me.'

The sudden change of both tone and subject shocked her. Alexander was like some exemplar of the power of confession, completely purged of guilt by the act.

'Please don't speak to anybody else,' she said. 'Promise me that.'

'Yes, yes.' Alexander walked, waving away the idea. 'Just don't expect me to come to some hole-in-the-corner wedding. He swung round abruptly. 'I have such terrible dreams, mother.'

'I can't think about it anymore today, Alexander. It's too much. We'll talk again tomorrow.'

'Oh, not just about Danny, though that's been bad. Since father died. You know, once I dreamed he came back to life again. I was so happy until I realised that he was still ill, that he'd have to go through the dying all over again, that we didn't know when it would begin or end or how awful it might be. That was almost more terrible than him being dead.'

Venetia put a hand on his forearm in comfort, though the truth was that Alexander had arrived too late and then kept himself too separate to really understand the dying: the beginning and the middle, the end that would not end. 'It made me think of how useless I felt when he was suffering so much,' he said. 'I should have done more for him and I didn't. I stayed in my room, left it to everyone else. Remember when Papa tried teaching me to sail up near the farm in Scotland? I dreamt about that too. He wanted to tell me something in the dream but I couldn't hear because of the wind and the water, then something changed and I could hear him perfectly.' Alexander turned to her. 'All along he was trying to let me know something terrible about you.' Alexander gave a wild little laugh, as if this second confession had freed still more in him. 'I shouldn't have told you, I suppose.'

The forest floor damp, frangible, curled in on itself. Layer upon layer of secrets. Sycamore branches limey in the slanting sunlight. A silver birch was ghostly and elegant among the great oaks. Here she could breathe at last, cool green air filling her lungs. She had flung back the lid of the cottage and run all the way.

Feet light but powerful, like a wary cat. Something was swelling inside of her, she could feel it, a deep muscle ache. Dropping to her haunches now; a hot spatter of urine among the leaves. Damp leaves turning darker, the hiss from the depths of her. Her feet looked so pale, the pink and white skin tender, like something raw, raised in darkness. Wetness clung to her skin. They would put her back in that box of blackness, push down the lid. She could still hear the terrible sobbing. Someone should shut that child up.

She hugged the fox stole to her, so beautiful, the fur dense and lustrous beneath her fingers. Forgot to be scared. *Goddess of the trees* someone had called her. That's what *dryad* means. Who and why? Her hair was too pale. Milky flesh of trees, axe-scarred, sap like tears, tears like sap. They would find her, put her back. Take handfuls, pale strands rubbing the bark of this oak. Giant leg rooted in the forest. Rough and tangled as the undergrowth now. A great strength flooding into her limbs which were not pink and plastic but pliable like branches.

Ahead. There the treetops thickened, like a scab along a thin wound. She heard it, filling the air with its coolness, damp tendrils touching her face. Like a cat, she moved all stealthy and camouflaged, and then she was close by. The roar of it, how it sung in her ears and the trees full of it too, canopies exploding above her head. You could smell the roses from here. Look. Danny Masters was a good boy though he had fallen to pieces in the water. *I don't want to hurt you, Lennie. I love you.* She could not be snapped in two just like that. Murderously strong, she was, her bloodbeat as powerful as the water. How it forced its nose through rock like a blind snake. Close at hand she felt it, just over that little rise in the land. Smell of wet, the scent of dark petals. On her hands and knees now, ground rearing up before her, goose-shit green. Scrambling through the undergrowth to the call of the river.

CHAPTER 59
Venetia, Spring 1955

I f there was no teddy bear on the plastic cup it might just have been possible. She would rather withhold water than push the spout of that cartoonish infant's cup into her husband's mouth, the only sensuous feature of his aquiline face.

She watched as Angus moaned to himself in whatever twilight world he inhabited, dry lips moving as if in supplication. He reached for the enamel cup on the bedside table. His hand fluttered, shook. He muttered in what seemed to be some nascent form of language, some proto-speech, then gave a little cry, dropped his hand back onto the sheets. Those hands that once reined in the strongest of horses lay useless and almost transparent in the late afternoon light. Still his lungs dragged in air, chest heaving like some awful machine, the air rasping in his throat.

Venetia stood. She took the cushion from her chair and stepped towards the bed. How long would it take to push him beneath the surface? His body might fight on, even now that the flesh hung loose on his limbs. What if she wasn't strong enough to overcome him? She hardly dared to think, knew only that she must act before terror undid her. She lifted the cushion, stared down at Angus's face in order to register any change in awareness. The cushion was sea-blue. It felt heavy in her hands, dense enough. She could feel the prick of a feather against one palm. What was she was waiting for? A miracle that would make all that had gone before a mistake, a terrible misdiagnosis? Forgiveness? Or just an imprint of his still-living face on her memory?

Angus's eyelids were like parchment and the whole room seemed to breathe with him, roaring in her ears, in, out, in, out. She lowered the cushion.

She threw it aside. She could not do it! She had been so sure, convinced she was strong enough. She had failed him as always. There would not be another chance, that was a certainty. Never again would she find the courage. She had failed him and she did not know how she could go on with that knowledge.

'Venetia.'

A voice in the doorway.

Her eyes were wild, she could feel it. She could smell her fear, the failed blood-lust upon herself.

'I can't.'

They gazed at one another, she and James, her husband's brother, a man who knew how to put an animal out of its misery, who had loved her all these years. Venetia bent down, plucked the sharp feather from the sea-blue fabric, offered the cushion to him.

They would never speak of it; how Angus's eyes opened just before the cushion descended for the second time, a last pulse of consciousness as he lay propped up on his pillows like some terrible, broken mannequin. How he gazed at his brother, standing over him, then directly at Venetia with the clear eyes of youth.

Three figures caught for a moment in the frame of time.

What did he feel in that moment? If he had been able to speak, what would he have said? Venetia was sure of only one thing: Angus understood exactly what was about to happen to him. And, though she would like to think she saw gratitude, acceptance, there was no evidence of either. She would not pretend otherwise to herself. There was no comfort to be had in lies.

Finding himself observed, James panicked, thrust down the

cushion with a desperate strength. Angus's legs began to kick like a panicking swimmer, his back arching from the bed, body still fighting for any kind of life. She might have cried out, though she could not be sure that the strangled sound issued from her own mouth and not his.

James came to her later. It seemed like hours. On the darkened landing, she lay huddled on her knees, dared at last to take her hands from her ears. He stroked her hair in the darkness. Silence. Somehow she stood, walked towards the guest bedroom. In the doorway she turned to James, unbuttoned her dress.

He hesitated, confused, but it was better this way, with no time to think. A deal had been struck and she would not renege. He moved above her in the darkness. Her back arched involuntarily. It felt as if they were the only two people left alive in this world.

No one could work out how Lennie had escaped the cottage unnoticed. All anyone knew was that she was seen entering the river with the Turkey rug trailing behind her. The children who saw her were from the village, knew better than to go in after her. They tried to rescue her by way of sticks and branches, following her progress a short distance downstream, almost to the point where the river lost its force quite suddenly, opening out into the glassy pool where Danny Masters had been found, a gentler place where dragonflies skimmed the surface, where the first autumn leaves drifted over the coppery shallows. Lennie did not seem to hear their cries or notice the sticks they held out for her. She reached up to the pendant branches of the willows as she passed beneath their shadows, made no attempt to grasp at them. The children could make no sense of it. Lennie was singing to herself as the water closed in, her hair floating on the surface for a moment like some pale water plant. No, said the smallest of the children, a girl of about five, she wasn't singing, she was definitely crying.

Such an exquisite corpse, poor Lennie, once they'd put her in her pretty cornflower dress and her bright hair had been dried and arranged. Sam Bracegirdle had pulled her to the bank just a few minutes after the children came running for him. There had been no time for the water to find its way beneath her lovely surface. Someone had placed a spray of stiff tea roses in her hands—Venetia would have liked to take it away, replace the bouquet with something less formal, some of the late-flowering scented damasks from the garden, even the roses from the river bank if they weren't finished, but there was no point trying to make things better now.

Alexander made a scene at the funeral, lurching towards the narrow coffin as it was lowered into the clayey ground as if to impede its progress, as if he wanted to attach himself to it. Part of Venetia felt desperate for him as he sank down, covered his face, the first handful of earth thudding onto the pale wood, yet why must he take centre stage when Lennie's own father was sitting beside the grave in his wheelchair, his face locked into a permanent parody of horror, and Thomas stood frozen in grief, his face set.

'Alexander . . . ' she coaxed, because others were joining in the weeping now.

'Stop it!' Thomas seemed to wake up. He stared round at the mourners, eyes black and angry. 'All of you. Is there no peace for her even now?'

Alexander smashed his fist against the greedy earth, oblivious; Venetia gave up, focused her mind on practical matters. They must find a nurse to live in at the cottage with Fairweather, it was the least she could do. She looked across the mouth of the grave at Thomas, who was weeping uncontrollably now, his head in his hands. He could not know it, but in time he would find resilience within himself, the urge to continue. It was the only wisdom she had to impart. Hardly wisdom really. It was more that her ear had become attuned to some communal human instinct to persist.

Wakes have a particular rhythm, thought Venetia, as the mourners streamed into the salon. She had attended enough of them over the years to recognise the pattern. The funeral has been endured, a feeling of relief follows. At first everyone behaves as if the taking of food and drink is a painful, unwanted obligation, a vulgar concern for the body's needs. There is no avoiding it though, this playing out of the newly updated division between the living and the dead. After a time, someone will smile, if only in the remembrance of some aspect or act of the departed; later people might laugh out loud for the same reason, and before long a celebratory mood sets in, albeit too intense, too heightened. All of it a distraction from a body lying alone in its cold grave for the first time.

Lennie's wake was different. The young people from the village came up to Richmond Hall as invited, but slunk away early, perfectly sober. The atmosphere in the salon remained hushed, never showing any sign of slipping towards merriment. Fairweather became distressed, was taken back to the cottage to rest by Nathan Lacey and his wife who offered to sit with him for a few hours, trying hard not to show the relief they felt to be gone. Thomas barely spoke to anyone and so Venetia, with some help from James, did what was necessary, moving between the small groups that had gathered in uncomfortable knots around the room to thank them for coming, to urge more wine or food on them.

Alexander was alone, standing by the fireplace in what seemed to be deepest thought. He had a glass in his hand but did not appear to have eaten. Venetia put a few small items on a plate, took them to him.

'I can't eat,' he said, registering her approach.

'You must try.' She set the plate down on the mantelpiece.

'It doesn't feel possible or right.' He looked up at her. 'I still can't believe she's dead, mother. I have no idea how to go on.'

There were none of the usual layers of meaning beneath Alexander's words, no archness. These were just statements of fact. Simplicity that was the opposite of childlike.

'Just today,' she said. 'Don't think about more than that.'

'I saw what happened with father,' said Alexander. 'I've been wanting to tell you.'

'What?' Fear pitched in her stomach, cold and certain.

'I was so scared of him dying in front of me if I was alone with him. I wondered if I'd know, whether you could tell without pulses and mirrors and all that. Then I saw him and I knew he was dead right away, even from the doorway.'

'But you weren't there . . . afterwards.' *When we came back.*

'I lost my nerve all over again. Couldn't even keep him company, just waited in the chapel until I heard Dr. Harrison arrive. I often wondered what I would do if the pain grew too bad for him to bear. I'm hoping you tidied up . . . *things* before he came?'

His voice remained flat, puzzlingly gentle. Venetia felt her throat constrict. He knew. Must have seen the cushion by Angus, guessed. *Oh Angus*, was all that she could think, because only he would know what to say about his own death, what to do. She clutched at the mantelpiece to steady herself against the true nature of his absence, permanent as stone, closed her eyes for a second and pushed her chin down into her chest. When she opened them Thomas was standing directly in front of her.

'You knew,' Thomas said.

Thomas was very still and yet something was happening beneath his skin, as if a vibration was taking place in some visceral part of his body, then making its way to the surface.

Venetia's first instinct was to ask him to go away. She needed time to absorb Alexander's words, his full meaning, could not be expected to fight on another front. The two of them had caught her with a pincer movement on this most dreadful of days, when she had invited mourners into her home. The word that came into her mind, quite bizarrely, was *ungentlemanly*.

'Reverend Jones admitted everything about my mother. Dr. Harrison was part of it too, keeping the whole thing quiet. You all agreed it was for the best.'

'Thomas, please understand . . . '

'How could you not warn us?' His voice rose, twisted into anguish. People were turning to look. 'I might have been able to save her.'

Venetia remained silent. No good could come of telling Thomas that his terrible temper, his moods, had taken up so much space. That his father had by turns placated and fretted over him all these years and in doing so had turned his gaze from the quiet storm in the very same room. 'If I'd known I could have protected her!' said Thomas. She took a step back towards the fireplace as he thrust his face towards hers. 'Even if the rest of you didn't care enough to bother—' spittle flew from his lips, landing on her face. Venetia tried not to flinch, then suddenly Alexander was there, filling the small space between the two of them.

'Stop it, Tom!'

'Did *you* know about any of it?' Thomas said. 'After all, you were supposed to be in love with her, so perhaps they allowed you in on our shameful little family secret.'

'Of course I didn't! Not till it was too late.'

Alexander had Thomas by the arm. For a moment Venetia thought their mutual agonies were about to spill over, that they might strike one another and for no reason except to make their suffering physical, finite, fight it out, right here in the salon. Tom stared at Alexander, seeking veracity in his eyes, his expression.

'Then why aren't you as fucking angry as me?'

'I don't know.' Alexander shook his head. 'I am.' They are not warriors at heart, Venetia thought. 'I do enough damage of my own,' Alexander went on. His face contorted as if he might cry.

'But all the lies . . . ' said Thomas.

He was obdurate, yet the rage had gone out of him. Venetia could sense it.

'All families have secrets,' Alexander said, and there was a steadiness in his voice that she'd not heard before. 'Maybe the truth was too difficult; people were just trying to protect you.' His eyes moved to his mother, holding her gaze for a long moment. 'How else are we supposed to go on?'

James came to find her when everyone had left. She was in the garden, cutting stems of fragrant phlox for her sitting room, when she glanced up to find him watching her. His expression was tentative, tinged with melancholy, just as it had been the night they met. Even then he seemed to apprehend that life would not be as he willed it or dreamed it to be.

'I came to say that I don't think we should carry on as we are,' he said.

Venetia put down her secateurs but did not rise from the flower bed where she was crouched.

'Because?'

'Because it's still Angus. I thought it would change, but it hasn't, it won't.'

How terrible that there was still hope in his eyes, a tiny flicker of it.

'No,' she said.

'I do understand, Venetia.' James nodded, gave a smile that was more like a grimace. 'I loved him too, of course.'

W as that all a family amounted to? A jumble of furniture heaped up on the Great Lawn like abandoned props on a stage, the curtainless windows
of her sitting-room an empty backdrop? Perhaps Alexander
was right, that day last summer when they walked along the
ridge. If so, then this was the beginning of the inevitable, the
dwindling down of the white-smocked broods in the old
portraits in the hallway; of Teddy and Thomasina, with their
solemn faces and stately bearing; Sir Laurie as a boy and
then again as a young man, with his wife Penny seated beside
him. All the way down to the three of them: Angus,
Alexander, herself. James too, of course, pictured alone,
seated at the farmhouse kitchen table. *We are a dying breed*,
Alexander had said.

Against her wishes, he'd given up any idea of finishing his
studies.

'I need to go away from here, mother. The army's as good
a bet as any.'

'One day when everything . . . ' She ran out of words.

'I don't know.' Alexander shrugged. 'I can't imagine wanting to live here again. Not without her.'

The farm would carry on as usual; Thomas would remain
at Gatekeeper's Cottage as long as he wanted. Venetia had no
difficulty persuading Alexander of that, though she was surprised when Thomas, sombre yet clear-eyed, came to tell her
of his intention to look after his father without any extra help.

She did not know where Alexander would settle once the army had done with him. Abroad somewhere was the most he could say. Germany for now. Venetia felt quite sure he would never return to Richmond Hall.

Lennie's grave was already hazed with green as if it were somehow more fertile that the rest of the churchyard. Venetia had cut early blooms from the garden, but the flowers that had seemed so pretty in her hands looked wrong when she stood at the foot of the mounded earth. Instead, she laid a handful of the blooms on the flat oblong of Danny Masters' grave, beside the small bouquet that his mother brought to him every Sunday. The remainder were for Angus. Venetia crossed the grass to his grave, leaving Lennie untroubled.

On the driveway, sycamore leaves bright and new above her, Venetia heard the rumble of a van approaching. She'd spent the winter making over a semi-derelict cottage on the edge of the estate, but most of the furniture from her rooms at Richmond Hall was to be taken to auction. The cottage was tiny, just one bedroom and two small rooms downstairs, and she had seen little point salvaging much for herself. She would live a smaller kind of life now: an almost-reversal of a journey she'd taken as a young girl and newly married. She had tried to hold onto all that she and Angus had built for themselves and failed. In the end there was only herself. But it was something to be alive, with spring bursting from the buds and a new garden in need of attention. Civilisations could rise and fall all they wanted, but no one could stop her going on if she chose. It was up to the rest of the world what it did with itself.

A housing company had shown interest in the Hall. Alexander had written of it in his last letter from barracks. Soon, developers would come to scrape the house from the landscape, making way for other lives. The river would flow on though, long after the earth had closed in around the bones of the past, and the land would become what it always had been: a palimpsest waiting for a new story to be told, which was always the old story, of love and loss and joy and grief.

ABOUT THE AUTHOR

Karen Powell was born in Rochester, Kent. She left school at 16 but returned to education as a mature student to study English Literature at Lucy Cavendish College, Cambridge. She lives in York with her husband and daughter.